THE NIGHT OF TREES

By Thomas Williams

THE NIGHT OF TREES

‹‹

THOMAS WILLIAMS

*Why, aren't we then thrust back
Into our senses' wily night?*

NEW YORK · THE MACMILLAN COMPANY · 1961

© Thomas Williams 1960, 1961

Chapters 5 through 10 were first published in
Esquire Magazine for May, 1960, in a slightly different form under the title "Waiting for the Moon."

A part of chapter 17 was published in *Good
Housekeeping* for October, 1961, under the title
"Christine."

First Printing

The Macmillan Company, New York
Brett-Macmillan Ltd., Galt, Ontario

Printed in the United States of America

Library of Congress catalog card number: 61-11952

PART ONE

Why should men love
A wolf more than a lamb or dove?

—Henry Vaughan

He had started from New York late in the morning, buzzed along over the wide turnpikes through Connecticut and Massachusetts, and now, on the long hill above Leah, New Hampshire, stopped to put up the top of his new little car. The sun was about to go below the hills, and October began to make itself felt again after a bright day. It was as if October and New Hampshire meant the same bright coldness; the sun went quickly toward the hills, and the horizontal light itself seemed cold against the vivid hills to the west, on which, even though they had lost most of their leaves, the hardwoods stood orange and black, struck out against dark green pine and spruce and hemlock, the green of these dark and yet so bright they amazed the eye, for behind them was a bank of cloud as black as the deepest part of the night. Not a speck of dust softened the air, and each tree a mile away, each bird shaking on the wind was all sharp edge; even the border of the cloud was honed sharp against the blue.

Night came with the shutter of the black cloud, and as he drove down into Leah, into an autumn as precisely right among the old New England houses and the fountaining elms as childhood's pure memory of autumn, huge clean dollops of rain splashed against his windshield and cleaned it of the acid grime that he had, it seemed, been living in all year until now.

He had owned the little car a week, and though they had told him that it was a racing car, not anything like the large sedan he had been used to, and that it might "bite" him, he didn't worry about that. He was a careful man, careful in the sense of preparation and research—not in the pursuit of limits. He drove fast, and used the machine according to the specifications of its maker. He had no desire to race: the little car was a present to himself of honesty and predictability, a reward, in a way, for prolonged confusion and unhappiness. His wife had left him. His son had quit school and was about to be drafted into the army.

But he was not a man enmeshed in lies, a man who considered himself betrayed. Rachel, his wife, to the best of his perceptions, had not lied herself away from him. If he yearned for honesty, it was more an understandable simplicity, perhaps, than honesty, that he wanted in her and in his son, Murray. He was not, and he knew he was not, a simple man. He had always been able to cope, able to see the complexities of life in such a way that they became, if not simple, at least understandable. He was a man capable of making up his mind.

And so he had given himself presents—the Arnolt-Bristol roadster, a new rifle from Abercrombie & Fitch, a new wrist watch— all expensive. There was no reason why he shouldn't. He had never collected *things*, had few of the intense and fashionable hobbies of the well off—no hi-fi, no sailboats, no horses, no other highly intricate sporting equipment. He had worked hard; he was forty-five years old, and his business, in which he was an equal partner with his father-in-law, seemed just now to run itself with an almost human instinct for gain. It consisted of ten dry-cleaning plants, two in each of the five boroughs of New York City, where the fallout of industrial soot was constant and profitable.

Now, in the sudden night, he drove toward the quiet center of Leah, the cockpit of the buzzing car functional, plain, yet illuminated by the glowing faces of the dials that were at the same time sensuous, warm, without the slightest lack of honesty and precision, telling him of his control, of the machine's faithfulness. Foolish, he knew, to depend upon a machine—and yet, why not? Machines

4

could not love you, it was true; but how rare was honesty, cold but absolute; if the machine stopped, you opened it up and looked inside, and there was the simple trouble.

He had two weeks in which to hunt and, he hoped, to try to understand his son. Murray was still at Dartmouth, and hadn't yet said definitely whether he would come to the lodge or not. But if he would, perhaps the things they had in common might lead to a solution of other problems. Richard had always tried first to simplify, then to include the necessary complications. He could not dive into the emotions, tears and loving gestures scattered God knew where. He was an effective man; a good shot, for instance, and he was a good shot because he took careful aim. He would plan and wait and see.

They knew he was coming at the lodge—Shim Buzzell and Shim's father, Zach—but he stopped at the Welkum Diner to call and make sure. Shim answered right away and said come on up, and Richard decided to have a cup of coffee while three boys in black motorcycle jackets went out to look at his car, then came back in to look at him, their faces hard and full either of respect or of possible mayhem. He couldn't tell, but drank his coffee and let them look. Either a hero driver or a fancy pants, he thought; he looked young for his years, and rather dignified in a large, lean, yet somewhat overclean way, like one of the models in magazines who tried to make long cigars seem highly respectable in their tapered, immaculate fingers. Like most healthily vain men, he knew what he looked like, and how he looked was odd in Leah, New Hampshire. A handsome man with a black mustache (his father's, worn as a memento, a bit of continuity; it was identical to the one in the old albums), and above the black mustache his bony British Grimald nose; above the high cheekbones pale, cold eyes of the color of robins' eggs. He never had to speak in order to be highly noticeable—even, sometimes, he felt, a little frightening.

The juveniles waited until he was through with his coffee, and casually followed him out. He was sure they liked the sound, and he enjoyed, with a certain amount of embarrassment at his own childishness, his fairly expert speed shift into second gear. The motor could seem nicely angry if one played with it. The juveniles, with delinquent tendencies now, leaped to their motorcycles, fol-

5

lowed him for a few miles until he turned off the tar onto the gravel, and then turned back.

In New York he had been conscious of the murky air—part irritation, part his business—but there was no such fallout—at least no visible fallout—on this New Hampshire mountain. His headlights shone on the dark spruce and turned them from black shadows into clean, lush green. The last few pretty leaves of late October's hardwoods, the leafy hummocks beneath the trees, jumped into light; sometimes little eyes, deep in under, stared him by. The wind blew; a sudden curtain of rain fell, and stopped completely, as if it had been tossed from a bucket. In front of him the little dials signified the temper of the machine as it sped upward on the mountain road, and told him that all was well. All was well, and the toy comforted him the way a toy might comfort a child who faced the coming of inevitable grief: a child lived in present time, and could not conceive of the end of any time longer than moments. He could, of course, knowing how short a time forty-five years had been. Yet it worked, this present to himself, and it did take just the sharpest edge away.

Bemused thus by the instruments of the car, he nearly hit the buck. Fortunately he looked up from the tachometer in the last possible moment, put his brakes full on, and stopped—in a straight line, he was pleased to see, even on the loose gravel of the mountain road. The buck, himself bemused by the headlights that held him so vividly against the dark trees, stared calmly down upon the little car. His thick brisket higher than the car's roof, he turned his tined antlers, his great head and all so easily, so smoothly it seemed to Richard that the huge complexity of armor and sense he carried on his neck was somehow suspended from above. Still he didn't move out of the road, and Richard's eyes moved over the deer with conscious avidity, as if he might collect and own such graceful strength and dignity. "Oh God, oh God, oh God!" he found himself whispering. Steam shot in narrow streams from the black nostrils, light collected in the wild eyes; the belly, flag, and chest were absolutely clean and white. The immaculate presence of the buck transcended his obvious stupidity in the face of danger, but of course the animal, on his nocturnal business, was helpless in the sudden, alien light. Richard watched, and watched, and then, with

6

reluctance overcome by a feeling akin to sacrilege, switched his lights off, then on again. The buck was gone.

His panic stop (he had felt no panic—this term was one of many he had scrupulously learned before he bought the car) had stalled the engine. Or perhaps his unfamiliarity with the disciplines of clutch and brake had caused it. But now he was in the woods, having seen so closely the greatest prize of the woods, and he was eager to get to the lodge and tell about it, to remember it, and to get ready to hunt. He started the engine and drove on.

He must look for Buzzell's sign, and take a smaller, steeper road to the left. And there it was, the sign, very high on its pole—he remembered it as it usually was, in the winter when he and Rachel and Murray had come up to ski, when the snowbank pushed up by the plow had nearly covered it. Now it seemed alone and out of season, and awkward, like a pile at low tide. The sign said: SKI, white letters on a graying board, the board nailed to a narrow hemlock pole, the pole, here on the ledge, held up by a small cairn of stones. SKI. The sign neither asked for patronage nor gave quite enough information—an affectation, maybe, of Shim Buzzell's. Another bit of consciousness revealed in that white paint: if the board had been new and yellow (it was pine) when the paint went on it, Shim knew how a few weathering days and nights would turn the wood dark gray against the white, the way a photographer, also expert in his subject, would know how dark could turn, with science, into light.

The road to the lodge, though narrower, was in better shape than the town road; the water bars were unbroken, the turns were carefully banked. Shim, although he used town gravel, had famously told the town road agent to keep his goddam grader off it. Since he lived there all year round, legally the town should have maintained the road, and could never, legally, have "throwed it up." But Shim said, always with contempt: "Look at the town road. Turns into a squirrel track and runs up a tree."

He followed the single lane and turned, trembling a little as he thought of the deer, into the small clearing next to the big white house. Beautiful! he could hear himself saying of the deer; and Shim Buzzell, who would ordinarily sneer at such a word, might even use it himself when talking about a white-tailed buck. When

7

Shim spoke of deer, something in his crouched, feral look called for abstractions. He liked them big and he liked them to eat, but he also liked them dead, so he could run his hands along their flanks.

Richard parked his car next to the barn that had been converted into sleeping lofts for skiers, took part of his baggage from the rack, and walked across the yard toward the big old house. Built above high pastures, it now found itself in the middle of the wilderness; it had outlasted nearly all its fields, and stood among the tall trees that had usurped its land, even most of its lawn. The pine and spruce came close, even touched in places the old narrow clapboards. The house was four stories high and had twenty-five rooms. Now most of its narrow windows looked straight into the darkness of the woods.

A bare light bulb hung swaying over the kitchen door, and as Richard came under its harsh light the door opened. Zacharia Buzzell, Shim's father, motioned him in with a shiny, arthritic hand, and without saying anything turned and stiffly walked back to his chair between the water-heater tank and the oil-and-electric stove. The copper pipes to the tank passed between the rungs of Zach's chair, an upright wooden chair, armless and painted blue. In it Zach sat bulky and straight. The pipes had been brazed on with the chair in place, and they always made Richard think of old barbed wire in the woods which sometimes passed straight through the trees that had grown around it.

He put down his bags and was about to speak to the old man, who had now settled himself in his chair on what appeared to be the same gray feather-leaking pillow he had used two years ago, but Zach shook his head. He didn't want to talk. He looked much older, and the first startling thing Richard noticed was a plastic bag hanging from a strap around Zach's neck. Zach pointed to it and again shook his head. In spite of his chunky body the old man looked more and more fragile, less dense, in a way; age had turned his skin pearly, translucent, babier than a baby's. The thin tendon of his nose seemed naked, flecked only with the wan, light blemishes of age. His white hair was like fine smoke over the slightly yellow skull, seeming to hover half an inch over the skin, and he seemed to have no beard at all.

8

Suddenly Zach's thin lips, speckled with brown, opened too wide, like those of a fish. *"Huch!"* he said, inhaling, gulping the word. "Operation. *Hough!* Got to talk. *Huch!* In a belch. *Hough!* Ain't wuth it." The words were made of air and hollow places, like the words of a ghost. After speaking, Zach turned straight ahead in his chair, the gesture suggesting a kind of inanimate arrangement, as if he had turned himself into a statue. He shook his head once more and was still. An old farmer and woodsman—in New Hampshire one was always both—Zach was not too different from many old men Richard had seen, silent beside a stove, in his overalls and leather slippers, his Carter's blue work shirt washed nearly white.

"Where's Shim?" Richard felt he had to ask. Zach motioned toward the mountain, Cascom Mountain, invisible but heavy above them. Then, without turning his head, he grinned, showing the edges of his perfect plastic teeth. But the little grin was evidently private, and lasted only a moment. Then he was still again.

Beside the modern restaurant sink, on the cork bulletin board, Richard found a note from Shim:

> BUZZELL'S SKI LODGE
> LEAH, N. H.
> 25 Oct.
>
> MR. GRIMALD:
>
> Hello. You get the room at the top of the stairs next to the new bathroom. Opal is in town (I married her this spring) and Zach does not like to talk. He has a laryngectomy now and has to suck wind, which he does not like. The little bag on his neck is for spit. You will get used to it. I will be back around ten.
>
> SHIM B.

Richard wondered who Opal was. He knew many people in Leah, but no Opal. And as far as Zach's little bag offending, the old man seemed much too washed and pure in his age to be offensive in any animal way. If a little bag were now part of his plumbing, his metabolism, so be it. He took his suitcases up the narrow staircase to the high, familiar bedroom. It was like going back in time; he remembered brass bedsteads, nostalgically sagging, and thick white pitchers and bowls on turned-legged, spindly bedside tables in his Midwestern youth. Then his father might have stood tall and fit in such a room, and unpacked his celluloid collars. He had none of those—just beautifully expensive Abercrombie & Fitch hunting clothes. But he looked into the oval mirror, the frame painted bright red, and saw the father he dimly remembered, mustache and all.

"Mr. Grimald," he said, then did not wish to fool with the idea. Such almost frightening whimsicality was inconsistent with his image of himself. Seemed to be, at least. He did not want to fool with equilibrium, a thing that had always seemed to him to be hard-earned and precariously kept in this world.

He washed next door in the new bathroom that was all lavender tile, the toilet seat also lavender with a little hooked rug over the cover, like a tea cozy. Two years ago the room had been a closet.

Relaxed and conscious of his leanness, he put on a soft flannel shirt and khaki pants. As he went back down the narrow stairs, his knuckles touched the wallpaper. Zach decided to speak again.

"Letter. *Hough!*" Zach must have had the first bubble of air prepared. "On the board."

That would be from Murray. With a feeling of excitement that was almost painful, Richard went quickly to the board and searched for the letter. He resented the power the boy had over him—and then, as the word "resent" occurred to him it turned to love. Murray, his son, to a man who liked craft and perfection in things, was the only perfect thing he had ever seen. And whether or not Murray would come, the letter would be modest and affectionate. He found it and sat down at the kitchen table to read:

DEAR OLD MAN,

I can see why you are somewhat worried about me, but don't be. I'm not flunking out or anything, as you know—really just a leave of absence. I have no honey I'm hot to trot either (at least outside of dreams), so don't get worried about that. Actually, I like it here. I suppose most professors are pretty dim everywhere, but there are a few good ones, and for that I'm thankful. It's not that, either. And of course I like to show off at sports. (If you think *you're* worried, you ought to see Coach Brackett!)

As you could see in my letter, and did see, I'm not too hot for hunting at the moment. Maybe I feel like hunting something else, or maybe I feel, right now, what with the army after me, like I'm the one being hunted. But I'll come for a week and try to get back my old itch for birds and bucks. Maybe Thursday. Are there many partridge this season?

About mother. We can talk about that later. But I suppose we won't. Maybe I can see some reason for it. Maybe I can't. All I know is, it doesn't seem right. Actually, it rocked me. But I'm old enough, I guess, to know that whatever the reason is, it's your problem— yours and hers, and that I didn't see it coming. It's like the sun, maybe—what if it began to dim? We measure everything by it, don't we? Your family is like that. Mine was, anyway. I didn't see it going bad. How's old Shim the Silent? (I just heard of an Anglo-Saxon king named Aethelred the Unready, but that wouldn't apply to Shim.) I always felt that he went out in the woods—way back—and screamed. And then, of course, brought back the biggest buck in Leah. Which shotgun did you bring for me? The 16? I hope so. See, maybe I am getting the itch again.

Shoot straight (I know you do, O.M.),

MURRAY

So he would come. And now that one problem was solved, Richard began to plan for the next. If he could perhaps talk Murray out of this ridiculous idea of a trip around the country, or at least find out just why the boy must quit school and take off on his own, without even a friend along—that would be the next. The army had given him a month. One month. To a twenty-year-old, he supposed, that would seem to be a long time. Of course, he could remember in himself that itch for adventure, but now, with Rachel's defection, he wondered with a kind of desperation if all people were meant, for reasons just beyond his ken, to leave him, or to disregard his loving plans for them. He was not a man to feel left—he never had been—and therefore he did not waste his time on self-pity or his energy on fear. He planned. That was the business of a father; not to rule, but to plan, and it was the business his own father hadn't had the time to do.

Zach breathed gently in his niche between the stove and the hot-water tank, a slightly moist, insistent noise accompanying the metallic *tick tick* the tank made, as if it were squeezing little bubbles to death. It must have been intolerably hot there, but there was no sign of sweat on Zach, who stared into his private evening—perhaps, Richard thought suddenly, with some envy of Zach's placidity, of fields and oxen and stone walls long ago. Evidently Zach no longer smoked his pipe. He just sat, and it did seem logical that a man who must always be conscious of his flues and openings would not fill them up with smoke. Richard, who could act upon any reasonable evidence, hadn't smoked for two years.

He put Murray's letter in his breast pocket (he would read it again) and went out to the car to get the gun cases and the liquor. The car, so gleaming and pretty, cheered him up, and when he came back to the kitchen he got out a bottle of bourbon and held it out to Zach: a question. The old man nodded and carefully walked to the cupboard over the sink. He got down a tumbler for Richard and a juice glass for himself; then he took a can of grape juice from the refrigerator and put some in his juice glass, his glassy fingers steady but seeming to hinge only at the first joints. Richard filled the juice glass with bourbon, then made himself a highball with ice cubes and water. Zach nodded and sipped his purple drink.

"*Hough!*" he said. "Ain't nothing. *Huch!* Wrong with. *Hough!* My hearing. *Huch!* Speak out."

"I know how you feel, though," Richard said. "I never like to have a dentist talk to me when I can't answer."

The old man, back in his chair again, nodded solemnly. "*Huch! Huch!* Pain in the ass." He nodded again and sipped his drink, the purple like ink on his pale lips.

Things had changed at the lodge in the two years since Richard had seen it. Like the lavender bathroom, the new built-in refrigerator and sink, here the modern was superimposed piecemeal upon the old. The house was very old, and except for a picture window in the living room through which Richard, wandering around with his drink, could barely see in the darkness some attempt to clear the trees between the house and a view of the mountain, the windows were narrow and small, built at a time when heat came from wood alone, and was precious. A modern, plastic-covered divan sat between two end tables of dark plain pine, luminous and dented. The little lines of dots from a tracing wheel upon their tops showed

12

that they had once been used for sewing. Shim had taken out the partition between the parlor and living room, and now the room was long and high. The stone fireplace was new, as were some of the mounted deer heads along the walls. Most were old. The glassy eyes were dusty and dull on some, and the hair dull, as if they had grown gray and patriarchal there upon their mounts. Even the neck hair seemed darker on those great bucks shot by Zach before the First World War. From their plaques of varnished birch they stared with great dignity over Richard's head.

The lighting of the room, consistent with the somehow pleasing hodgepodge of furniture, seemed western: all down the long room wagon wheels fixed with shaded bulbs hung from the ceiling. Only the two near the center were lighted, and the deer looked upon them with their usual gravity, mixed, too, with a suggestion of fright in those wide eyes and stiff ears, the antlers pointing heavily forward and up into the cobwebby darkness of the ceiling.

A car turned into the yard, its lights bright for a moment against a white birch, and he went closer to a window to see it. At first he thought of Murray, but Murray wouldn't come until Thursday —if then. It was a Jeep station wagon, and that must mean Shim's new wife. He hadn't liked his immediate and irrational thought that it might have been Murray, and he was slightly irritated with himself as he went back to the kitchen. As he entered the room she was at the door, and as it opened to the noise of paper bags he thought, with surprise at his own surprise, Shim was *married?* This with his first sight of Opal, nearly hidden behind her shopping bags. His first impression, before he realized that she was very small, was that to carry such large bags and still have a finger or two to open the door, she must be very strong—and as Shim's wife she might have to be. But she was small, less than five feet tall, and the bags took on their proper size. Her heels hit the floor with a *crack crack crack* as, with a small woman's jauntiness, she marched in. She had to bend backward in order to raise the bags to the table. As she turned to look at him her coat flared open, rather gracefully, and she stood with her high heels firmly on the floor and said: "You must be Mr. Grimald. I'm Mrs. Buzzell. New here," she added in a cool, schoolish little voice, and he saw that she faced him, and perhaps the house and the old man, to whom she had nodded over the groceries, with some defiance. Richard asked if he could get anything else from the car, and she said yes, there were two cases of beer, "But I could get them all right."

"I'll get them," he said. She didn't smile. She was very dark, almost olive in complexion, with a soft, rounded little face. She seemed younger than Shim—in her twenties—and yet her rimless glasses were surprising, and predicted elderliness. So it was a surprise to see her move as she took off her coat, and to see the precise good taste of her clothes and the gracefulness (he was surprised at his thought) of her little body. She was not chunky, but somehow narrow-boned, as if she were all in miniature.

"Thank you," she said unwillingly.

As he went out to the jeep he decided that he didn't like her very much. She gave him the impression of an old-maid schoolteacher, for midgets. Then he remembered who she was, Opal Perkins, and that she had been a schoolteacher. She'd taught Murray high-school English that winter they'd lived in Leah. She must be nearly thirty, then; not so much younger than Shim. They made strange mates, but then he couldn't think of Shim having anything but a strange mate. And she, no doubt, was the genius of the lavender bathroom.

When he came back with the beer he saw that she had moved his four gun cases over to the wall, where they stood in geometrical order, evenly spaced, short to tall, with no chance of their falling over.

"Would you like a drink?" he asked.

"No, thank you," she said rather primly. She had put on an apron and tied it tightly around her tiny waist. The word "jaunty" occurred to him again, this time as her perfect little rump bounced, and her smooth little ankles flashed as she put away the groceries. She seemed a funny little bird, fascinating as a bird might be, not quite believable, with something about her of the quick-quick-stop, and when stopped, the total immobility of a bird. Then *trot-trot-trot* again as her sharp little heels jabbed the linoleum.

He made himself another drink, intending to take it up to his room, where he would read Murray's letter again. By then she had put away the groceries, and she said, "But I'll have a cup of coffee with you in the living room." Her eyes, although it may have been a glint from her lenses, barely flicked toward Zach, then toward the coffeepot. "On this stove we have a quick-heat unit. Infrared." She turned a knob, and the coffeepot seemed immediately to be sitting on red fire. "Extremely quick," she said, and it was.

Holding her cup and saucer in both hands, she led him into the living room where, with remarkable strength, she adjusted a great birch slab of a coffee table with one hand. She sat down on the plastic-covered divan and had to adjust three throw pillows behind her back so that her feet could at least hang over the edge.

"Well!" She stopped to reach for her coffee—a sitting-up exercise, her knees straight. To give her credit, he thought, she did not seem to want to be cute; in a world slightly too large for her she had to be pretty limber.

"I've never met you, but I remember your son . . . Murray?"

Slightly fake, he thought; she did feel defiant.

"A very bright student," she said.

"Yes, I remembered that you taught in Leah high school." He sat down at the other end of the divan, and for one giddy moment it looked at least ten feet long.

"Shim says he's an awfully good athlete at the college. He reads about that sort of thing in the paper."

"He seems to be good at everything he tries," Richard said. "He's quite a boy." And he thought, What a foolish thing to say about Murray, and what a sardonic grin Murray would have for such a statement. "Obviously a chip off the old bone," Murray would say, or something like that. He seemed, at least at present, somehow steadier and more purposeful than anyone, in spite of his desire to take off. His letter (at that moment Richard wanted to go up to his room and read it again) did show such wise and easy toleration of his parents' troubles. He didn't want to sacrifice a week of his trip, either, and yet he would come. Suddenly Richard wondered if Murray might be coming, not just to humor him, not just to reassure a father of his son's sanity, but to console a man who had been deserted by his wife. He felt a great weakness at the thought. He didn't want to think such things.

He hadn't been listening to Opal, and she had formally taken her turn to talk. He smiled, hoping it to be an answer, and she looked a little surprised. Her little red lips came open, and he had a glimpse of a white tooth, lined delicately with gold. But he never did find out what she'd said, because just then they heard the kitchen door close and Shim's soft, inflectionless voice.

"Seena cah, Pah," Shim said in the kitchen. Richard could almost see his meaningless, but rather nasty grin: he had told his father that he had seen Richard's car, and therefore knew that he was here, and implied that the fancy foreign car was exactly what he might expect Richard to be driving. Shim was, really, fairly literate. He had gone to Dartmouth after the war, and graduated.

Opal scooted herself off the divan, and Richard followed her into the kitchen, taking one step to her three. Shim bent over the sink, washing his hands and face with Boraxo. He wore his usual uniform of green chino—he didn't like to be seen in the woods. His hair, cropped close, was all reddish gold, and tawny, and he looked around as he wiped his head dry, grinning—his most characteristic expression—as if everything in the world were just slightly smutty.

"What you got for guns?" he said to Richard. They would examine the guns. From Shim's hip pocket protruded the stock of the tiny Stevens single-shot .22 he always carried, with which he had shot, among other things, two wildcats. This he pulled out and unloaded; then, his grin unchanging but his yellow eyes straight upon Opal, he presented it to her. She backed away, a watchful look on her face. Shim placed the pistol on the edge of the table. The old man watched, it seemed to Richard, with eagerness. As he unzipped his gun cases he glanced up at the people by the table. Zach had hitched forward in his chair, and Opal watched Shim. She stood close to him, but with a certain alertness, as if she were afraid she might touch him inadvertently. Shim's yellow eyes were for the guns, and Richard brought them forth one at a time.

"Ah," Shim said. He had never seen Murray's 16-gauge Browning over-and-under, and he took it in his rough but thin hands and swung it to his shoulder. As if one quick sight down the barrel had been enough for his imaginary bird, he put it down upon the table—one smooth motion. There was no sound as it came to rest upon the formica table top. He had seen Richard's double-barreled 12-gauge, and this he merely opened and shut, listening appreciatively to the solid click of the English locks. Murray's rifle, the Mauser, had always pleased him. He ran his fingers down the receiver over

16

the stamped swastika and wings, and pulled the bolt back slowly, his ear to it as if he were bowing a long note on a violin. Murray had shortened the barrel and refinished the Wehrmacht's laminated stock, but had deliberately left the rifle its military character. "I like the irony of it," he'd told Richard—this at seventeen. "Irony is a very nice word."

Shim's comment would have pleased Murray: "Ugly, ain't it?" he said, his face showing nothing but aesthetic delight. He admired the new rifle Richard had bought ("Five hundred *bucks?*") at Abercrombie & Fitch. It, like Richard's shotgun, was English. But he went back to the Mauser. "Those krauts!" he said admiringly. He himself used a military rifle, a shortened Arisaka he had converted to .30-06. This he brought out from the hall closet and placed next to the Mauser.

They all stood back to look at the guns. Upon the bright table their long, blue-black barrels and ugly, honest actions manifested a kind of darkness in the mind. Such perfect tools they were, so adequate, so startling and honest in a world complicated by ambivalence. Murray had written a poem in college about that same simplicity, and Richard remembered the lines,

No ambivalence can trifle
A mind as simple as a rifle.

If he could, in the week ahead, simplify and rest his own bothered consciousness, perhaps it would be like a sleep, and when he awoke the answers would be clear to him. He thought of Rachel—saw her clear and beautiful for one second—then deliberately attended Shim, who had taken the Mauser and who now held it out to Opal. She didn't back away, but wouldn't raise her hands to take it.

"Take it," Shim said. "See if you can heft it." He grinned, and the pupils of his eyes, to Richard's quick glance, might have been slit vertically. Opal seemed to hide behind her immobile, dark little face. Her mouth was a little open, and she breathed through it.

Finally she said, in a practical, rather harsh voice, "You know I don't care for guns."

"Take it anyway."

The rifle was awkward in her little hands, as if she held some-

17

thing as long as a ski. She quickly put it down on the table and went to the sink to wash her hands. "Oily, greasy things," she said.

"You ought to git to like them," Shim said, his voice still soft and monotonous. He turned away to grin.

Richard surprised a little smile upon the old man's face, but it quickly went away.

Breakfast would be at six-thirty, and he would try his double on the ruffed grouse. One more drink had made him drowsy, and he lay in the hammocky big bed listening to the wind down from Cascom Mountain hiss slowly through the pine beside his window. Now he should sleep, and not plan, and not remember. He heard Shim and Opal use the bathroom, then go on down the hall to their own room. Zach slept downstairs. The house, moving according to its own rhythms, sighed now and again.

He should not think of Rachel, and yet he kept building upon what had been an obvious little dream—kept inventing little details. *Rachel, Rachel,* he called, seeing her as he had often, lately, in his mind, her back turned to him as she walked sadly away. He called, loving her, but she did not understand his language. *Murray is here, with me,* he called, but she would not understand. He called again, and finally she turned and in a thick Yiddish accent he had never heard her use—was sure she couldn't even imitate—said, *Vatchu vant!* It wasn't his beautiful Rachel at all, but an old Jewess with a mustache, busy with her business, busy with troubles he would never understand.

 2

HE WOKE up hungry, to the delicate scent of the morning woods, as if the clean air had washed every old taste out of him. He went to his little window and stuck his head out. The October sun was bright and cold where the trees let it cross the house, and the few leaves left on the maples turned dryly in it, reflecting and filtering it, yellower than the sun where the sun touched them, red-speckled in places as if they had just been sprayed with blood. The black arms of the pines moved slowly as their pale, dusty green needles swayed in the wind.

It was six o'clock. No one had called him; his eagerness for this day had awakened him. "I can hunt," he said out loud, and he knew just where he would go—up the right side of the open slope next to the rope tow, where blackberries grew alongside a deep grove of spruce, up into the taller spruce, and then where the birds led him. His limit was three, and they would be quick, difficult shots in the deep thickets where the partridge hid.

He was the first in the bathroom, and he had coffee going by the time Shim came down to the kitchen. Later, in ski season, Shim would have extra help, but now, as he had written, "It's get what you want and stack your own dishes." Zach came in and washed at the sink. He had been to his outhouse; he wouldn't use an inside toilet, even on the coldest winter day. "I never took to shittin' in the house," he had once explained. Shim, who in some atavistic way was highly pleased by this, kept his father's little house in good repair. As a further indication of his good humor about it, he'd hung a little sign on the door: MAN—since only Zach used it. Or, Richard wondered, he might have—witness his grin—meant some comment upon mankind in general. With Shim, one could never tell.

Opal didn't come down for breakfast. As he ate Shim's good, greasy, country-fried eggs, he told them about the buck he'd seen the night before. Shim immediately began to glow, looked straight into Richard's eyes with his hunter's yellow ones, and questioned him carefully: "Which way was he going? At what time? How many points?"

Richard couldn't tell how many points—eight or ten. Shim nodded, and kept nodding for a while as he ate. Deer season would begin in a week, on the 1st of November, and such information was valuable in Leah, where it would be carefully collected. Zach nodded too, but Richard, watching the old man's speculating eyes, knew that the maps he saw in his mind were long obsolete; what

19

had been fields and crossings where the deer ran or skulked were now grown back into woods.

After breakfast Shim walked with him to the base of the rope tow. Shim complained about the porcupines, and how every year they ate up his ski tow and he had to build it over again. He'd tried putting hot pepper in the stain he used on the supporting logs, hanging a block of salt nearby over some old boards—but they preferred his scaffolding. He'd shot eighteen already that year, and had received fifty cents for each, from the state. But now the money the state had appropriated for that purpose had run out. "You shoot any of them quillpigs you see," he said to Richard. "I'll give you a twelve-gauge shell, any size shot—what d'you use, sixes? Sevens-and-a-half? You just blast the bastards, and I'll give you a shell for each. Just tell me how many. You don't have to bring in no noses."

He left Shim at the bottom of the tow. He had in mind that he would do his own preseason scouting for deer, and he would watch for sign: ruffled leaves beneath the beeches where the deer had pawed and nosed for the little nuts, saplings rubbed by antlers where the bucks had removed the last of their itchy velvet, the pressed grass and leaves where the deer had curled up to bed. There were many old apple trees on the mountain, craggy, arthritic-looking trees, with dead limbs fallen crookedly to the trunks. But they still gave sweet, dwarfed fruit, and he would look around their bases for sign, or for the revealing absence of it.

Feeling light and strong in his new clothes, his red cap jaunty as a cock's feather, his shotgun balanced nicely on his forearm, he climbed the hill. At any moment a bird might explode into the air —behind, at the side, in front—and he felt himself to be precisely ready, and deadly, ready to move smoothly into the pattern of the swing of flight. As he came to the top of the open ski slope, the first bird flushed unexpectedly from the upper branches of a spruce. He had time to see its nervous jumping as it made up its mind, but when it flew it seemed to lose any of the panic its foolish chirping and jerking had indicated. On short, whistling wings it beat its way directly through twigs and needles, straight away from him, keeping the tree between. He could not see which way it turned, but moved slowly along the tangled path the bird's noise had seemed to follow. He circled for half an hour and never flushed it again, but as he sat down on the warm needles beneath a balsam fir he heard, from below, the soft rush of wings and the stiff whistle of the bird's glide away. There were more partridge in the woods above, and he would let that clever one alone today.

As he lay back on the needles, he saw, through the chinks between the radiating green branches of the fir, the fresh blue sky. Not a cloud in the high, cool blue. On a maple sapling as thin as his wrist one single red leaf twirled in the light wind, and untwirled, and wound up again. As he watched, it wound itself too tight, and airily let go to swoop lightly down, like a child's unbalanced airplane. He heard the *tick* as it came to rest, and it seemed to him that he had been allowed to hear one beat of the season's clock in that leaf's final, graceful flight.

Before he left that spot, a tiny white-footed mouse came crashing through the dry leaves and stopped in front of him. Its myopic little eyes popping like black pearls from its head, it seemed to listen with its whiskers. The barrels of his shotgun lay across his toe, and he raised them slowly with his foot until they pointed straight at the mouse, who peered into those long black holes with nervous interest. Richard wondered why his first reaction was to point huge death at the humming little creature; he would never shoot, never.

"Bang," he said, and the mouse ran straight out for ten yards before he got his wits together and dived under a bush. Richard smiled, and stopped—it seemed a bit of a dirty trick. He hadn't expected to frighten the little mouse quite so much.

He climbed, when he left the place beneath the fir, and as he climbed he came to familiar places, those hollows, aged trees, tangles in the middle of the woods that had no name but a haunted, familiar greeting for the returning hunter. Because they were nameless, and changed only according to the slow movements of growth and rot, they presented the hunter with his other self: time was woods time, and he remembered with shock the woodsman he once was, and his eagerness or fatigue, or perhaps his desire to run, which was the constant submerged feeling of a civilized man in the irritating, mindless irregularity of the trees—their lack of order and geometry that could seem wickedly deliberate.

He had intended to go in a nearly straight line, and even though he knew this was not always practical in the woods, he had made up his mind to reach a ledge he remembered on the shoulder of the mountain, where he could see across the valleys. Having this goal in mind, he took pains to cross blowdown, to duck under low branches he would ordinarily avoid. And so it was a familiar frustration when he came, after crawling beneath the progressively lower branches of spruce in a grove he did not remember to be so deep, to a wall of striated granite, too high and mossy to climb. He should have known that it was there, and the sudden presence of it, adamant, massive, seemed a gesture of the earth itself. He had to turn away, and he did not want to. He impatiently pushed the leathery branches of a pin cherry sapling aside and forced his way through them: again he was reminded of his awkwardness, his alienness, his tenderness in the woods. One branch came back and flicked his cheek with such force that he was blinded for an agonizing second by tears, and he doubled over to rub his face.

He would get better at it. It took days, even with his health and strength, to master his energy and impatience in this dark country. Most difficult was to be aware all at once of all parts of his body and their proximity to each stub, twig, thorn, rock, trunk—to see beneath his feet as if with his feet, to feel the sharp, potential whips before they struck, even to fall and, while falling, to think.

And so he stopped and waited until his rhythms slowed, until he once again realized with all his body that the trees themselves would grant him his proper speed. A partridge burst up at his feet and flew hissing, spiraling up, and he shot and got it. He didn't know how his gun came up, how the safety was taken off, how his eyes and arms could have joined in the proper pattern. He went forward to get the bird, which had fallen fifteen yards away. A few soft, gray-brown feathers drifted against the trees. The bird was hot in his hand, and through the insubstantial feathers on its breast the huge flying muscles pulsed against his fingers and were still. The little head swung lightly against his wrist, a drop of blood like a ruby at its eye.

He put the plump bird in his game pocket, and then ran his hand along a branch to wipe away the few feathers that had stuck to his fingers. The wild thing was in his pocket. In his pocket rested this wild thing of the woods, and later he would draw his knife through the deep white breast meat, an inch thick, that had been wild muscle. The ruffed grouse was a bird of the woods, and could not be domesticated, could not be raised in any kind of captivity. This one, at dinner, he would assimilate.

He loved to climb, to go to those few places that were like islands above the forest where he could rise to the surface and see back down the hills, green upon red upon brown upon blue, where the rolling state was open to him. He had reached the ledges, and as he looked out and down, the low mountains seemed at any moment as if they might begin to move like slow, gigantic waves. Up here he came out of the dark woods, and was for a moment precariously above them. Still surrounded, as he wanted to be, he breathed slowly and deeply before he descended again into their luminous twilight.

A hundred yards below he came to a long-abandoned orchard, and found that the deer had been there. They had circled each tree in order to see if the apples had fallen. Some had, but it would take a good frost before the apples would turn to pulp and the deer, with their one set of browsing teeth, could eat them easily. He went through the brush from tree to tree, tasting the hard, cold fruit until he found one ancient tree whose light yellow apples were as pure as springwater to taste, delicately flavored and just a little puckery. With a pocketful of these he looked for a place to eat the bologna sandwich and the can of sardines he had brought for his lunch. He found the place he wanted beside a recently used tote road—used in the last year or two, to judge by the bruised alder and the weedy brush in it. Shim must have done some logging, maybe to get timbers for his ski tow.

He could see some distance down the road, and he had learned in the woods to find a place where, when he was not noisily moving, he could watch. If he saw an animal, any wild thing, without being seen, then he seemed really to be in the woods, and part of them. To be quiet, and watch—it made him part of the trees, and for a moment he would have the illusion of not being an alien. As he sat eating, he did look carefully, but all he saw was a furious red squirrel, who had seen him first, and who screamed and jumped up and down, tail snapping in miniature anger as he broadcast what seemed to be the complete description of a dangerous man. Trying to ignore this barrage, Richard ate his lunch. Once, when he was much younger, on a deer stand, he did shoot a red squirrel—theoretically to keep him from spooking the deer, partly because the squirrel said some unforgivable things (who wants to be called a foreigner?), partly because the squirrel made such a terrible racket. That time a bullet almost as big as the squirrel's head had taken his head right off. This time Richard humbly took the calumny, ate his lunch, wiped his mustache, and moved on to quieter places.

By three o'clock (on his gold Omega wrist watch—another of his recent purchases of predictability) he had flushed two more partridge. He had a shot at one and missed clean when a finger-sized sapling had maliciously reached out and stopped his swing. The other bird flushed just out of sight and flew back up the hill, where he didn't want to go. He followed the one he had missed, jumped it twice more and finally, on an easy straight-away shot, looked down the black barrels at the bird, fired, and saw it spin down into a blackberry patch. It took him a few minutes to find the bird, but he finally did, and emerged from the blackberries with only a few scratches on the backs of his hands.

As he straightened up, he realized for the first time that he was tired. In the wilderness each step was a calculation, full of possible surprise, and though he had walked only a mile or two his bones seemed to slide wearily under his flesh. It was lovely to be weary: he had taken two birds with three shots—a highly respectable score —and the most bothersome things he had to look forward to before he could have a long drink—a drink both long and tall, he thought—were a short downhill walk and the business of cleaning the birds, which, with grouse, was not hard. For a moment he lay back on the clean leaves and looked up to the sky. What he saw, ten feet above him in the white birch at his head, was the black face of a porcupine.

When Richard got up, the porcupine knew it had been discovered, but there was nowhere to go. First it backed up and started down the other side of the tree, but when Richard merely stepped around the tree the animal gave that up and sat in the crotch, head out, his sullen black face watching, waiting.

"Tough luck," Richard said, and then wished he hadn't spoken. The black marbles that were the animal's eyes moved as Richard moved. It was a big old one, fatted up for the winter he would never see. Richard raised his gun and looked over the barrels at the face. The quills lay flat upon its shoulders. Black, with white sheaths, they could not stop an ounce of Number Six shot which, at that range, would skin the face and blow the backs out of the eyes.

Richard lowered the gun. The black eyes watched.

"At least I'm alone," he said, and again wished that he hadn't uttered words. The animal should, probably, be executed—but there, again, the wrong word came. There should be no words, just the shot and the declaration of death. Again the wrong words: execution, post-mortem, certificate of death. The porcupine (quill-pig, hedgehog, he thought) was, according to man, harmful. Now it moved its head slowly from side to side, as if it were impatient. One of its long yellow teeth showed through the black lips. An ounce of Number Six shot would grind those lips right off the bone, and shatter the yellow tooth. The animal started to climb higher, then thought better of it. Richard remembered that John James Audubon once had a pet porcupine who would never raise its quills to someone it knew.

So? Well, he would shoot, and look upon the corpse. Wrong word again.

Rachel's sister, Ruth, had said once, "You're teaching the boy to be a *killer?*" Safe in her city apartment, with her standard enlightened philosophy, she could be quite nasty.

Saul Weitzner, Rachel's father, had been there too. His ugly, patient face was a little perplexed, of course, but he said, "Now, Ruth, this is an experience we know nothing."

"How can you deliberately kill a gentle thing?" Ruth cried.

"Sometimes I can't," Richard said mildly.

Somewhere in that discussion (Rachel was silent all through it, and Murray was away at school), Ruth had called him a cold beast, and implied that precisely such monsters had run the furnaces at Bergen-Belsen.

No answer had come to Richard's mind. Saul had come furiously to his defense, charging ignorance on Ruth's part, but in

Saul's gentle, perplexed mind, which would not conceive of giving pain, he found no way to justify Richard and Murray's hunting. Richard could understand why, to a man who had seen so much cruelty and agony, any death at all might take on the color of murder. Irrational, but the surprising thing about Saul was that he had any rationality left. That he was at all tolerant, to Richard, seemed almost supernatural; but he did not judge Saul as he did other men. When he thought of Saul his emotions ruled that ragged area where grand abstractions accompanied pains in the back of the throat, and eyes that threatened to shed tears. Such goodness either made Richard want to weep, or, more often, want to turn into a deadly, berserk protector. Enough of Saul, he said to himself.

Later he did think of words he might have said to Ruth, and he would find himself mouthing things like: "Why? Because I'm a man, animal and instinct both, and I have my eyes in the front of my head—predator's eyes, and nothing's very simple. I admire your heroes too—Gandhi and Schweitzer and all—very much. But I'm none of them. Another thing is that I was brought up by hunters, and they were kind and humane. As long as I remember them I won't turn, like you"—here, he chose and arranged and re-chose his adjectives—"into a treacly glob of sentimental clichés, ready to pulse at a word." But of course the words hadn't come in time, and even if they had he would not have said them.

The porcupine looked down and harshly ground its teeth, for a moment looking as though the effort had made him cross-eyed: he was making the most horrible face he could, and Richard knew that it was all sham. Those long teeth were good only for taking the bark off trees, or for gnawing shallow grooves in wood. Again Richard raised his gun, and the dim eyes looked into the two big holes, waiting. Richard saw the column of shot as it would fly, hardly spread, as if it were a ray of light arrowing from the barrel, and knew the mayhem it would do to the beast's flesh. It would not be painful, and this was simply an animal (who wasn't? he could not help thinking) whose natural enemies had been reduced by man. Pain he knew, having been wounded himself, was somewhat overrated—most of it came later, and there would be no later here. The argument about the porcupine's place in the balance of nature was highly debatable, because every expert had his own balance of nature in mind. If it were a question of porcupines in general, however, the choice would be simple: he would shoot. Unfortunately the real defendant in the case was *this* porcupine, whose life, for him, must have a certain value. Think: no more of the succulent cambium layer of bark; no more of that excruciatingly touchy copulation; no more of the thick heat of the sun on a fat, satisfied belly. The small joys of a congenital dullard, perhaps, but ones Richard himself could appreciate.

The barrels of his shotgun had been lowering, and now he held the gun across his forearm. He could give the animal a Mexican trial—walk away and then shoot him as he tried to escape—but that was not his style. If he shot he would bear the vision to the end, and certify to his conscience that death had occurred. He raised the gun again, rested his finger upon the trigger of the choked barrel, and aimed down that barrel, sure of his point of aim—the black nose between the black eyes. The porcupine ground his teeth again, and made a fearful face. Richard waited until the grinding had finished. He would see what an ounce of Number Six shot would do to the composition of that head, how disarrange it. The pressure of his finger grew, and in his blood a pressure, warm, powerfully pleasurable, also grew. There would be an end to this, and it would be the only end, and he would be the agent of it, the doer of it, the ruler of it, and it would be destruction.

<<<<<<<<<<<<<<<<<<<<<<<<<<<<<<<<<<<<<<<<<<<< 3

"You don't look Jewish, Mur," Shelton said.

"Neither do you."

"I know, but my name and all . . ."

Murray looked at Shelton, who didn't think he looked Jewish. What, exactly, was it in that dark hair? How it grew where it grew?

And that pale skin whose hollows were just a little too hollow, the flesh in its angles just a shade too acute (or obtuse?), the skin again, saying *heavy beard, but tender, transfixed me;* and more things, of course: the pimple below his eye, where the skin still oiled adolescently—wasn't that a Jewish pimple, the dark red of it Job's anguish, the pus in it Jewish, straight from the cornucopia of suffering? And more things: an expression a thousand years old and at the same time callow, sallow, vulnerable. He was a Jew at ten yards, at a hundred yards, and he didn't think he looked like one.

"You little kike," he said, knowing that the love in his voice was precisely, accurately received, stereo-hi-fi. What a preamplifier in this nervous little animal! Shelton turned, his pimple blushing, to his book. Once, when they were freshmen, shortly after they had met and become, immediately, good friends, they had gone to the library to look at the Orozco murals. "Lookit Christ!" Shelton said, and they looked up at the violent creature painted in an agony that seemed nothing meaningful, but vindictive, cruel, as if the injured Christ were as blindly vicious as his tormentors. "Wow!" Shelton said, "this Orozco . . ." and as he had taken to doing, he hung his hand on Murray's shoulder and then hung on it. Murray, without thinking, turned and said, "Don't *lean* on me, will you?"

They were cool, then. Friends, but cool—and that coolness had never quite gone away, as if Shelton had said to himself, "OK, ½ goy, 50 per cent goy, .5 goy: we can live with strangers. That's not new."

But now Murray wondered, and asked himself, "If he doesn't know he looks Jewish, is that good for him, or bad for him?"

"I'm just part of a percentage—a quota. You know, just so many Jews in this Ivy League," Shelton said bitterly.

"You must be smart, then," Murray said.

"Sure, what with all those eager little Jewboys pushing up."

"Then what about me, Statistic? I'm not even here. What quota did I come in on?"

"Your old man's quota, butch boy. One hundred per cent Amurrican," Shelton said.

"They saw the dirty fact on my application, Ikey. Dear old Mom's a sheeny from Jew York."

Shelton looked at him and burst into whimsical, bitter laughter. "You're a kike-o-phrenic, you are, with all your Anglo-Saxon muscles. What does it feel like? Which is the poison, the Jew or the goy? How the hell can they even breed? I think they're different species. You're a tiglon, a mule, a freak—probably sterile. Don't your guts go two ways sometimes?"

"My Hebe friend, let me tell you. I am the true American, and I refuse to go neurotic: everybody else is cake, best friend (one of my *very*). My father is a hunter, and knows which way is north north *north*east, and he-and-his settled and fought bloody for this country. My mother is from the city of the world, that first and most cosmopolitan city, named Ghetto, where the walls echo to civilized violins, and howls. So up yours, Dr. Selkoff, you wig shrinker, I wear no rug."

"Nor no tefillin, nor no New Testament . . ."

"No, both. I've got a supplicating arm and a sanctimonious hip pocket, both.

> "Oh, the Moskevitch Ramble is cool, that's all,
> So come, let's have a matzoh ball!"

Murray sang as he jigged lightly from chair to bureau to desk to floor.

But was there just a little, just a *leetle* bit of want and wonder about certification that was absolutely pure? *My father's antecedents, man, are old and almost noble. Viz. Nicholas Grimald. 1519?–1562?, scholar, preacher, author. In Tottel's miscellany of Songs and Sonnets. Treachery toward Protestant cause during the reign of Queen Mary. Viz. that! And though my mom, well . . . match the old man for stud, bud. I'm no bastard, no accident, either. I saw it on the birth certificate. Hard to tell about you, love chile.*

He sat down at his desk and began a letter to his father:

DEAR O.M.,

Expect me soon if O.C. (Old Car) makes the mountain. Maybe we won't be able to talk (I always write easier, anyway) and maybe I won't send this letter (I don't send easily). But I wonder myself why I want to go look at the country. I know, we've *been* to Illinois,

29

California, etc.. But I want to go with no credentials but my face and the price of a hamburger, and see what they do where they live

Here he stopped and thought of a line of poetry that had been going through his head: "The music of windy distance." His poem, of course. The line made him think of the eerie crackle and singing on a long-distance telephone circuit, or the just heard radio stations across the plains and mountains late at night: the music of weather and faint human cries and electricity that was the real hum of the lonely country. Always reaching out a little too far, and at the mercy, really, of God knew what: *My country*, he thought. And then, with a grin self-conscious in the presence of his sense of humor, he thought, *My girl, my honey*, because he would be looking for her, too—for the one in a dream he'd had about the end of the world. Maybe he'd have to hurry. He crumpled up the unfinished letter and tossed it in the wastebasket.

"Let's go over to the house," he said to Shelton, who could not look up because he was making a neat arc on graph paper with his compass.

"Eff the fraternity," Shelton said, and made his arc.

"What an attitude! Boy, this ain't like the old days."

"I don't like to be a walking tolerance, at which they can point with martyred pride and secret disgust, so eff the frat."

"You're a bleeder, patient Selkoff. My diagnosis is that you have Hebe-o-phelia, an old cut that refuses to coagulate."

"And you have goy-tre, which is a thick neck, the upper part of which you call a head."

They were both silent, in some awe at their own wit, trying to think of more. More didn't come, so Murray jigged again, this time jumping from floor straight to the top of Shelton's bureau:

"Oh, the Moskevitch Ramble is cool, that's all,
So come, let's have a matzoh ball!"

"Watch out for my picture!"

"Slippin' an' slidin' up an' down the mantelpiece,
Spittin' through my yeller teeth. . . ."

30

"Save it for the crowds, halfback!"

"Your picture?" Murray reached down and picked up the gilt-framed picture of a girl, a sweetly humble, drooping little girl who looked about fifteen, very soft; not pretty, but tender. "Ah, Leilani, sweet Leilani," he crooned, holding the picture in his arms. "I kiss thy pure and limpid brow, thou child of passion! Leilani, Leilani Schwartz!"

"You know what her name is!" Shelton's pimple waxed very red this time—a danger signal. His voice had risen and grown just a little querulous.

"Shel, now. Hoo, boy. And you know how charming I think she is, too. So whoa, there, and don't become Semitic warrior, what?" Shelton subsided a little, and Murray said, "If I can't bait you, Jew, who is the Jew I can bait, *nu?*"

"Well, I know I'm sensitive."

"*Sensitive!* You? Well, I won't go on. . . ."

"I just get tired of it, Mur." This time serious, having gratefully given up, because Murray was his friend, who could be trusted (almost).

Murray looked down from the height of the bureau as Shelton went back to his analytical geometry. The narrow bone along Shelton's shoulder seemed so pale, so fragile, and the pulse in his skinny neck so tentative, as if it had no real rhythm and might suddenly, for no real reason, do the cha-cha-cha, or stop.

"You're OK, kid," he said, and Shelton's hands stopped fiddling with his protractor for a second. He was still, tense, very moved, Murray knew. Stereo-hi-fi, all right: preamp, amp, tuner, changer, tweeter, woofer, high decibel range. But so fragile.

He leaped from the top of the bureau to the door, and the room shook. "Hey!" someone yelled down the hall.

"See you later," he said as he opened the door.

"Grüss Gott," Shelton said without looking up.

Murray went down the stairs two or three at a time, not really running, just pleased with the swiftness of his feet, their nice sense of control in the air. It felt as though he were floating down, just touching a step here and there for fun, not for support. He could even go down backward this way, and turn around and around as he descended. "Hi!" "Hi!" people said to him as he went by.

"Hi!" he answered. He liked to jump hedges, the fenders and even the hoods of cars, to run up a tree as high as his head and then fall back with a twist and land on his feet. Sometimes he felt that if he had to he could run to Kansas, jumping fences all the way. No one could catch him on a football field; no one tackler, at least. They all seemed to be in slow motion, like the puffing steam engines he had seen when he was a little boy, and all he had to do was to step off the track for a moment and they'd go right on by, their eyes glazed with exertion and staring as inflexibly toward where he wasn't—where he used to be—as the eye of a locomotive. Whenever he started around end, he'd give a little jump and click his heels, just for joy, for neatness, for the love of his confidence and lively knees; and the run itself, no matter how long, he would foresee and then remember as a fine series of loops and side steps and curves, like flight. Even in his dreams he ran and jumped. He could glide—take a little run and jump and keep going all the way down the sidewalk a foot or two above the cement, then gently come to earth, still moving lightly on. Sometimes he would jump too high in these dreams, deliberately, and find himself in the air above the trees, with too long a way to fall. Still in control, though worried, though sometimes even painfully scared, he'd know that when he hit, it would hurt.

By the time he reached the common he had danced some of the demanding energy out of his legs, and he walked past the subdued street lights, out, away from things into the middle of the wide common, where he stood with the stars turning over him. Cars drifted around the edges, and the few neon signs of the business street at one corner were muted, rather Ivy League themselves. But that street led to America, to the center of things, to Murray Grimald without titles: not a student (that limbo), not a football, basketball, skiing, weekend-houseparty star. He never wore his varsity sweater, for instance, unless he was required to, and *never* inside out with the stitches so modestly showing. To hell with it all, and with it the expressions of admiration, guarded regard, jealousy—all the necessary bric-a-brac he had to carry with him at school. He wished there were nothing, nothing but possibilities, things to do, and each a different thing to do. Nothing seemed impossible to him, and because nothing seemed impossible he felt the responsibility to learn, to achieve. In this enormous, inchoate list still dreamed the fantasies of childhood. They sneaked in on the back of his energy and youth. He wanted to write a book, to make a movie and a play, to paint a mural bigger than Orozco's, and twice as shocking, to sail a sloop around the Caribbean, wearing nothing but shorts and sneakers—no socks—and a rigging knife at his belt and a Tommy gun stowed in the paintlocker, to play the guitar like Segovia, to play Hamlet, to meet and love and marry the most lovely and intelligent girl in the world, to win the *Deutscher Preis* against Mercedes-Benz in a Grimald Special, to build a house, to raise a son. He was willing to learn, and he wanted to start right now.

He lay on his back in the grass, looked up at Orion's belt, and began to compose a letter to his father:

DEAR O.M.,

Have you ever been sitting around, not knowing what to do, and all of a sudden you realize just what's bothering you—you don't want a drink, you don't want to go skiing or drive a sports car—as a matter of fact you suddenly have a clear, honest streak—and what you want is for someone to tell you how goddam good you are? Well, so have I, sometimes, but not any more. Not right now. I'm sick of being a B.M.O.C., O.M., sick of it. In the army, at least, I'll be a plain soldier, with just my face sticking out of olive drab. That's all right, but what can you do in the army? It'll be over after a while.

I want to *do*, O.M., not *be*. You see what I mean? I may be wrong, but I think I'm a man now. Like you in some ways, not like you in others. I *hope* I'm like you in some ways, O.M., and I only wish you knew I hoped so, because I'll never write this letter, O.M.

With respect, admiration, perplexity,
Your son,
MURRAY

P.S. What is wrong between you and mother? Answer in 25 words or less.

M.

33

"AND I killed a porcupine," Richard said to Shim, who had cleaned one of the grouse for him.

"I'll git you your shell," Shim said.

"Never mind the shell."

"Said I would. By God I will." Shim went to the hall locker where he kept all his guns and ammunition, brought back a shell and placed it on end in front of Richard. They sat at the kitchen table, Shim with a beer and Richard with his long drink of bourbon. Zach had accepted another one of the purple ones, and sat in his chair with the little glass held upon his knee. Opal, standing on a little platform so that she could reach the sinkboard, flashed her smooth little calves at them as she prepared supper. They would have partridge pie, among other things, and she skillfully stripped the meat from the bones.

"If they ain't enough bird meat we might have a little wild veal," Shim said, his face carefully blank.

"You've got some?" Richard said. Zach grinned.

"Maybe. Maybe not. You find a bullet in it, it's wild." Shim chuckled, and then with his thin hands squeezed his beer can and easily bent it over upon itself before he tossed it into a basket next to the sink. He went to the refrigerator and got out another.

"It's too dangerous," Opal said.

"Good eatin', though. I notice you like it some." Shim turned to Zach. "I was practically raised up on venison, warn't I, Pa?" Zach grinned, showing his too perfect, bluish teeth. "One time Zach got two deer and a elk—one season." Zach nodded, looked as if he wanted to speak, and then composed his face for silence. "Didn't we have meat!" Shim said.

34

"Elk?" Richard said.

"Every so often we git a herd on the mountain; then the state is supposed to keep the herd down to size. Easy to kill, you find the herd. Ain't like deer. Zach, he didn't have no permit, though." Zach smiled and nodded.

"It's not worth it," Opal said in her clear, practical little voice. "Look what would happen if you were caught."

"If they caught Shim Buzzell," Shim said proudly, "they'd really bear down. That young Spooner now, he's *hot* after me! Oh!" Shim said, laughing, "you ought to see him come nosing around. Bet he's out there below the open slope right now. I know where he hides his car, too. Don't he think he's some cutter in the woods?"

"Ever since what you did to him," Opal said.

"Oh, dear!" Shim said, and whacked his hand on the table. "You got to hear it! Ain't I a mean son of a bitch? You tell him, Opal."

Opal didn't care for such goings on, and she disposed of the story as quickly as she could. She turned around on her little platform as if she were going to recite in class, like a little girl, and said: "Shim found the game warden's car where he had hidden it. He was on a stake-out for Shim, and Shim did something to the tires—smeared bacon grease on them—and in the next week the porcupines ate all four of his tires."

"He never could prove where it was done!" Shim shouted. "Oh, dear me! That Spooner!" He leaned back in his chair and purred, his laughter low and mellifluous, and continuous, his white teeth showing between lips that were slightly redder than the smooth orange bristles that covered his face like stiff fur.

This time some amusement did appear on Opal's dark face. "He had to walk home twice, once from Switches Corners to Leah in the middle of the night."

"Seven miles!" Shim said, for a moment halting his moaning laugh. "Oh, dear. The poor little Boy Scout in his fancy uniform!"

Zach himself had been rocking back and forth from the waist, heaving and smiling, his cloudy little bag wagging like a goat's beard. While they were honest in most ways, the Buzzells, like many hill families, felt that game laws were amusing, and to be played with. Dangerous play: the standard penalty for jacking deer was a $500 fine and the loss of every article connected with

35

the act—usually cars, guns, flashlights, even tractors and trucks. But the dangers were accepted and never railed against. The law was there, and one disrespected it at fair peril. Many of the game wardens, coming from the same hill-farm families, had been poachers themselves and they knew most of the tricks.

Now Shim seemed very open and talkative, and Richard felt that because he had shot the two birds and the porcupine he was in good favor.

He could still see the porcupine after the shot had wiped him out of the crotch. His fat body bounced like a bladder full of oil when it hit the springy leaves. The face was gone, bone mashed. He pushed the plump flesh, quills askew, into a hollow and kicked some leaves over it. The woods would take care of it. The image was there, of this destructive act, but it was not all unpleasant. The violent act was a certain one, at least, and its symmetry—the form of the giving of death—called, in a satisfying way, to an impulse 'way back, and deep. He would not romanticize himself by pretending, by pumping up in his modern conscience any great symbolic, moral drama. He did not feel any different, and he trusted how he felt. He was alive, and a man could keep his secrets without letting them fester. If, next time, a porcupine crossed, with a porcupine's fat and sullen crawl, the place where his own body rotted—so be it. And of course it would be so, some day. Meanwhile, the bourbon tasted good, and his mortal bones proclaimed their well-being by being justly weary.

"It *was* mean," Opal said. "Seven miles."

Shim grinned.

"He even likes to listen on the car radio to 'Strike It Rich.' You ought to see him."

Shim grinned wider.

"All those miserable people crying," Opal said.

"People," Shim said. "Just poor old plain stupid nasty weeping bitches. They pay to see each other! I think it's funny as hell."

"You're a misanthrope, Shim," Richard said, and then looked Shim in the eye so that he wouldn't pretend not to know the word.

"Maybe I got some people I like," Shim said, but he approved of the title.

After supper, at which he saw no sign of wild veal, Richard got

36

one of the books he'd brought with him and went into the living room to read. In the kitchen Zach had brought out his portable television and set it up in front of his chair on the kitchen table. For a while Richard had watched it too, fascinated by the old man's strict, inscrutable attention to something called "Private Secretary." Zach didn't laugh at the jokes; he just paid attention, and the canned laughter, coming in little waves, left him solid as granite.

From the living room Richard could barely hear, now, the soft whirls of giggles. His book, a satirical novel about commuters, failed to interest him very much: the jokes were so self-confident, the villains, the middle-class boors, too powerful and too stupid. It was as if the author had given him a wink and said, "You're a cultured man—get it?" And he got it, but it seemed so familiar. He sipped his coffee and thought of making a fire in the great stone fireplace.

He went to the kitchen to ask Opal if she would mind, and she turned on her platform and said eagerly, "Oh, let me make it, Please! I love to make fires! I'll be through in a minute." He watched her rinse out and stack the rest of the dishes (he'd asked her if he could wipe, but she said she never wiped, and besides, he was a paying guest and didn't come to be domestic), deciding that she knew he was watching and thinking about her, and that she didn't mind. Possibly the movements of her arms, hips, shoulders, and the cant of her well-kept little head, were just a little exaggerated. She, too, knew what she looked like. He wondered if he would have so obviously watched her if Shim had been there watching *him*. She *was* being consciously female in his sight. A strange little bird.

She wore a plain, light-blue denim dress, like a toy dress, a play dress; she must not have had many of those plainly mechanical troubles with straps, belts, and plackets that larger women had. And he thought of Rachel and her long, tapered thighs—a man-sized woman: he shivered, shook all over for part of a second, for Rachel, and saw her again in the dream, walking sadly and gracefully away from him.

When Opal had finished the dishes and wiped up the sink, she turned toward him on her platform and held out her arms. He didn't really have time to think before some immediate, polite nerve made him reach out for her—it seemed so much like a little girl's saying, "Help me down." And she, too, had a choice; really she was only straightening out arms that must have been cramped from her work, and at the same time sliding her plastic apron off her shoulders. Her choice might have been one of courtesy too, since his gesture was too obvious to go unexplained. She let him take her by the waist and lift her to the floor, her face warm and confused. She seemed to give off a little buzzing sound, then tried to smile and say, "Thank you," with the proper, light inflection. It came out hot, low, and embarrassed.

She weighed nothing—nothing because his reaction to her tiny weight and lively waist was unexpectedly, immediately male. He hadn't expected it at all, and the surge of strength that caught him in the arms and belly made him for a moment unable to undo her embarrassment. And so the moment for explanation went by, and between them as they walked into the living room was a thick, irritatingly exciting sense of possibility.

Now she walked demurely, without any suggestiveness at all— although with his quickened sensitivity to her he wondered, *knew*, that this indicated that the femaleness of her (*Stop that!*) was alive and churning. She bent her knees and squatted to get the paper and kindling, the hemispheres of her behind like a small, inverted heart below her narrow, narrow waist, and tight beneath the fabric of her dress. He could see the line where the hem of her panties circled around and down: *dark hinges*, he thought, this from another poem, not Murray's. And then of course he said to himself, *Stop that*, grinned in the middle of a yawn, felt like sneezing, did. *Stop this!*

She had the paper and kindling arranged in the andirons, and again he was impressed by her strength as she placed two birch logs, *crunch*, on top. A matter of leverage, he supposed, in the short, neat shafts of her bones—their fulcrums—the round arms full of firm muscle. She had to go back to the kitchen for a match, and he sat back into the davenport to look at the unlit fire. Just a match to the neat little triangle of paper she'd left sticking out, and it would burn nicely, well curbed by the stone and firebrick; a pretty fire, economical and well planned.

When Rachel built a fire, into it went everything (this in the city, where birch logs cost fifty cents apiece because they were pretty—others cost twenty-five), milk cartons, kindling, usually with paint or putty on it; *New York Times Magazines* whole, so that they merely curled and charred, and stopped the draft; plastic odds and ends that just wrinkled and dripped. Sometimes half the paper and kindling would go on top, and she'd light the whole mess from the top, like a candle. But he liked to repair Rachel's fires, and get them going again, and he thought she liked to have him take over and do it. That's what he'd thought once upon a time: *Can you get pleasure out of doing something badly? Have it sit and stink? Do the things you, you lovely woman, are beautiful at doing!* He loved her, and all of a sudden, now, again, this crazy thing he thought she'd got over, this going away from him.

And when Opal came back he was free, at least, of the tingle in the nose he'd got from Opal's dark places and new shyness. He had troubles he had come here to solve, and the adventures he wanted were the pure and tiring ones that had to do with the other part of him as a man. "I'm *not* an indoor hunter," he said to himself; "*not* an indoor man." He'd done his work and his fighting and his hunting outside living places, in his plants, in the army, in the mountains, and come home to Rachel, into Rachel, loving Rachel: he had thought himself to be such a lucky, lucky man.

Opal turned on her little haunches, after she had lighted the fire, and quickly looked at him.

"That'll burn very well," he said. "A very nice fire." His voice calmly erased the embarrassment that had been developing between them. As far as he was concerned, the situation was one that was, usually, easy to control. He feared only that Opal might want him to keep it up, and that would be a bother. He had never played around that way, not really. Certain tensions had developed between him and other women—his friends' wives, one or two of his employees—but he was by nature faithful, and those tensions had eventually cured themselves. He knew that a woman had to be asked, and he would not ask. After having decided, almost by habit, not to fool with Opal, he looked at her again as she stood aside to look at the fire, and wondered what it would be like. He had never considered such imaginings to be acts of unfaithfulness.

So different from his Rachel! She was so small, this tiny replica of a woman, that she made him feel big, extremely strong, and he would probably have to wonder if he might hurt her. But enough of that. Even if he did pursue this foolish twinge of desire it would lead to no more, probably, than a young wife's pretense at outraged virtue. Messy and unnecessary, he concluded, no matter which way it might have turned out.

Later that evening he had to reconsider these resolutions.

He had noticed in Opal's attitude toward Shim certain odd things: she would move toward him, for instance, but would not touch him, as if he were fascinating to her, yet basically abhorrent. Richard's first impression was that perhaps she thought of Shim *in toto* as she might a naked phallus, and that his masculinity itself attracted and repelled, like the guns she wanted to watch but didn't want to touch. They had been married for six months or so, and by that time, presumably, they must have decided who would do what to whom. But then he thought of the homework he had done during Rachel's analysis, and though he found much of it hard to believe—who knew? His own sexual "adjustments" had never seemed like "adjustments" at all—they were just there, and hadn't needed any adjusting. And neither had Rachel's, as far as he could see. Until he read those cold translations, each of which was written in what he took to be the most inhuman and unsurprised of Germanic prose styles, he had considered himself to be a usual man. What had seemed to him to be the rather fine animal desire Rachel had at certain times to be thrust into with nearly brutal strength—a strength she gave him—turned out to be "masochism." This he interpreted to mean a desire to be hurt. But it didn't hurt. He asked her, "Doesn't that hurt?" and she said no, it felt good. If it felt good, wasn't it good? *Neither good nor bad*, the cold voices implied, *but . . .*

He read them—Freud, Jung, Krafft-Ebing—all that were recommended to him, and dutifully learned the new language. It had even been suggested that he undergo analysis too. He'd answered: "Just ask me what you want to know. I'll tell you straight off, as well as I can remember." He didn't feel quite interested enough in himself to take all that time and spend all that money. There were so many other interesting things in the world to do and to learn about.

What happened, later that night, seemed almost to have been arranged; sometimes he thought it had been, sometimes not. Shim had gone off somewhere, probably to work on the old automobile engine that ran the T-bar ski tow, and Opal, after watching the fire for a while, went back to finish up in the kitchen. He tried his novel again, and in spite of its strikingly visual caricatures Richard could not get interested in it, so he decided to go for a drive in his new car. He told Zach and Opal that he would be back at ten or so, and left. The dew was almost like mist as it fell, and along the car's black flank it had gathered in little silver beads, like the eyes of frogs. In spite of the cool night's dampness he put down the top. The car started nicely, held him firmly in the leather bucket seat, and he drove slowly down the mountain on the gravel road. When he reached the asphalt the engine was warm, the little dials informed him of the car's health, and he began to drive faster, to hold his speed on the banked corners of the Cascom River road just a little more than he would if he were simply going somewhere. He drove and thought only of driving and the subtly changeable purchase of his wheels at speed. After an hour of this intense exercise he headed back toward the mountain, his head cold and clear, his upper body actually cold, but pleasantly so because the heat of the engine warmed his legs and feet.

When he came back into the parking space he sat in the car for a moment, letting it cool at idle, then switched off the engine and lights and sat for a while, his hands on the wheel that was suddenly unresponsive, listening to the creaks and sighs of the cooling engine and the faint bubble and hiss of the radiator.

Then he heard, from the barn, the cry of a cat. Low, humming, as if it had originated as a hiss, it deepened into a hum with overtones of the higher scream that always seems to be a response to pain. Then it turned human, and stopped short. A light was on in the converted barn, and he stepped quietly to one of the small, original barn windows and looked in.

In the middle of the bare room between the triple-decker bunks, the light shining bright and harsh upon bare pine and the uncovered mattress ticking, Shim and Opal stood side by side, not quite looking at each other. Neither moved, and Richard thought immediately of a terrible fight he had once seen between a cat and a raccoon who had stood thus for whole seconds, then, as if at a signal, struck, yowled, and resumed attitudes of extreme quietness and attention again. The cry he had heard suggested a previous moment of violence.

He didn't think of going away. He watched with the same sense of discovery and privilege he would have had at observing wild animals in the woods. And some woods sense must have been operating here too, like the quietness that means invisibility to animals; he knew that the window screen would keep him from being seen.

Shim spoke, but Richard could hear only the lower ranges of sound—a hum. Shim's arm suddenly bent at the elbow and then viciously skewered the air, his cuff open so that the arm and fist shot out, shining and golden, from his green sleeve. Opal didn't move, although the fist had come past her cheek. Richard felt that if it had hit her it would have struck her dead. She circled toward the door on precise little feet, and Shim jumped like a dancer in front of her. Then they were motionless again. Shim spoke, and this time he pointed with a spasmodic arm toward one of the unmade bunks. Again they danced the taut circle, she in little steps, he in a quick leap that brought him beside her in the last possible moment before she reached the door. She didn't seem to be afraid, just watchfully cool, and she seemed cool even when he grabbed her and threw her into one of the bunks; it was still like a dance, and she bounced on the mattress, against the wall, back to the mattress all contained and prepared, as if her flight in the air had been rehearsed. Shim leaped onto her and began to tear at her with both hands, and Richard had time to think, My God! The man is raping his wife!

But it was over too soon for that. Upon the mattress there occurred the hopeless, disorganized movements of Shim's need. He pulled at her clothes, at his clothes, bared her dark thigh and tore at her, tore at himself as if in a rage of self-destruction as she quickly, efficiently covered herself up again. He pried her legs apart, but they would not stay apart for him. Then Richard heard again through the wood and glass the same cry that had brought him to the window, this time, too, full of pain, but with a high keening in it that suggested sadness and desperation. It came from Shim, who vibrated with a paroxysm entirely and hopelessly in-

42

dependent of the woman he covered. He rolled off the bunk onto the floor, and lay with his face pressed to the wood.

Opal daintily swung her legs to the floor and pulled up her skirt to rearrange herself, her legs apart, her lips wide, her eyes, behind her strangely undisturbed glasses, wide and straight upon the window, as if she meant to look straight into Richard's, and to be seen by his.

He ran swiftly to the house, ignored Zach as he made himself a quick drink, and was sitting guiltily with his book in front of the dying fire when Opal came in. She walked past him and dabbed at the fire with the brass poker, then turned and said, "Did you have a nice ride?"

He thought: My God! I should be appalled, I should be revolted, I shouldn't want to touch this with a ten-foot pole. But he looked at her, and felt himself grow. No! he thought, No! But as he answered, he wanted to sneeze, and out came the kind of ambiguous comment he must not dare make. "Very nice, but cold. Cold."

"Don't you have a heater?"

"Is Shim back yet?" he asked, trying to lie.

"He went out to the woods," she said.

"At night?"

She shrugged her straight little shoulders and bent gracefully to the fire. He felt that he had been entered, against his will, in a competition, and while he did not want to, his body, like some uncontrollable monster, got ready to try. But then, he thought, it won't do anything I don't tell it to. It never has yet.

 5

THE OCTOBER wind was cold at Murray's back and around the edges of his clothes, pleasantly cold because he was prepared; that was what his new hunting jacket had been made for. And the fire at his feet, his father sitting against the bole of a blowdown pine, these also were measures against cold and loneliness and the silence of the black mountain. His shotgun, too, where it gleamed along its barrels, breech open, might have been reassuring; but the day's hunting was over, and with the day his right to be a hunter seemed also to be over. Now, in the dark, wind-filled valleys of Cascom Mountain, better hunters moved.

He had arrived at the lodge at noon, spent an hour playing with his father's new car, and when they left for the mountain it was late, for October. They had hunted too far up the mountain, and by the time they had their limits of grouse the light had gone.

The fire was old and hot, and he thought: dark fire. Dark because it seemed so native to the dark hills, no interloper, no illuminator of the private night, but another view into the wilderness. One chunk of birch glowed clean through, and it took the shape of a bear in agony. In the wind the ashes brightened, and as if the great beast suffered its death right there before him, the brutish mouth opened and slowly closed. It seemed to him that he could feel, all at once, the weight of all the pain that had ever been inflicted, out of need or pleasure, upon the dumb beasts of the earth. It was just a little frightening, with a night full of animals at his back. He took a stick and poked the bear out of shape.

In the resulting flame his father's face stood out against the columns of the trees. The long, handsome face with its black mustache seemed native too, and translucent as the fire; in it he had also seen unpleasant things. Right now, as his father glanced at him, an expression of muted, calm, yet deep worry seemed to have lodged there—worry and a question to which the face had small hope for an answer. He knew his father well enough to know that the man was unaware of his expression, and would never ask.

"Pretty soon we'll have a moon—part of a moon—to see by," his father said, but his voice revealed his preoccupation with other things.

They were at least a mile from the house, but it was like his father to know that the moon would rise tonight and help them find their way back. It was like his father, so precise and knowledgeable about the physical world, not to feel the reasons for violent gestures. His father blamed himself for Murray's having quit school, and that was because of the possible divorce.

44

Neither of them had mentioned the separation; neither had mentioned wife or mother at all. They had spoken, with elaborate dignity, going to great lengths never to invade in the slightest each other's private thoughts, of the army. Never a word about the separation.

Now, as his father stared into the fire, Murray looked again at the spare, bony face. There was no other face he knew, in the family or among his friends, he would not fearlessly startle with a remark, then speak the truth. He might say: "Look, you ass! It's not your fault!" knowing that his father would respond correctly, with a smile, and they could then talk. He might, but he could not.

<<<<<<<<<<<<<<<<<<<<<<<<<<<<<<<<<<<<<<<<<<<<< 6

RICHARD GRIMALD felt his son's eyes upon him, and thought, The boy is being delicate with me. His son hadn't mentioned his mother. The thoughts that, uttered, might have led to the mentioning of her name were wholly avoided, as if they both were as expert as chess players at seeing a hundred impending choices. It was as if, in his son's delicate avoidance of her name, her name itself had become something of questionable taste. *Mother.* The word might so easily have sneaked into the air, but it had not.

He saw her face in the face of his son, especially here in the windy dark, the firelight evoking memories of the deep and tribal strength of her Semitic face. Rachel in Murray, her back to the mountain, her face turned to the eternal, protecting fire. He had seen her turn from him as if he were the alien and threatening mountain: he knew when the moon would rise, where the bear denned up, that the night wind fell downhill. He did not really know why she had left him, except that the psychiatrist's queer language did, sometimes, seem plausible. Plausible, but to his mind no cause for divorce. What it all amounted to was that he had too strong a character for her, they said; that he took care of everything too well; that she coped with too few problems; that, in fact, her personality was not in the process of disintegration, but of disappearance.

"Nonsense!" he had said, and at the word they (the psychiatrist and Rachel's sister, Ruth) seemed to be reassured of their prognosis. The old-fashioned word did not cut through their technicalities. He could not think in that language. Suddenly it occurred to him that they were both Jews, the doctor and the sister. Their faces hardened, became secretive, initiate; he had had to resist the temptation to think of the whole business as a plot.

Rachel, at forty, hadn't lost the highly vivid muscularity that had first struck him with such lust. Her long legs still revealed beneath the dark skin all the beautiful articulations of muscle and bone; her breasts were still high, still impossibly symmetrical, the great black dugs like cruel eyes; yet they were not cruel, just burned upon his own eyes so that even now he could see them, feel their touch upon his chest. Her face he knew, but did not see so clearly; round, black-browed, wide-mouthed, with large gray eyes—he saw more clearly the body with which she best expressed her presence.

And his child, delivered of Rachel, had from the first been physically perfect, mentally unquenchable. The birth itself was nothing to her, and her care of the infant was as calmly efficient and instinctive as that of a mare for her colt. She possessed no nervous modesty, and when the child was hungry, no matter where, let fall the side of her nursing blouse, stunning observers with the sheen of the tumid flesh, the nipple seen suddenly for what it really was, and put the avid mouth to suck.

The fire reddened; a yellow spout of flame whipped about in the wind and went out, then came on again like a lantern light. Suddenly, with blunt, deep pain, as if his flesh were tearing, he was filled with desire and love for his wife. He sat it out. He had experienced many such quick and agonizing upwellings before.

His son leaned back against a bank of pine needles, his long legs stretched out before him with the clean and awkward grace of a colt's. Murray was as big as his father, and at any time Richard might be startled by certain of the boy's gestures. It was like seeing himself from outside himself, or seeing—perhaps more often this

—Rachel if she had been a youth. In the boy, in his bones and violent grace, he and Rachel became one.

And now, in Murray, he found some of Rachel's talent for terrible and irretrievable negation. Why? Why? Nonsense! he wanted to shout. How could a part of his flesh be so reckless? All for a gesture? For revenge? For what? And was it all, as the psychiatrist so earnestly implied, his fault? No, it hadn't actually been his fault; that would have been, in itself, too rational a verdict for them. It was his father's fault, his mother's, his grandfather's— who knew? No one's fault, in the end, and so—nothing could be done. The final triumph of science: no one was responsible.

They thought him cold. He could see it. Cold, that a man could organize *his* science, all his resources, even in desperation? Cold, that he argued straight for love, that he could not, with a melting, too sympathetic face like the psychiatrist's, utter words so organized, so dialectical that they had lost all heat and meaning? Not cold: he had saved them the sight of a man berserk.

When Rachel first left him, four years ago, his logic had sufficed to bring her back. At least her father had been on his side—Saul Weitzner, that real and honest man.

And now his only son, held by a promise, waited for the contract to expire. Richard held himself together as coldly, as rationally as he could, and waited for a sign. The wind, sharp and clean, moved through the needles of the pines and fanned a spark up into the air, then tossed it until it winked out. From the corners of his eyes he saw that Murray had turned his face back to the fire.

<<<<<<<<<<<<<<<<<<<<<<<<<<<<<<<<<<<<<<<<<< 7

"It was a good day, wasn't it?" his father asked.

"Great!" Murray said, feeling that he had put too much enthusiasm into the word. His father could not be fooled. "That shot you made on your first bird," he went on, trying to amend it, or perhaps to justify it. "Tremendous! Damned if you didn't shoot right through a hemlock. You couldn't see the bird when you shot, could you?" As if a question—any smokescreen—could fool his father! He wanted to say, *God damn it! Let's cut the shit!* What did his father want to know, and how did his father want to find out? He might tell him of the dream he'd had at school, the beautiful dream about a girl, but that could not be told.

"I shot where I thought he'd gone," his father said. "Just luck."

"Calculated luck. That's the best kind." Something he'd once heard his father say. But his father was no professor eager to hear a young voice assert an old philosophy. Now he was making a bad impression; the embarrassment, the fakery. He thought: The man loves me. I am his son, and I act like a stranger.

Did his father know how much he imitated, how much he admired him? Even the legends of that old and musty war, the war of Stukas and B-17s and the Bulge, were part of it. The medals, especially the drab brownish one with all the tarnished stars on it (that was a campaign ribbon, he'd found out), were part of his feeling about the man; that he was capable of the bravest and most heroic actions ever done. Even the long-dried blood and the nostalgic knowledge—somehow nostalgic, although Murray had been six or seven years old and mostly indifferent at the time— of all the drama and shabbiness of that war, its glory that sneered at glory, the massive pain of thousands and thousands of wounded men, killed men, men afraid, merged in his heart and became as deep and moving as the sea. In the old battles his father always walked, kind and brave; in them his father's worth was struck permanent.

Though wiser, more sophisticated in the youthful world, though quick to see a certain brittleness in his father's mind, secretly he felt that his father was made of nobler material, that his guts were harder, his tendons stronger, his honor more durable than his own.

And perhaps it was for these reasons he couldn't tell his father about the dream of the girl. Anyway, he knew too well the usual diagnosis of such a dream, and maybe in a way the usual diagnosis was accurate; there had been that stiffness in his pajamas in the morning. But to him the dream was not at all funny, not even now.

He was on his trip. In the beginning he saw a huge topographical map of the United States, only this map was not really a map, but the real thing. The Rockies were rock and they were actual Rockies; the Great Lakes were blue and fresh and cold; the cities were dark, smoky, and full of inviting rooms; the plains were soft with corn and wheat; the deserts were hot to the touch. He found himself in the city, in that gray and somber place that was part of all the cities he had ever seen: City. Deep in buildings, on narrow streets where it was always night, some doors were dark and private; from some came music and laughter. He entered one of these. The girl was the beautiful blonde singer, and in the way of dreams, danger, without source or explanation, made everything tense and precious. After she sang he followed her up to her room, which was a moody high place, one side all clear glass—a huge solarium of a room, except that a full moon hung in the frosty crystal night sky.

With infinite strength and gentleness he took her upon the wide bed; they made moans, her arms about his back. They loved each other, and would be married. Their love was perfect, and in that sudden love, as is the way of dreams, not the slightest reservation could exist. Even now, although he felt it still with the power of a shock, he could only describe it in abstractions. It could not be told, for a smile would murder it, and he didn't want its power lessened. Even now, remembering it and what happened after, he began to melt.

With his arm around her, her arm around him, her hand, in that most loving and familiar way beyond modesty or fear delicate against his ribs, they walked to the great window. "God, I'm happy!" he said, and just then the moon exploded into fragments which came, hugely phosphorescent, slowly, massively turning, down. This knowledge was immediately in his possession: the earth was over. Man was over. He knew the exact meaning of it all because he then lived it. In a few seconds there would be no more history, no more hope, no more love. Then the great loudspeaker system came scratchily, booming on. The voice of the head of the Atomic Energy Commission, or perhaps that of a general, screamed hysterically into the last moments of earth and mankind: "*Hymie did it! I didn't do it! It's all Hymie's fault!*"

That was the dream, and it had left him with the deepest, most

49

immediate feelings he had ever known. There had been crises in his life—when his mother and father first separated, for instance, when he was sixteen—but never had any experience reached him in so sudden and encompassing a fashion. When he found out, in Aunt Ruth's apartment, about the first separation, there had been in operation that cold and protective ability of a child to disregard too great decisions. It worked in, though, after a while.

But the dream—even now he felt an infinite sadness for mankind, for all the sufferers of his father's war, for those who had been hurt in all wars, all fights, all little squabbles and arguments and sudden woundings everywhere back in the time that he had seen come to an end. For all artists and scholars whose work came to ashes—infinite sadness. Even for Hymie, even for the last petty voice screaming blame. Even more for love, poor love; perfect and wasted and gone.

The trip he was about to take would not, he knew, find him the dream. There would be cities without danger, cans of beer drunk alone in hotel rooms, pictures of lovely women in magazines. The women he met would not be the women he wanted; none would be the girl of the high glass room. And perhaps, even if he did find her, the world would not end.

Yet in spite of this dense, romantic urge to go, to search for fulfillment and destruction, he felt himself to be his father's man. *When this is over,* he thought, *when I get all this romance crap out of my system, why, then we'll be at ease again.*

<<<<<<<<<<<<<<<<<<<<<<<<<<<<<<<<<<<<<<<<<<< 8

In the southeast, over Brown Mountain, a certain cold light grew. Richard Grimald looked at his wrist watch and calculated the time before the moon would rise. His calculations made, he put another rotten birch log on the fire.

"A while yet," he said to his son.

The boy looked up and smiled at him; smiled, he knew, half out of amusement at this odd knowledge of the sky. Half, he hoped he knew, out of affection.

He had been a father, now, for twenty years, and he wondered when the condition would, if ever, seem his normal lot. His own father he could hardly remember. History belied, of course, his vision of Wall Street on Black Friday, the bodies of ruined men dropping down like bats to the pavement, but his father had not long survived that day. He remembered only a handsome, well-dressed man, who wore a black mustache. This man and his mother, who died a year later, always in his memory sat at a wide table: their mouths moved politely but no sound came out. He could not remember a sign of affection between the two.

His idea of what a father should be—the father he tried to make of himself—he had found mostly in what he had read. He had found it easier to rule in a benevolent way, however, than to be "whimsical and gay." He was no one's pal, certainly not his son's. Nor was Rachel's father, Saul Weitzner, anyone's pal. Strangely, this man had been to him much more than father, certainly more than father-in-law. Ugly, old, so washed and cured by life one couldn't think of him as being anything but judicious and fair, the man had become mixed up not only with Richard's idea of a father but also, by some mystical process, with his idea of a paternal, kindly God.

He and Rachel had been riding in Saul Weitzner's car on that September day in 1939 when they heard on the car's radio that Hitler had invaded Poland. Even though Saul hated Hitler and could, perhaps, have seen in the coming war Hitler's end, the idea of war had made him immediately and violently ill. He had to stop the car, and was sick in the gutter of Sixth Avenue. When Richard saw the ragged food come from the old man's mouth, it seemed to him in one twist of horror that in that moment there was more sacrilege, more blasphemous violence done a good and gentle man, and in Saul all good and gentle men, than had ever before been done in the world.

Although he had been an American citizen for twenty years, Saul had been caught on family business in Berlin in 1938. It hap-

51

pened on a night called *Reichskristall,* and before he managed to get out he had been, among other things, dragged by his heels for a block and taken into a lorry full of S.S. bravoes where, with several other people, he was robbed, stripped, nearly beaten to death, and left naked and bleeding in the middle of Krausenstrasse. He was then put into jail for indecent exposure. After six months, a period he would not ever talk about, he was released through the efforts of the United States Embassy. Richard hadn't known Saul before this time, but according to the family he did not look the same when he returned; he was hard to recognize, partly because of a crushed sinus in his forehead, partly because of certain spinal changes which had caused him to lose about two inches in height.

And it was to this man, so much a part of all men, so responsible for all men, that he gave the compliment of imitation; yet he felt few of Saul Weitzner's social obligations. He just didn't feel that way. They were all mad, the organizers, the petitioners as well as the governors. What could a sane man do? When his business let him, he came to New Hampshire. Here he knew, at least, the comforting, reasonable patterns of the seasons.

Saul had always been involved in his causes, and his causes were not always fashionable. Once he even found himself allied with the League of Navy Wives, an organization hardly liberal in Saul Weitzner's mind, because he believed, with them, that the right of the citizen to bear arms should not be infringed upon. In the presence of these ladies, before the City Council, Saul found himself, who had never fired a shot, arguing against an unenforceable gun law. In his thorough way he became a competent authority on ballistics and bullet identification.

"You should go. You know these things," he said to Richard, who could only hedge. "Yes!" Saul had shouted, "next they take your guns away from you! They would disarm only the honest man, not the criminal!"

Senator McCarthy gave Saul deep sorrow; he felt that he could do little or nothing, and yet he signed his inevitable petitions. "Why don't you do something?" he asked Richard again and again. Finally, with much shame, feeling like a bragging, ineffectual little boy, Richard said, "I won't do anything now, but if that man takes over my country I'll get my rifle and kill him."

Saul shook his head, his large, bristly, and worried head that in emotion always seemed to have a slight wettish patina over the dull skin and iron hair, then looked again, and sharply, at Richard's face. "You really mean it," he said, and added thoughtfully: "It's nice people like you we argue to protect. You would be killed."

Richard suspected, in his son, a greater depth of feeling than in himself. Perhaps Murray had inherited a strain of social responsibility from his grandfather, and the wandering he wanted to do was not the result of detachment but of connection. If it were, he did not know the language with which to ask. Idealists were so sensitive, so quick to condemn forever a slip of syntax—a violation, really, of their own dialectic, whatever it happened to be. What was the boy? He was quite sure Murray wasn't a Communist, although he suspected that any political language would be held in abeyance in front of a parent. Not a Communist, God forbid. Sex? He shivered. The boy might be a homosexual. He didn't think so, but God only knew how to tell that sort of thing. A beatnik? No, he had heard Murray say of them that they ought to have stamped upon their foreheads, *as advertised in* Life *magazine.* He might be anything—anything that he wouldn't tell a father about. And a father could not ask.

He hadn't really known the boy for such a long time, not since Murray first went off to prep school, seven years ago. When he and Rachel first separated, Murray was sixteen, and Rachel wanted to take him back to New York and send him to the High School of Music and Art. Thank God that had never come off. If anything, Murray had too many talents; everything came easily to him. He never had to *work* at anything. He was too damned bright, too damned handsome, too damned well coordinated. He'd never been gawky like most teen-agers, never had many pimples. The Dartmouth freshman football coach once told him that Murray was the best natural football player they'd seen in years. He was also a fine wingshot. Who taught him that? He looked across the dark at his son, who now stared thoughtfully into the embers, his square hands supporting his jaw. Strangers for so few reasons,

53

Richard thought: age, and because I am his father and he is my son, and what else?

Among Jews, Richard had always felt himself to be—an uninvited yet permanent feeling—more efficient: if it came to violence, he believed himself a more handsome and deadlier animal than they. His violence, of course, would be for their protection. And if he sometimes felt in them envy and resentment, he didn't mind it, for on the fringe of his practicality, his pragmatism, he gave to Jews, nearly all Jews, intuitive powers. He thought of them as intellectuals, as critics. Even those middle-class Jews who seemed to have perfected their caricature of materialistic bad taste—something about them made him pause—perhaps it was the mark of torture on them all. To himself he reserved certain virtues of the wilderness; of the world as he saw it straight beneath the civilities, the brittle, thin civilities that masked the animal in man. Though he was not pugnacious, seldom raised his voice, and never fought, any really serious argument that did not end in blood was, to him, a kind of miracle.

As much as, in a deliberately unformulated way, he admired them, he felt that they needed him more than he needed them. They usually came around to liking him. He knew, too, that if he ever tried to put his feelings about Jews in order he would end with self-disgust. Prejudice in other gentiles usually had the same effect upon him as the sight of gratuitous cruelty: he became cold, furious, and hard. Since he understood very well the stupidity of the Semitophile as well as that of the anti-Semite, he would then coldly convict himself. But these were vague thoughts, seldom acted upon, seldom anywhere near the surface of his mind.

Murray confounded him. In the presence of his son, his flesh and blood, a bright and complicated and alien mind, he found no security in his own imagined superiorities, for he could see none, feel none. His love for Murray, unlike his love for Rachel or his love for Saul, was unprotected, and made him in many ways a coward.

His son moved restlessly. With a stick Murray pierced the punky birch log, and steam hissed from the boiling wood. As he stared into the fire his young jaw tensed, teeth biting down on teeth—on nothing but the vague shape of an idea, perhaps; again Richard yearned helplessly to know.

Over Brown Mountain a white haze grew. A long cold cloud pointed east and moved toward Maine and the sea. Soon they would not be blind in the night, and could start back. The trail, the straight path he knew, would be plain enough; back in the trees, where it was still black night, the shadows and hollows would seem deeper for the moon's clear light.

<<<<<<<<<<<<<<<<<<<<<<<<<<<<<<<<<<<<<<<<<<<<<<<<<< 9

His FATHER looked toward Brown Mountain, where the light of the moon, that cold and ominous planet, began to separate the earth from the night sky. His father seemed alone. He had always thought of his father and mother as two large and complete animals—gentle, strong animals—and if he no longer believed that beneficent Providence or God or Fate, or whatever it was made the world the generous and nearly perfect place it was in his childhood, if sometimes he could no longer believe that the act of creation was one of intelligence and love—still he felt that they should be together. The symmetry of the universe, of which his family was the microcosmic symbol, must not be tampered with; else, perhaps, the moon, its orbit bent, might fall, cold and gigantic like a great honeydew, and end the world.

Ah, love, let us be true to one another! He moved his lips and caught his father's wary glance. *And we are here as on a darkling plain.* . . . Yes, he accepted that; he'd known it all the time. (And who hadn't? The instructor had been startled and a little upset when the whole freshman section agreed perfectly with the poem.) But where was his love with whom he could stand warm, fulfilled, and bravely, sadly watch the falling chunks of moon?

If he had always thought of his mother and father as strong, handsome animals, he had also found it possible and not fright-

55

ening that they slept together, and had that knowledge of each other that was dark and primitive, the flesh its own mover, thighs spread and urgent. He had felt the rhythms of their love in the night, and found himself alone.

When he was sixteen his mother came to take him out of school, and he hadn't thought to ask why. He'd been told that it was not permanent, but not by his mother. Mr. Skillings, the headmaster, had very lengthily and kindly, in the shining Georgian office, explained to him that his marks were so good he could take this necessary vacation. The Head, who had always seemed so remote, smiled at him for the first time, and it seemed to Murray that the smile was fake. He was never told why the vacation was necessary. Strange, he thought then—but only for a moment—that it was not his father who made the arrangements.

"Murray," his mother said, her beautiful moonlike face a point of embarrassment to him, and yet of love in the cold, boy-noisy halls of Dexter-Benham. She did not go with him to his room.

Though he was barely sixteen and hadn't a license yet, she let him drive the car on the country roads until they came to the outskirts of Manchester, New Hampshire. "Maybe you won't want to go back," she said hopefully. She had never given him a direct order, not even when he was a little boy. The car was his mother's old Fleetwood Cadillac, ten years old, polished until the white metal shone through at the edges of the door panels, yet slightly grimy from its last long rest in storage.

"We're going to stay with Aunt Ruth for a while," she said, "and I want her to see your latest paintings." He was still slightly annoyed that she had collected all his paintings, without his permission, from the school art room. Aunt Ruth taught at the High School of Music and Art, and for a moment he was worried. He didn't want to leave Dexter-Benham, and he knew that he would not be made to leave it against his will; knowing how susceptible he was to flattery, he was a little afraid that he might make the choice himself. He was as vain about his drawing as he was about his athletic ability, and for a giddy, unreal moment he wondered if the High School of Music and Art had a football team.

Once, on the Merritt Parkway, he asked, "Why are we going to stay at Aunt Ruth's?"

"We're just going to stay there for a while," his mother said.

" 'Way uptown like that? Why don't we go home?"

"I'll explain everything," she said.

"What's the matter with now? We've got plenty of time. It's only Hamden."

But his mother drove carefully on, and wouldn't look at him.

Aunt Ruth lived in a tall old building on Riverside Drive, and her apartment had rooms as big as barns. On the high walls of every room hung expensively framed reproductions of the *fauves*. In her own bedroom were her two originals, a Mary Cassatt pastel, and a tiny Inness in which vague figures did agricultural things in the middle of a dark night. In the place of most dramatic honor, at the end of the long, narrow living room, a full-size copy of Picasso's *Guernica*, done by one of Aunt Ruth's students, agonized. To Murray the place had always been the center of the violent and perfervid world of Art. At sixteen, however, he had begun to guess that Aunt Ruth, in spite of her intense blue eyes, blue smock, and blue-black, straight hair, her dab of paint like a caste mark somewhere on her face, her exciting odor of cobalt and turpentine, had been passed by. He had an unsure feeling about his own talent, and had also begun to suspect that youth and time might not act always in his favor. She grabbed him too eagerly; her eyes dashed from his canvas to his face too often; she marched, with little cries, too often from the easel upon which she had put his painting, back to him. Tall for a sixteen-year-old, he looked down into her collar at the chamois flesh of her chest.

"The boy has talent!" she said dramatically, "but he needs discipline!" as her round, plump face, the color of zinc, moved with excitement that seemed to him old, old and somewhat desperate. His mother, he could see, believed. He wanted to, and at that point of delicate balance when passion itself, not quite entered, seems to lie all clear and predictable ahead, he coldly foresaw that he, too, could believe.

Then the buzzer: Aunt Ruth backed reluctantly toward it, her eyes still on the canvas, and spoke to the little box. "Who?" She turned conspiratorily toward her sister and whispered, "It's *him*."

His mother said nothing, and Aunt Ruth turned back to the wall to shout, in sudden and extreme rage, "We don't want any!"

His father's voice, tiny from the little holes in the box, said clearly, "Push that God-damned button."

Murray went forward and pushed it. He listened for the opening click of the outside downstairs door, then left off ringing.

"Murray," his mother said in a voice of sorrow and lost hope. She began to cry, and he, more confused than sad, cried a little himself.

When the doorbell rang he let his father into the apartment, and the tall man, lean and vivid as a rooster, took charge. "This boy should be in school," he said, and they all felt guilty. Aunt Ruth seemed really afraid of him. He looked at Murray, at his wife, and at the canvas, in which Murray saw all at once the fakery, the imitative facility of the amateur; it was a clever New Hampshire Cézanne.

"Rachel, I want you to come home. Just for a while, anyway." Richard Grimald motioned toward *Guernica*. "We can discuss this better without that God-damned ruptured horse dying in our faces. Murray, come with me now. I want to talk to you."

Murray followed him. They never did talk. They walked downstairs, across the street, and under the West Side Drive to the river, then stopped near a husky man in nothing but a jockstrap who tried with mighty heaves, a wrecking bar and science to pry a huge stone block into the water. It was September, and cool, but the man, his strong face dedicated and stern, glistened all over the orange fuzz that covered his muscular body down to the crack of his behind.

"For Christ's sake," Richard Grimald said. "For Christ's sake!" The next day Murray went back to Dexter-Benham.

‹‹‹ 10

THE MOON had appeared, gigantic among the pines, cold and near above Brown Mountain. They buried the remains of the fire and pissed on it: steam flowed along the ground in the October wind, through the bare stalks of the October brush. Richard handed Murray his gun, and as the boy took it and carefully snapped the action to, he looked straight at Richard's face, and smiled. In the darkness of the dead fire, even in the cold and sober light of the moon, the smile seemed to Richard a warm fire itself, like a flame against a vast bank of cool snow.

As he led the way down through the black shadows, the smile was like a mote in his eyes, and superimposed itself, sentient and warm, against the false passages, the deceptive corridors of the night of trees.

‹‹ 11

MURRAY HAD taken the new sports car for a drive, leaving his old Volkswagen in the parking place, and Shim was again out in the night somewhere. Zach sat at television in the kitchen.

Richard again tried to read the novel, but in spite of its pretty dust jacket, its crisp binding, and a look about it as fresh and appetizing as a canapé, his eyes kept going to the hardwood fire, to the fireplace's weathered fieldstones set in dark mortar, to the gaunt, ancient bucks who gazed from the high walls.

Opal came in and stood in front of the fire, then said with difficulty, "I'll take that drink you offered." *Almost*, he could see in her face. She must, he realized, see in him the world of sophistication she could only read about or see in the movies or on television. She'd *almost* said it right, and saw that she hadn't. He went quickly to the kitchen to make the drinks, feigning, out of his embarrassment for her, much pleasure at the idea. She was very smart, and probably saw that, too. Knowing that he shouldn't, that he should not play with danger, he made her a stiff one, decided to take that one himself, then at the last moment, as he saw her again so strange and womanly, handed it to her. He sat a certain distance away from her on the davenport—a distance he saw her measure and file away—and watched her drink. She shuddered and took another, smaller sip, then pulled her little legs up under her so that she could sit comfortably on the wide cushion. She had prepared for this—changed to a narrow yellow Chinese dress with a modest slit that showed the incredibly smooth skin of her knee. He thought of poor Shim, but with a kind of triumph, and wondered, and wondered.

"You live in Manhattan all the time now?" she said.

"Yes. That winter we lived in Leah was sort of a vacation. My business is all in New York."

"I know. It must be quite lively there," she said, and he noticed her choice of the word, and again saw that she was smart, and a learner.

"It's dirty, and that's good for my business," he said, and smiled at her. She smiled back, her little heart-red lips just open, and took a sip of her drink. The glass looked enormous, as if she were drinking from a pitcher.

"You should have brought your wife along," she said. "Or maybe that isn't done on hunting trips."

"We're separated."

"I'm sorry."

"It happens," he said.

"But I thought you were such a happy family. Such a wonderful boy. I remember your wife, and I thought she was . . ." Opal thought for a minute, then tipped her head to the right, then to the left, as if she had a choice to make between this word and that word. "Beautiful."

"Yes, she is."

"Do you love her?" Her voice grew small at the enormity of the question.

"Yes, yes," he said, again painfully seeing Rachel.

"I don't mean to ask like that," Opal said quickly, "but I've been married for just a little while . . . Shim. I just . . . wonder about marriage. I'm thirty . . ." Her expression asked, please don't let me finish, and he said:

"Don't you know by now?" Kindly—he was full of sorrow still. "Aren't you happy?"

"I don't know," she said, and her face went darker. "I'm not a fool. I know nothing's the way a girl wants it. But how can it really be?" She took a long drink, for strength. "I didn't mean to talk like this."

They sat for a long time as the fire consumed the logs with a yellow, rather avid, smooth wrapping of flame, silently except for a little hiss, an occasional *tick* as the charred squares upon the wood contracted. From the flue came a windy rumble. The ice in their glasses was very loud. Without asking he took her glass and made two more drinks, hers this time not so strong, the reason being that he had begun to like her a little. He had, he decided: yes, and to see her—that common weakness—as a person (that old joke).

"I mean," she said when he returned, "it scares me. I'm small." She looked at him, daring him to smile. "I'm small, and I've always puffed myself up, like one of those funny little fish. Against the big world. You know, strutting. But I used to think when *he* came along . . ."

"Shim?"

"Yes, Shim. Whoever he was. What a romantic!"

"Mr. Right," he said, smiling.

"Oh, I know all that. By the time I got to be thirty and an old-maid schoolteacher, I wasn't so particular." She thought for a second, and then said, "Me? An old maid?" She couldn't believe it.

"I wouldn't believe it either," he said. "You're pretty."

She blushed darkly. "I love this," she said suddenly, and blushed harder, then moved her glass in a circle as if to take in the davenport, the braided rug, the fireplace.

He had a sudden, reckless desire to tell her that he had watched her and Shim in the barn, but fear and caution stopped him.

"Does she love you?" Opal asked, her voice small again.

"Yes, I think so. I know she did once."

"How? How did you know?"

"I don't know how. I don't know." He had never talked about it to anyone, never put any of it into words before. He turned to her. "Do you really want to know?" All right, he thought, what do I know about it?

61

"Yes," she said, and with the fear that he might not know, or that he might find that he knew what he didn't want to know, he tried to tell her. She leaned toward him eagerly.

"I know because of the way she waited for me, and needed me. No, wait: more like this! The way she looked, all soft and devastated by me. This was a long time ago. She opened up to me, everything, every way. I don't know. Don't you know how a woman loves a man?" He was very depressed, and wished he'd kept his mouth shut, his secrets to himself.

"Only in dreams," Opal said.

"Shim?"

"Sometimes I think we're a different species," she half whispered, shuddered, and took a drink. "You don't have cigarettes, do you?" She got up and went for a cigarette, came back with it lighted and tossed an empty book of matches toward the fire. It hit the andiron and bounced back to the hearth. She knelt unsteadily, tossed it into the flame, and stood up, laughing. "I almost asked you why I was telling you all this."

"Maybe because I look old and wise."

"Sometimes I wish I were a man," she said as she leaned back against the big stones. He smiled.

"I do, though," she said.

"You make a good woman, Opal," he said.

"No, I don't. I want to, but I don't. Oh, my God! I'm going to be sick!" She staggered toward him, and he jumped up and held her.

"Don't fall into the fire," he said. She laughed bitterly, gagged, and said, "Front door. Front door. Not the kitchen. Won't be seen."

He picked her up and carried her through the hall and out the seldom-used front door, into the trees. "Oh, God! I'm sorry," she said. "What a mess!" He put her on her feet and held her over as she was sick, took her glasses and put them in his pocket, then held her over so she wouldn't dirty her shoes. His hands, only because it seemed the best way to hold her, cupped her soft little breasts. As he held her light, racked body he looked up through the branches, saw a star, and felt terribly strong and for a moment unbearably tender.

62

"Isn't this stupid? Isn't this awful?" she finally said. "Oh, I hate to be sick!"

"Who doesn't?"

"That's kind," she said, still hanging over. "You're kind." She put her hands—they were cold from the shock of nausea—over his as they covered her breasts.

"What do you expect a gentleman to do?" he said.

She laughed and retched. "This is hilarious. Oh, God!" Her chest heaved, and the tearing, choking sound was muted, absorbed by the dark trees.

"You're just sick," he said. "There's nothing wrong with that. Everybody gets sick. You're not used to whisky, that's all. Can you stand up?"

She still held his hands, and after the last fit of nausea stood up and leaned back against him, her shoulders just above his belt. "I've never let myself go against a man," she said. "I mean even leaned like this, even with Shim. And look where you have your hands," she said wonderingly. He started to take them away, but she held them against her. "My God! Look what I'm doing! I feel like I'm going to melt." She threw his hands away and ran unsteadily to the house. He heard the front door close softly.

"Oh, oh," he whispered. "Oh, oh. Now what?" He was shaking. "Bad, Grimald. Bad, bad, bad." He stretched, and walked slowly toward the house. He felt pity, and he felt love for this unhappy little woman; but he felt curiosity, too, and much fear. Dammit, Rachel! he thought, you *left* me. Where are you? With your psychiatrist? Are you getting therapy? Rachel, where are you? He was jealous and excited and cautious; he felt like a kid.

In the entry hall, half hidden against the wall, there was a gleam of yellow, and his excited pulse thumped in his ears.

"You've got my glasses," she whispered, and her cool hand came out and touched his. He gave them to her and she put them on as she came out into the light. "Look," she said, "I'm sorry and I didn't mean to tell you anything or *involve* you at all." Her face was wet.

"That's all right, Opal," he said.

"No, you don't have to be kind. I've got my quills up and working again."

"Well, you've been crying here in the corner," he said. He reached to pat her, to be gentle with her, but she slipped past him and hurried up the front stairs. At the top she turned once to look down at him, her dark eyes half hidden by glints of light, then disappeared.

Richard sat in front of the fire for a while, intending to go to bed soon. He and Murray were going to take an old trail in the morning to a long-abandoned farm where there were supposed to be many partridge among the surviving apple trees. They would start early and take their lunch with them. Now, as he watched the last of the fire, getting up occasionally to poke the severed, diminishing logs together, he thought of Opal and Rachel, recognizing in himself emotions he hadn't had for many years.

First exhilaration, power: himself as a man, a stud of a man, and the idea of seducing Opal in this context seemed right, and the plurality of women highly exciting. Rachel, Opal, then another lovely, needful woman, and then another in whom he should deftly plant his seed. And after that idea came fear, the desire for neatness, predictability, lack of complication in his life. And after that, the ebbing of the wave, an odd, guilty, *moral* awareness of his long habit of faithfulness to his wife. And then sad anger at Rachel: she left *him*, didn't she? Perhaps even now—he looked at his new wrist watch—at eleven o'clock, a man he did not know, or a man he did know? arched his alien self over his, Richard Grimald's, loving, lubricious, soft-mouthed Rachel. She had a little brown mole with three silky hairs on it high up on the inside of her left thigh, and this submarine would heat it with his goatish jerks. Jealousy made him ache, and at the same time sexual excitement made the ache terrible, insupportable.

And then back to Opal: he must. Then Shim: toward Shim he felt only (at this moment) the careless pity one feels toward a cuckold. Opal: he would. He would gentle her until he could go all the way, and she would then truly melt. Rachel: again he saw her. He thought, *the beast with two backs.* But what man could have the back to cover her? No man was worthy of her after him. *No man,* God damn it! Perhaps it was irrational, but he thought of

64

her psychiatrist, Dr. Goldman. A burnished, plumply muscular man of Richard's age, with a sun-lamped face and neat little feet—could it be him? Was it anybody? Did she need, somehow—or was she told she needed—a good, well-fed, circumsized Jewish go? Her Semitic id needed reaming? Her ego rejuvenated by a ten-thousand-year-old seminal connection?

And then he thought: I do not know her because I love her. Because I love her I could not see her. She is a woman, and I am a man, not a believer of crazy myths and prejudices. Maybe Goldman is a better man. That bastard! That *dirty bastard!*

He found the pretty novel in his hands, raised it, squeezed it, and almost threw it against the fire. No. And good that he didn't, for Shim had come up behind him and stood there dripping wet and grinning.

"Rained. Caught me smack dab in the middle of the woods. Where's Murray?"

"Raining?"

"Quick's a wink, but it's over now. Where's Murray?"

"Out driving my car."

"Hell! Wanted to show him something. You want to come see? Ten-minute walk."

Shim was excited. He looked as if he were going hunting. "It's rich! Oh, it'll be rich! Come on."

He could not say no to Shim now. At first he wondered if Shim had seen him with Opal, and even though he knew Shim to be a deadly man he was not frightened at the thought. He knew how silly and rather primitive it was, but he had always found it difficult to be frightened of any man who was smaller than he, as if guns did not exist, or hadn't yet been invented. A strange thing—it had been true even in the army, when everyone was armed. But he could not say no to Shim, and some guilt, probably, was the reason for it.

It would evidently be a stalk; Shim had him put on his light leather boots and soft pants; then, before they left the house, went to his arms locker and got out a huge Very pistol—a souvenir of the war—its short barrel as big as a water pipe. "Rich!" he kept saying, "Rich!" He put two G.I. magnesium flares in his jacket pocket. "Come on!"

They went around the barn and immediately entered the woods. The ground was wet and relatively silent; the stars were out again, but the moon had gone down. Both of them instinctively crouched as they felt their way through the trees, Shim leading, both quickly feeling their way with all their exposed skin and with the soles of their feet. They stayed in the softwood, where the quiet, acid needles had smothered out much of the underbrush.

Whenever he walked with another man in the woods, Richard thought of the war, and of the constant patrols that were his most indelible memories. Not so different now, either, because he didn't know where he was going or what he would find when he got there. He guessed it had something to do with young Spooner, the game warden, but he would wait and see.

Shim stopped and whispered, "You're pretty quiet in the woods."

"So are you."

"Ought to be," Shim said, and that was true. Like most of his kind, he had grown up in the woods and in the war had joined the Tenth Mountain Division. "We got to cross some hardwoods now," Shim whispered, "so we got to be real dainty. He just might have moved. Even if he does hear us, providing we sound right, he'll think we're deer. So do like me." Shim moved off in the blackness that was just a little less dense here in the starlight below the bare hardwoods. In spite of the rain the fallen leaves were loud underfoot. Shim took several quick steps, since it was impossible to be silent, then stopped. Richard waited for a moment and then followed, keeping the rhythm of his steps broken, one following quickly upon the other, then a slight pause before he continued: a man in the woods could always be told by the steady tramp, tramp of his feet. This way they crossed the leaves and reached another band of spruce. They seemed to be circling the lower open slope in order to come upon it from the south, but Richard knew better than to trust such an idea implicitly—that was a good way to get absolutely confused and then to crash, under the tyranny of any inflexibly civilized idea, into the patternless trees. He knew he must never, never decide, but feel and look. He could just see part of the Big Dipper and so found north, but in the enforced detours made of blowdown and woods tangle and ravine the Dipper might swing like a crazy top before he glimpsed it again.

Even though they were woodsmen they were loud and clumsy,

of course, but they stalked a mere man, as insensitive as they, not a native of the dark trees. He remembered an instructor at Benning saying, "Unless you are fighting an animal, fight in the dark." There were no men who were at home with the woods and the animals of the night. When even the most skillful and knowledgeable hunter entered the woods, he was there as an intruder: noisy, clumsy, observed. This he knew, and at the same time, following Shim by Shim's delicate and deliberate sounds, he knew that man not only began in such an alien place, but prevailed in it and upon it. A man could feel its hollows and traps, hear its rhythms in his own heart, and know that though he was not the cleverest animal in the woods, where intelligence might not count as much as sense, he was the fiercest of all the animals: so fierce, so insatiably full of lust that he must even rend himself, fight for fighting, kill for killing. For a second Richard missed the stubby comfort of an M1 carbine, and the insurance of dark grenades. Then he followed Shim more closely. They crawled, now, beneath the low, dead spruce branches which tapped their heads and touched their backs like skeleton fingers. The dry needles, crushed and ruffled, slid aromatically beneath their chins.

He heard the field rather than saw it. Starlight again, but an openness of the ears more than the eyes. Shim edged close and breathed into his ear, then whispered, "You 'call that pasture pine out there? Big one, trunk wide as a man's shoulders? He's sitting against it, I *think*. Was, anyway." Shim peered into the blackness, and whispered again: "He thinks I don't think he's there, because of the rain, so he figures I might be out jacking deer. Now, he also figures I'd be coming along with a light, so he ain't really tensed up. He's looking this way, if he's there, thinking we might be deer. Only thing is, Spooner's what you call a butt fiend. He's just *got* to smoke a cigarette about every fifteen minutes, so we got to wait until he can't hold off. O.K.?"

"O.K."

"What I' d like to do," Shim whispered, "is leave him set and go take a whack at his wife. Y*ow!* would I like a hunk of that. Built? Stacked? He got her over in Texas he was there in the Air Force. Man, she just *draw*-wuls slow an' *eeea*sy. Give me a blue-steeler to look at her."

They waited for five minutes, and Shim said: "We either got

here when he just indulged, or he's moved. I think he's still there, but I'm going to move on up a ways and see if he's around the other side. You stay here and watch the fun." Very quietly now on the slippery needles, Shim moved off.

Richard propped his chin on his fists, and waited. He could not really watch, for there was not enough light to stimulate the optic nerves, but his eyes were open, unfocused, blind in the night, waiting for the flare of a match. He remembered many such vigils in the war, when the eyes, like shutterless cameras, waited to let a flash expose them. He did not think much any more about the war; he had served well enough so that the grand words upon his discharge evoked no irony. He might be caused to remember a scene, a sudden flare of action, the way a man once died before him with a sleepy sigh, the *pluck pluck pluck* of his carbine, softened by the after-silence of a gigantic blast into whose fumes and dust he had jumped to fire. But that war had been over for thirteen, fourteen years. What an unbelievably long time that was! Half as long as it had been then since the First World War, and once he had, with a sense of somber, imponderable history, killed three men on an ancient battlefield. There had been an echo then, too, of hunting, and he remembered a sign riddled with playful bullet holes:

ZONE DES BATAILLES
DANGER DE MORT!

riddled just as the stop sign on the Cascom River road had been riddled by frustrated hunters. It had been on a hill above Verdun at a place called Fort de Vaux, a battered mound, half cave, whose outlines had nearly merged with the chipped slate and the dead earth plowed and killed by artillery in that dull, stationary war when a round million men had butchered one another in one small valley above the drab little town.

It was night, cold, half freezing, and he was a first lieutenant leading a three-man patrol through scrubby, poisonous-looking brush. The Germans were supposed to have left. Rather carelessly they followed the mounded old trenchworks by flashlight; once he examined a curious object his foot dislodged from the clay. It was a jackboot, shrunken and green, and out of it protruded a rain-whitened shinbone thirty years dead. He was thirty-one years old, and he carried a carbine in order to shoot young men who might now wear jackboots of the same design.

They came out of the brush onto the fort itself, and were surprised to find a light in a small window next to a white door. After elaborate scouting to see if the light were not a trap, enfiladed and waiting to light a curious face, they looked in to see a plump man in blue, obviously French, eating bread and drinking *le gros rouge* out of a tall green bottle. He let them in at their knock and proceeded to sell them picture postcards of the place. He was the concessionaire, he told them, and congratulations, they were the first American tourists since 1939. They all had a drink out of the bottle. Richard couldn't now recall the names of the men who were with him, but they were good men, pretty good men, he remembered. One was named Smith. Smith, yes, because they looked at the wall and saw, written in pencil, the names he always would remember. Not the names of the three young Germans he soon killed, of course, but in his mind the three dead men were struck forever with names, and because of the names, humanity. Unfortunately, in this case, they were not the Jew baiters, the Jew killers he so coolly hunted for Saul—without Saul's permission:

> Willy Rosor   1942
> Hans Pietsch   1942
> Werner Schmidt   1942

—tourists from earlier days of German victory in France. The last was remarked upon by Corporal Smith: "That's kraut for my name!" Smith was later killed in a jeep accident at Metz.

They heard the shots as they examined the Spartan room of the hero, Commandant Reynard, his sagging wooden wire-covered pallet and his ramrod military photograph, everything stained by damp rot. And the concessionaire screamed, "*Bosches! Bosches!*" then added, strangely, in German, "*In der Kaserne!*" and then, "*L'infirmerie!*" He screamed all this down the dripping, white-washed hall they ran through, and they found him, his black goatee quivering with indignation, just able to point to a black square hole of a door in the wall before he vomited blood, bread, wine, a little smoke from his Gauloise *bleu,* and died in a puddle. At least he was dead when they got back to him and found little machine-pistol bullet holes like extra buttonholes in his shirt.

What they did instinctively, out of much patrolling in alleys and among walls, was to duck away from the black hole. Weak light bulbs with jiggling, nervous filaments like little nooses in them were strung up and down the corridor, and they could just read by these the diagram of the fort one of them had bought. There was no other way out of the room the Germans had so unfortunately entered, but in it were defilading walls that would make grenades doubtful. They needed something like tear gas, which of course they didn't have.

"Kommen sie hier!" Richard yelled at the hole.

"Screw you, Jack," said one of the Germans, and that was not so startling as frightening, because it told them that the Germans were veterans like themselves, and the odds changed a little. Veterans, the Germans would also be making plans. So Richard climbed up and tore out the electric wire, and they were all suddenly in that underground blackness that is thick, almost like velvet against the eyeballs. The cistern, cellar smell of the fort became denser in that darkness, and they heard the Germans searching for a way out of their room, and the drip of sweat from the stone ceiling. He knew he must act while the Germans still had hope of finding another way out, so he grabbed his two men, brought their helmets with a clank against his, and whispered directions. They remembered the diagram all right: like rats in a maze they had learned swiftly, cleverly, almost instantly, a diagram of such importance to their lives. They must go in fast, and find the right walls immediately, and *not hit a wall* with their grenades. First they placed the Germans as well as possible by the furtive scratching of their hobnails, then said, "OK?" and slipped inside. The grenades popped, hissed, bounced, and echoed stonily just before the simultaneous blast: Richard had missed his ears with fingers that had become entangled in his hanging helmet straps, and then it was, partly deafened, that his carbine made the soft *pluck pluck* sound. The Germans were nicely caught in the flashlights as he stepped toward them. All three were still standing, but one was bright red all over his face and arm, the rest of them white from the pulverized whitewash stirred into the air by the blast. *Pluck pluck pluck* went the carbine, and the three stunned, black-mouthed faces, two white, one red, began to fall. One of the soldiers—the one on the left—fired a burst of three shots (softer, even, than the sound of the carbine; for some acoustical reason Richard heard the metallic ring of the Schmeisser's bolt more clearly than the explosions themselves) and the soldier fell out from under his face. Or so it seemed: the body took the slow carbine bullets, each raising a little puff of dust on the belly, and began to keel, but the face, like a weird balloon, kept hanging there before his eyes, cheeks white, mouth black, eyes white and blind as though they were laced with cataracts. The face seemed naked as genitalia.

Finally they all ended their unjointing and thumping and were drably dead, the greenish uniforms being shaded by a slow powdering of whitewash.

> Willy Rosor
> Hans Pietsch
> Werner Schmidt

—not them, really, but three very young veterans of an old war, now dead as their fathers in a place dedicated to death. It seemed so natural there, and yet, as he moved the bodies with his boot, he was afraid—really, shudderingly afraid for a moment—that they would be painfully remembered corpses. It was like murder in a tomb, a tomb in which all the corpses were young men like himself. And he thought, *What am I doing feeling so normal and natural in a charnel house? Am I not a civilized man, a sapient, tender, feeling man? Wasn't I once? Will I ever be again?*

Now, his nose near the sweet spruce needles, his eyes open in the black, he wondered again how it should seem so normal to be stalking, and how no objections, no sense of the ridiculous came from his deepest nerves: they would have to be called, those objections, from lessons superimposed upon his alert mind. He had no time, however, for his waiting eyes now registered a faint glow from the middle of the field, and from that glow alone the field oriented itself, and he began to perceive distance. He heard from above the *phut* of the Very pistol and at the same time a screeching banshee bobcat yowl he knew to be Shim's—a scream like a woman hysterical with pain, like a girl being ripped apart. Then the white, ghastly daylight of the flare on its little parachute, and the man in the green uniform running like a rookie from the protecting tree, his face big as a buttock in the white light, staring like a perfect fool at the blinding light, his mouth a black hole. More of Shim's hysterical laughter, and the man fell in a woodchuck hole, then got up to rubberneck some more. Led thus, and thus, safety off, just to the right of the green flap of his uniform coat, he would have been a dead, dead, foolish young man. Richard's arms did not move in such a silly pantomine of aim, but again, deep in his reflexes somewhere, an old, thick satisfaction registered.

 12

AT BREAKFAST Murray heard about the successful stalking of young Spooner. Shim purred and laughed all the way through his meal, and Murray took this new, talkative Shim to be the result of marriage. He didn't know for sure, but he supposed marriage could do funny things to a man. Who would have thought Shim would marry Miss Midget? But there it was. In school that year they'd spent in Leah—he always remembered it as the year he didn't learn anything—he used to sit in Miss Midget's English class and think what an odd, unhealthy (because she was so old) but thrilling thing it would be to undress her. Gluh! Now she treated him the same, in a sort of proud, motherly way, not seeming to realize that he was grown, now, and pretty experienced. He wondered if she and Shim did it, and then realized what a childish thought that was; of course they did. The image that came to his mind, however, was not erotic at all, but rather sexless, and strange, as if the two of them simply wrestled.

"You should of seen the damn fool," Shim was saying. "He run, his gaumen big face hanging out, and fell flat. Oh, Jesus! You should of been there, Murray! Stepped in a woodchuck hole. He won't be telling that story around!" Shim laughed low and long, his reddish face creased all over. "Oooo, hoooo!" he said.

"It's funny they didn't teach him in the service not to look up at a flare," Richard said.

"Air Force," Shim explained.

Murray looked at his father and found him trying to be amused for Shim's sake. It wasn't necessary; Shim never seemed to care. Half the time he laughed alone, out of his own bitter frame of reference.

"Well, I wish I'd been there," Murray said.

"Oh, you should of been there!"

Zach, too, rocked and rumbled with pleasure. "Ah, *hep!*" he said.

Richard made some more pancakes, and for a while they ate. Shim felt so good he was going to go hunting too. It was the last day before deer season, and he said he never bothered with partridges when he hunted deer, so he might as well try them once more. After breakfast he wanted to shoot a few clay pigeons so that he wouldn't disgrace himself on the birds.

"Come on and try a few," he said to them, "I got a whole case some sport left here last year—didn't cost me nothing." He went to his arms locker and brought out a big cardboard box, his automatic shotgun, and a hand trap. "You ever throw these things?" he said to Murray, and handed him the little wooden-handled trap.

"Once," Murray said. "I guess I can throw some for you." Shim laughed, and seemed very pleased with him. On the evening he had come Opal said that Shim had been following his "progress in football" and that Shim admired him. He had never seen Shim quite so friendly.

But he didn't really care if Shim were friendly or not. Once, when he was younger, he cared very much—when Shim's hunting, skiing and woodsmanship were so admirable to a boy. Now he was impatient, and wanted to be somewhere else, not up in the woods on a New Hampshire mountain, but into the stream of things— down on the plains, deep in the cities where adventures were happening, and he wanted to go there while there was still time. Even

73

now, as they walked toward the little field behind the barn, he wished himself there, in the city of the high glass room, and the golden girl, and the dangerous moon.

"Screw down that there wingnut," Shim said. "Gives the right tension. Not too tight or you'll break the bird, not too loose or it'll just fall off the trap."

Murray slipped one of the fragile little discs into the trap. Shim loaded his gun, got set, and said, "Pull!" Murray swung the trap out on a stiff wrist and the little disc, black with a yellow center, spun out into the air and rose toward the trees. Shim fired, and the disc was a black fuzz of powder in the air.

"Dead on, by God!" Shim said.

"Good shot," Richard said.

"Couple more like that and I'll know I ain't too rusty."

Murray loaded the trap again, and when Shim was ready threw the clay bird lower and faster this time, so that it began to rise farther out, the way a jumpy partridge might flush ahead of a man. Shim fired three times, but the bird sailed on and on, unperturbed, almost insolent, entered the woods, and disappeared. They heard it smash against a tree.

"God damn it! Toss me another!" Shim stuffed more shells into his magazine.

"Where do you want it?" Murray said, sensing that he had made a mistake to ask.

"What!"

"High, low, where?"

"Any goddam place!"

Shim shot twice before the undamaged bird sailed into the trees.

"Must of run right through the pattern. I was dead on, both times." No one could say anything to that. Shim broke the next bird, and felt a little better. "You try it," he said to Murray.

Murray loaded one barrel of the over-and-under, and when Shim threw the bird he easily found it over his barrel, and fired. The bird turned to black dust. He got the next three, and on the fourth Shim threw so hard the bird came off the trap in two flopping halves. Before they hit the ground Murray chose the largest half and powdered it.

"That's shooting," his father said quietly. Murray looked up,

74

as if his father had meant it as a hint, and watched Shim carefully. He was aware at once of the tension in Shim's face: a redder, darker line crossed his eyes like a slash of paint, and the little yellow irises were bright in its dark shadow.

"I think I'd rather shoot these than live birds," Murray said.

"You *would?*" Shim was truly incredulous. Perhaps he understood that it had been a pacifying remark; actually Murray would rather have been doing something else entirely. "What I can't understand," Shim said, "is why, since you do everything so well, you ain't a hunter."

"I guess I don't have the blood lust."

Shim laughed. "Your old man's got it. What happened to you?" He looked slyly at Richard, then said seriously: "You know why I can't hit them damn clay pigeons? They don't give me no blood lust." He laughed harder.

"It looked as though you lusted after that first one you missed," Murray said, carefully smiling.

Shim may have hesitated for a second, but then he chose to grin, and said: "They do sort of take on a personality, don't they? The little black bastards. Here, throw me one more! Urrrr," he growled as he got ready. He hit the bird before it had gone ten feet from the trap. "See? I got to get my blood hot first."

"Wait till tomorrow morning," Richard said.

"Oh, the *deer*," Shim said, rubbing his hand delicately over his orange brush of hair. "Murray, how do you feel about the deer?"

"I'd like to get one, I guess."

"You'd *like* to get one you *guess!* Murray, you're a strange one, you are. You're a rang-dang weirdball sometimes."

Murray's father looked at him too, but he couldn't tell what kind of speculation or judgment lay there.

Shim threw some more clay pigeons, and his father broke three out of four. "Wait'll we see some hot-blooded birds," Shim said. "Course, if we do see a deer we can't shoot—even if it's close enough for birdshot." Shim laughed meaningfully, then added seriously: "If young Spooner warn't so hot after me, I'd try for a little camp meat. Always carry a slug and a double-ought buckshot in my belt anyway."

When they brought the trap and the clay pigeons back to the

house, Opal was standing at the sink on her little set of steps, doing their dishes. "I hope you get your limits," she said. Murray noticed that she did not look straight at his father, and in her not quite looking there was excitement of some kind. It gave him a little shiver, and he tried to decide just what kind of shiver it was, but he could not choose between fear—not fear for his father's possible entanglement with her (what a strange thing that would be!) so much as a fear that life might find *him* up here in the mountains where it could not be as romantic as he wanted it to be—and another choice, even stranger, but stronger; he saw Opal as a girl. For just a second she was no longer ten years older than he, and had never been his teacher. He was aware of her silky legs, and of possibility—slight, tiny, ridiculous possibility. Ridiculous, all right. Then they went hunting, and he almost forgot about it.

When, at noon, separated from the others by at least a half-mile of trees, he shot a partridge, he half remembered it again. The vividness of death, even in the bird, again suggested possibilities. Here was death, and it was like taking off his clothes, like opening the wrong door and being ready, even though embarrassed, to see the naked woman standing inside; shock, response; not quite shock, too much response. He sat against a maple tree and looked at the gawky-necked dead bird. He began to think of Opal again, and thought, *Ridiculous!* Then, because the bird was still warm in his hand and yet very still, except for the skinny neck which rolled meaninglessly over his fingers, he went straight from the possibilities of dreamy sex, straight, as he usually did—as he usually tried not to do—to reality and fright, as if he had within him a horrid ability to perceive morning-after—a previewer. And this unwelcome memory had to do with life and its little visitor, wee death, too. But he was younger then. . . .

It was in the spring of his freshman year, when he had just become eighteen. His Aunt Mae called him from New York.

"Murray," she said, and her voice, usually a rather mellow, effected alto, this time was touched by a hysteria that came clearly all that way, through all those circuits. He thought first of tragedy, and it was the thought of his father that came down upon his head and all at once crushed him, made his neck bones ache. He pulled the telephone booth door closed against the ringing of the dormitory hall, and asked, with dread in his voice, what was the matter?

"Oh, Murray, I'm sorry I scared you! Nobody's dead. But we need you."

"Me?" He'd just come from a poker game—penny ante, and he was triumphantly twenty-one cents ahead. "Me?" He had never before been needed for anything, and the penny-ante game, he thought suddenly, might even be considered the measure of his serious life.

"Murray, I can't tell you over the phone. But it has to do with Sophie, and we've thought it all out, and we do need you to help us. Can you come, and tell nobody? Do you need money? Not even your father or Rachel? Will you?"

No adult relative had ever pleaded with him, had ever needed him. He could not refuse, but he might simply turn inadequate: the child's choice still powerfully occurred to him, with some shame. Aunt Mae's tone of voice had made him pretty sure he knew what was wrong with his cousin Sophie, who was just a kid—fourteen or fifteen—but how could he help that? For a horrible, trapped moment, he wondered if the family were planning to trap him into child marriage. With his first cousin?

"What's the matter? What can I do?"

"I can't tell you now, Murray." He had never heard more love, more respect directed toward him. "You come and we'll pay for your trip, and then you can make up your mind—we won't try to make it up for you, Murray. Please, Murray."

He liked his Aunt Mae. Her husband he disliked with such nervous intensity that he could hardly eat anything in Aunt Mae's house. He hadn't seen any of them for two years, and then Sophie was a plain, plump little girl in the eighth grade. But he liked Aunt Mae, and she began to cry into the phone—unlike her to be so unstable—and suddenly he felt very strong and wise.

"Aunt Mae. Mae!" he said sharply, and impressed by this new voice of his, also aware of its staginess, he said, "Now don't you worry. I'll be there tomorrow morning. I'll get the night train to Boston, and I'll fly from there. I've got enough money. Just don't you worry, Aunt Mae. Just take it easy and I'll be there." He could not see her even in his most recent memory, and the reason was that she had always been firmly, justly adult: he recognized in her voice another person, a stranger who was his flesh and blood, full of the need for comfort.

"Oh, Murray! I told them. I told them you were a peach, Murray, even if I haven't seen you for a year and ten months! You were always my boy, Murray. God bless you!"

"Tomorrow morning."

"All right, Murray. God bless. God bless."

He didn't go back to the poker game to cash in his twenty-one cents' worth of chips, but went straight back to his room. Shelton, wise in this emergency, with a grave face that showed to Murray his understanding and delight, said he would tell the professors that it was so sudden and such an emergency that Murray could have had no time to ask for leave from his classes. Also two exams. He did not ask Murray for details; that would have been beneath the fine gravity of the moment.

Murray packed a small bag, and in the alternate moods of fear and a benevolent, proud feeling of real experience, took a taxi to White River Junction, a train to Boston (it seemed to take very little time), and another taxi to the airport. With some superstition he calculated his chances—somehow they were worse because of the nature of his journey—for crashing. He couldn't stop, of course, and then worsened his chances again by buying $10,000 worth of life insurance from a coin machine and making Sophie Gelb beneficiary. That would help, if he could not.

How serious, how wise he felt as the plane labored up from Boston and circled like a giant silver cross! This, he felt, was life; mixed, risky, breath-stealing life. He was honored by it—a rescuer. But then came the small thought that held him quickly, again, in its smallness like a nest holding an unfledged bird: what did they want him to do? Could he make himself do it? He had diarrhea, and had to go to the rear of the plane, to the hissing little cubicle, and spray his childish, babified nervous mess out into the cold, the iron cold, real night.

He got out of the taxi in front of Orson Gelb's house in Floral Park, Long Island. The modern little house was solidly made of brick, just like the house next door, and just like the house next door to that, and in the suburban, secondhand dawn that was all gray, in which even the dew was dirty on wood, cement, brick,

asphalt, the number of the house, silver on a little black plaque—
1488—was the only indication he could trust that this was Orson
Gelb's house. And because of such deliberate duplication of everything—even the picture window swathed in its gauze glaucoma
around the oversized table lamp was the same up and down both
sides of the street—it seemed to him that trouble and possible
tragedy were waiting for him just beyond the front door of any
house he chose, or that whatever was wrong with Sophie was number 1488 in the canon of trouble.

Sleepy gray dawn, tired grass in the little front yard, the short
driveway to the carport just two cement strips so that some more of
the precious, soiled green could exist in the middle; but everything
now, in April, was just a shade or two removed from the dirt of
winter. His eyes were tired from his trip, during which they had
only closed to blink, and they felt as if they, too, were covered by
dreck; his eyeballs itched. The dew was drying on the trunk of his
uncle's new Chrysler—on the taillights and on the huge, dirty fins
that nearly touched the side columns of the carport.

The knocker was an aluminum anchor, not really meant to be
used. He pushed the square plastic button of the doorbell and
heard, deep inside the house that seemed somehow thick, thick-
walled, thick with sleep, paint, panelings and joinings, the heavy,
soft chimes. Inside there were wall-to-wall carpets to absorb that
sound, and solid doors to stop that sound and all the necessary
sounds of arguments and toilets and bed squeaks. He pushed the
button again, and the chimes, deep inside in the still, heavy air,
rang slowly.

Waiting, he looked at the sky. Light grew, but though there were
no obvious clouds, he could not tell east. The sky lightened as if a
bank of fluorescent lamps straight overhead came slowly on—as
if the whole suburb had been set up on the floor of a huge, dirty
loft. One of the plane trees that had been planted up and down the
narrow street had died, in spite of the wire cage that protected its
frail trunk. It was spring for all the rest, even if they did remind
him of animals in a zoo—the kinds of animals who must be protected by cages from the people, instead of the other way around.
But they were the only real indication of spring. The trunks of the
trees were soiled like the calves of children who have played in

79

dust—in rings and little islands—but the little leaves were quite young, and still bright.

The door opened, and a big girl in bright green pajamas stood smiling at him. Upon the tall green creature's neck was Sophie's head, no different than it had been upon the little eighth grader he remembered; the face was seriously open, incredibly open, as if it could never hold a secret. The face was plain, with a wide mouth, a narrow forehead below black hair thick as wrapped velvet. Sophie just smiled. "It *is* Murray," she finally said. Her eyes were hazel, and the whites of them were too large, so that the irises seemed unsteady, and moved as she spoke, smiled, and examined his face. They moved too much, with what seemed to be too much freedom, too much affection.

"Come in, cousin," she said, and stepped back. He felt the warmth of her sleep as he passed, and the smell of her, even the sight of the odd little wrinkles in the gaudy silk of her pajamas, reminded him of his own bed and his own innocent sleep.

When he turned to look at her again, in the living room among the solid, crowded furniture, she said wryly, "I've grown, haven't I?"

He smiled. He wanted to say something nice—that she was pretty, for instance—but she would not take that. She looked like a fifteen-year-old who was just a little too tall for her age, a plain girl who would never be very much else until she became ugly, whose spareness and cleanness were now attractive as all young are attractive—even young heifers—but whose bones predict surplus.

"How are you, cousin?" she said.

"Fine, Sophie. How are you?"

"Don't you know?" She was amazed.

"Not really," he said. "I just had to guess."

Her pajamas were such a primary, blatant shade of green they could only have been the property of a Chinese whore or a little girl, and he was now not sure. She seemed so innocent, she smelled so sweetly of sleep; even the tiny dark hairs upon her awkward, childish wrists were virginal.

"Well, I'm pregnant, that's what."

"Oh, hell," he said, consciously imitating her bravado.

"And don't ask me how it happened. Honest to God, cousin,

the next person asks me how it happened, I'm going to explain the whole process."

"Little Sophie," he said admiringly, and she saw, with those ever-moving big eyes, his admiration. "Where's Aunt Mae?"

"Mom and Dad? They took Nembutal. After last night's screaming session, you know. Matinee in the afternoon, continuous performance in the evening. You hungry?"

He nodded, and followed her into the kitchen. "How do you feel?" she asked him, then turned serious as she looked at him. "Grown up, or not?"

"Right now?" he asked.

"Now, and then, too, Murray." She smiled, and he saw a woman's wry twist upon her smooth child's lips. "You know what? We're both teen-agers, cousin. I figured that out."

"I don't feel any older than you, Sophie," he said, and knew, out of his own fear, that soon she would have to stop being so old. She began to make scrambled eggs, and he sat at the chrome-legged table and watched her. All the kitchen fixtures were of mauve enamel, and her green pajamas, moving against the mauve, hurt his eyes. A child, she was, with another child inside. Her hips were still too narrow—or at least seemed so on her gawky body—and her breasts, though possibly large for her age, were nothing to what they would be later. One didn't see—or mean to see—such things as breasts and broadness upon her yet; her body's attributes were all in length, and slimness, in her sharp shoulders and narrow thighs. She would look more natural running and jumping. And yet something grew in her womb. Here she was, in her ridiculous whore's pajamas, an immature girl, and he found it hard to imagine the "process" she now knew all about. She did not yet seem to have the glands for it, and her flesh did not suggest at all ripeness, or oil, or the dark hollows of sex.

They ate their scrambled eggs, and it was as if they were playing house, he the father and she the mother. She didn't think to make coffee; they drank big glasses of milk.

"I don't have morning sickness," she said. "I looked it all up. Thank God for small favors, at least. That's what Mom says. I wouldn't know it, really, if it wasn't for the other thing. And the frog test. Boy, did I flunk that one."

"You don't seem too shook up about it," he said.

81

"That's what they all say. What do they want? So I should scream? You couldn't hear me over Dad, anyway. He's impossible."

He shivered.

"Amen," she said. "You'd think *he* was the one, really." She went to the cupboard and got a cigarette. "They don't seem to mind these any more. Again thank God for small favors." She lit the cigarette and expertly inhaled. "The loose woman has her vices."

Her thick black hair was bound into a ponytail, and as she swung her head to clear away the smoke, the big brush, too large for her head, whisked through the air. "You want a Kent?" she asked.

"I'm in training," he said.

"I'm so glad you came, Murray!" She did not startle him; he had seen himself in her too clearly.

"Of course I came, kid," he said.

"I mean I always liked you, cousin, even when I was a kid—loved you—you know, like the family insists until you get to believe you even love Aunt Ruth. But I mean I've wanted to *talk* about it. They made me swear all over the place not to tell any of my friends about it, Murray, and I was about to *flip*. I mean it. You've just got to have some other human being to talk to!"

"Yes, I know," he said, and filled, suddenly, with love—or as suddenly emptied of fear—he reached for her hand, and took it, and they were both silent as they looked for a long time at the two hands joined firmly upon the mauve formica.

Everything was made for silence in that house—everything except Orson Gelb, whose private image of a man of the house he screamed and bitched about and tried out all his life. He meant to be bluff, hearty; it came out querulous, precarious. He meant to be good-natured, to imply, through his bluntness, that it was all a huge joke; it came out not merely loud, but dangerous. He now appeared in the kitchen, after having rammed the swinging door with his hip, in striped shorts and shaving lather. "Huh! The college boy!" he shouted, then went back through the house and up the stairs yelling, "Mae! Wake the hell up! The college boy is here!" His deep voice seemed a falsetto, and had a falsetto's lack of expression. To Murray his Uncle Orson had always seemed mad. As a child the man had frightened him; now, because his uncle had always seemed on the edge of purely physical violence, and Murray was bigger and stronger, it simply made him nervous.

Sophie looked at him commiseratingly and said, "I thought of saying that Daddy is really a dear, underneath, but Daddy is really a drip."

"I've just never quite got used to him," Murray said.

"So who has? God! I'm glad you came."

Now Aunt Mae appeared in the swinging door. She was as tall as Murray's mother, but had a plainer, more disorganized face. She'd worked on it some already that morning, but it was softer in spots where her sister Rachel's face was firm and burnished. She had the same large gray eyes, but they seemed unanchored, and her nose was her father's; something about the hinge of her jaw was Saul Weitzner's, too, and her face must always have been a foil to her beautiful sister's, as if some principle of symmetry, the subtle organization of beauty, were just plain missing. Else, Murray could not help thinking, she wouldn't have settled for Orson, that shlemiel in the skin of a shlemozzle.

She'd been standing there looking grateful, tearful, pumping up the glorious, deedful moment: Murray had come! "Murray, you came!" she said dramatically.

"Said I would," he could only mumble. He felt like making that hand signal which is used in construction work: *Slow it down, now, slower, easy.*

"Sophie, you didn't make coffee for Murray! Murray, did you have enough to eat? Here!" She tightened the belt of her housecoat and rushed to the electric coffeepot, then came over to him. "I'll bet you didn't get any sleep at all, poor boy. Now, did you?" A warm, fluttery hand against his cheek.

"I'm not sleepy," he said.

"You're nervous, darling. You don't know why we dragged you away from school."

"Not really. Sophie and I talked some."

Mae shut her eyes and pretended to faint—pretended to catch hold of the table. "Oh, isn't it a mess?"

Sophie looked on, seeming to be quite alert and calm. Mae then insisted that he talk about college, looking sharply at Sophie now and then, as if to say, "See? See what Murray does?" and he knew that part, at least, of his duties was to make Sophie want to go to college. She was only a sophomore in high school. He knew he'd better wait until they were alone before he brought that up.

Orson slammed something in the living room, by way of announcing himself, and then charged through the swinging door, his eyes averted from Murray, his pot now disguised by the pleats of his suit pants. Eventually, Murray decided, Orson Gelb would turn into a smooth white egg, like Humpty Dumpty. He shaved so closely and carefully his skin looked burned out, like bone ash, and even his forehead was white and fat. And yet he was not roly-poly; he looked somewhat manufactured, like a vegetable grown under optimum soil conditions, but in artificial light.

"I suppose he knows all the dirt!" Orson said in his gruff, toneless shout. Mae got him his breakfast—orange juice, toast, tea and Alpha-Bits, and as he spooned up the little letters he seemed to be carefully reading them. He never once looked Murray in the eye, or spoke to him directly. "I don't know," he said. "All I do is earn the money! Why the hell should I know what's going on? Jesus Christ! All I do is pay the rent around here!" He drank his glass of warm tea and then struck the glass, deliberately, upon the table as he put it down. He hurried into the living room, and they heard him shout, "Where the hell are my cigars? Somebody stole my cigars!" Mae went in to find them. "Had a five-pack!"

Sophie shrugged her shoulders and pretended to faint, as her mother had, then grimaced in the ugly, contorted way young girls do. More shouts from the other parts of the house: "Has she started smoking cigars, yet?"

Later Murray would remember that Orson really meant to be funny; later, though, was always too late.

Orson had to be off to work—"to buy the goddam chow around here." He made a good living, surprisingly enough, selling life insurance to gentiles. His Chrysler fed past the kitchen door, yard by yard of it, slowly. He was a careful driver.

Aunt Mae said to Sophie, "Go take a bath, with plenty of hot water."

"It won't work," Sophie said. "You want me to fall downstairs?"

"I want to talk to Murray, dear. That's all."

"Friday they took me riding, out to King's Point. What a kick!

Daddy fell off his horse three times, *walking!* You should have seen him, cousin. He'd start to list, like a boat, and then pretty soon he'd have both hands around the horse's neck, and then he'd be hanging right down between the horse's front legs, holding on like mad!" Sophie laughed, with some hysteria; they both watched her anxiously, but she got over it. "OK, OK, I'm going. Me and my loathsome disease."

Mae waited until they heard the bath water start. Then the door to the bathroom closed, and in that sound-proof house they couldn't hear the splashing. A pipe in the kitchen wall hummed, but that was all.

"Your grandfather knows, Murray." Mae slowly stirred her coffee, testing with her spoon for the saccharine tablets. "Nobody else knows. I know it sounds bad to ask you not to tell Rachel or your father, but I ask you, Murray."

"I won't tell. Don't worry."

"I know you won't! You're one of the best people I know!" Tears grew in the corners of her eyes, and another highlight appeared in each iris. "If only all boys were like you, Murray!"

"Take it easy, Aunt Mae. Take it easy. I'm no angel." To put it mildly, he thought, remembering his careless cruelty to girls—the common, careless egotism of boys, and the girls who had to wait and wait and couldn't ever do anything about it.

"*Well,*" Mae said, drawing in her breath with the word, "I just want to tell you that your grandfather agrees. We've got to have an *abortion.*" She could hardly say the word, and it worked its way out of her mouth shudderingly, as if the syllables themselves were little abortions. "The reasons are . . ." Here she began to list upon her long, nervous fingers. "Sophie simply can't marry at fifteen, and she couldn't marry this boy anyway. His name, God strike me dead, is Patrick Flaherty, and he's a Roman Catholic." She spoke the two words carefully, he knew, in order to distinguish between that and Protestant, which Murray vaguely was. "But aside from that he'll never amount to anything. Sophie even says that. She doesn't love him. Says she doesn't know why she let him—she just *melted,* she says. Oh, *God!*" Here Mae ran out of fingers and breath.

"Anyway. Anyway," Mae said, "if she has to stay out of school she'll end up a year behind, and that's bad, and then there'll be a baby. A baby . . ." She pronounced it, with horror and tenderness, "bay-bee," and ran right out of breath again.

"So, Oh, *God!* I hate to ask you, and you don't have to do it, and nobody will blame you, but we've tried to find a doctor who'll do it. It's simple, very simple, really. Anyway, things are tight right now. They're 'cracking down' on that sort of thing, and unless both parties appear nobody will touch it. It's got to look just right, or they get suspicious. The boy doesn't know, and we don't want him to know, or his family to know, you see? So we want you, Murray, to—oh!—pretend it was you. Now, we've got these names —Saul got them—your grandfather got them, somehow. And we just want you to take Sophie to these doctors. . . ." She shuddered so that she spilled her coffee.

And he had a matching *frisson*—a beaut. For a moment he felt like running; remembered exactly where he'd left his overnight bag, and had it all planned how he'd run into the living room, grab it by its familiar, comforting plastic handle and run, run right out and down the street, the identical blind picture windows ticking off his speed like telephone poles along a road.

And then he thought of poetic justice, and how lucky he'd always been, especially with Gretchen, who was so irregular. Well, it had finally got him, by proxy. He smiled. Mae, who couldn't interpret the smile, looked as though she'd been stabbed.

"Murray?" she quavered.

"Of course I'll do it," he said.

"Don't if you hate it!"

"I hate it, Mae," he said, and he cursed the tears that threatened his eyes—tears of appreciation of his nobility. "But I love you and Sophie, so that cancels it out."

"Oh, Murray!" And this time she let go altogether, and sobbed so hard it sounded as if she retched.

Sophie came downstairs clean and young-looking. Every time Murray looked at her he got a chill for himself and, for her, a sympathy pain in his crotch. She was now very meek, subdued, and when his grandfather came she sat mildly by the old man's side.

Saul Weitzner was, even more than his father, to Murray a kind of prow that steadily and capably thrust into the outside world—

that brutal, noisy place outside school and family. He was old, but never infirm. He was solidly the head of his family. He either knew everything or knew where to find it out, and Murray had never seen a man treat him with disrespect.

He was the color of beaten iron, and lumpy, as if he had at some time in the past been clubbed and mashed and bludgeoned for months at a time. What was left was ugly, but purified; there seemed to be no room left in Saul for impatience, for meanness, for cruelty, for any of the small weaknesses of ordinary people. Anger, maybe; Murray had never seen him pushed by anyone, but there did seem to be a place in his grandfather's soul for gigantic wrath. He was a strong man, with a short, wide back, and whether he said so or not—for he was mild, usually—he judged sternly. Murray knew, too, how important Saul's opinions were to his father, even though his father had never really let himself become too much a part of the Weitzners. And this, he felt, was not because they were Jews, and thus strange, but because his father had no family (except a cousin in the import-export business in Buenos Aires whom they never saw) and did not know how, or did not want, maybe, to know how to become part of a family. Murray had been told, too, that the only reservation Saul had made when his daughter Rachel wanted to marry a gentile was that after the civil ceremony they be married by a progressive rabbi.

One time, when he was in grammar school, Murray saw on television some old movies of the liberation by the British of a concentration camp—an extermination camp—and he went through streets full of monsters, butchers, torturers waiting to catch the poor skinny big-eyed Jews—went to Saul and told him, bawling, that he wanted to be a Jew. Saul told him to be a man, like his father, and to be whatever his father wanted him to be. Murray said he wanted revenge; he was thirteen years old and he understood that if he were a Jew he would already be a man, and could fight. Saul told him, with pride, and also with a kind of perplexity that seemed akin to sadness, that in the Second World War his father had killed men enough for those crimes. "Your father is a warrior," he said, and coming from Saul Weitzner it sounded like a great, echoing judgment out of the Old Testament. On the way home Murray looked the people coolly in the eyes, but it was some time before he could again look calmly upon strangers and think of them as possible friends.

Saul now took Sophie's narrow hand in his wide, grayish, salt-and-pepper one as he spoke: "Our little girl has been foolish. *Stupid!*" he added sympathetically, with a deliberately startled expression. Sophie giggled, and without knowing why Murray laughed too. He remembered that in spite of his grandfather's wise leadership, he himself had to do something very unpleasant. And then, just as quickly, he was ashamed, because Sophie faced something a hundred times worse, and she was just a girl.

Saul had just looked in, he said, and would come back later, for dinner, and they would get all the details straightened out. They all seemed to have decided that night was the time for shady doings, and that after dinner Murray and Sophie would go see the doctors. They would all go in the car to Saul's apartment, and Murray and Sophie would take a taxi from there; the doctors were in Manhattan, and neither was very far from Central Park West. To give them strength, they would have steak for dinner, Mae decided.

"Your father was looking good this morning, Murray," Saul said. "In the tiptop of health. Someday I will tell him what a good boy. You don't have any idea how much this is to Mae and Sophie— and Orson. Mae told how we could trust you and depend on you. I believe it."

"I always said so!" Mae rushed over to Murray and put her arms around his shoulders, and for a second he had trouble keeping his balance. He felt surrounded, suffocated, and he thought with nostalgia of his dormitory room, with its dented furniture and its hard, impersonal bed.

When Saul had left, Mae became anxious that Murray have enough sleep. He was in training, all right, as far as she was concerned, and she sent him upstairs to take a bath and then to lie down in the guest room. He found that he could, at least in the bathtub, forget for moments at a time what he had to do. But then it would come back, and he was sure that the abortion part of it was not the thing that bothered him the most. It was the asking part, and even the money they would pay the doctor did not make it any less an act of begging. He had no reservations about the abortion; that was a simple operation and had no bad connotations to him, nor did his having to pretend that he had made a girl pregnant; that was life, and perfectly normal. But he would have to sneak and ask, and he was horrified by that. He could never sell, and could never ask for things which might be given only grudgingly. He had to have a clear and perfect right. If they all thought he was a good friend to them because of *what* he had to ask, rather than the asking itself, then he was a hypocrite. That was too bad, but he would suffer enough just the same.

They would go to the two doctors' offices—providing they couldn't get the first one to do it—without the imperative of sickness, without the proof of disease or the broken bones that give one a clear right to ask for cure. He rubbed his hand over the unfamiliar bedspread's little cotton tufts, and they felt like nipples, where he shouldn't have had his hand; he felt the way he did just after he had first successfully masturbated; a feeling of excruciating shock, as if a current of electricity were constantly running through his body. That, and the horrid but fascinating thrill of possibility. That, and the desire to run back to comforting childhood. In part it was the penalty for growing up, and would be there no matter how wonderful were the rewards.

Later, when Sophie came in to find him lying there in his shorts, he didn't want to see her. He wanted to hide himself, but was embarrassed to cover himself up with the bedspread. He couldn't tell her to go away. She brought her portable phonograph with her, and made him listen to a singer named Herky Fleming, who was fifteen years old, and whom she was mad about.

She handled the record carefully, her face dedicated; she really wanted him to like it too. The music, when it started, seemed familiar enough. First came the coarse rock 'n' roll beat, brutal and simple, and the blatting saxophone in mindless, repeated bursts as crude and unmusical as a belch. Sophie moved to this rhythm, her feet tapping, with an expression on her face that was nothing like her—it was an imitation of an imitation of joy; if it had been wholehearted it might have been more believable, but alone, in Murray's doubting presence, she was subdued, and her little gestures were tentative, even faint. Fingers and thumbs touched, but made no noise; eyes stared back up into the head in imitation of unconsciousness, but remained open, as if they were looking at their own brows. After a while she looked at him questioningly and he shrugged.

"Wait—wait—wait," she said rhythmically, and then, knowing the record by heart, she said, *"Now!"* and suddenly the rock 'n' roll stopped, and one thin, high note of an organ, so clear and sustained it brought to mind the long nave of a Gothic cathedral, gradually increased in volume, as if the listener approached the altar. Far in the distance, hushed at first by the holy atmosphere of the place, came sweet, virginal strings—violins, cellos, all clear and pure, bound together by a flute that did a dainty obbligato. Only then he realized that the flute and the violins were restating the rock 'n' roll theme. More instruments were added, and the organ and delicate chimes indicated high holiness and grandeur. Far away a chorus of what must have been vestal virgins sang alleluia, as faint and inevitable as wind, and they faded as the voice of a boy—a voice that was at the same time weirdly immature and yet as smooth and experienced as an elderly *castrato*'s, sweetly innocent and yet perverted, half sang, half reverently whispered the words:

"My girl has changed from cotton to silk,
    And now she melts my heart.
    The *adults* do not understand
    She's taken a new part.

"Though just teenage, she has grown up
    Into a lovely thing:
    No matter what they say I will
    Give her a golden ring.

"When we go to our wedding hop,
    With all the Dee Jays there,
    Then our folks will understand
    We make a perfect pair."

Then the chorus of virgins began to rise again, in litany, repeating the words, and subtly the wedding march from *Lohengrin* appeared, faded, turned minor, and was sustained and finally assimilated by an insistent beat, as if the vestal virgins had begun to stomp. The belch of the saxophone was then appropriate, and came triumphantly down the aisle as the original high A-flat of the organ rose, not to compete, but to join in. Higher and higher the volume and the excitement rose, until the cathedral rocked, and the priests blew hysterical saxophones and fell to their backs to blow crazy, and the choir had bongos. Baal was in the church, gyrating, grinding, ecstatic—and then it was over except for the thin high, holy note which suggested eternity and which faded imperceptibly in the distance, through the years, diminishing until the faint hiss of the needle on the record was all that could be heard.

With the quiet, subdued air of an undertaker adjusting a necessary crank, Sophie removed the needle; then, still trancelike, she hummed the melody, and swayed. Her dungarees were belted tightly, painfully around the waist, and her boy's shirt was freshly starched. Murray got up and put on his pants.

"Well," Sophie said, "isn't it?"

"Isn't it what?"

"I mean it just *is*, isn't it?"

"Well, it didn't quite make me puke, if that's what you mean."

"Oh, Murray!"

"I don't understand you, Sophie. Sometimes you seem pretty grown up, and then you go for that sickening goop."

"You're too old, Murray. You're getting too old," she said sadly. "All the romance has gone out of your life." But she didn't seem too angry about it. "You're just mean to say that. It happens to be my favorite record!" Then she immediately suggested that they go out in back of the carport and play basketball, and they did for a while, under a basket that had been set up on one of the uprights, until Murray found that the only pair of pants he'd brought were getting dirty. Sophie never hesitated to give him some solid and illegal body checks; she was pretty good, and she wanted to win.

Dinner wasn't too painful, although at times waves of actual, physical pain—waves that came with a disconcerting lack of cause —seemed to dash up against him, like ice water, whenever he looked forward to evening. Orson got out an old, half-full bottle of Scotch and made Murray a stiff Scotch and soda before they ate.

He had finally managed to be able to look Murray in the eye and to address him directly; he was proud of his seltzer bottle in which he carbonated his own water by means of little carbon dioxide cartridges, and he made much of this process. He didn't drink very often himself, and so made much, too, of the hearty business of mixing the two drinks.

Saul had a beer. He had come out on the Long Island Rail Road and by taxi, and would ride back to town with them in Orson's car.

Murray made himself eat the steak, but the pudding was too much. By the time of the pudding they were, under Saul's leadership, talking so determinedly about something other than Sophie's problems that they hummed and hesitated right in the middle of words. Perhaps most difficult was that occasionally Murray would look up to see Mae, who had, like a woman, moments of hideous truth she had to act upon in spite of the manufactured talk, staring at him out of wet and loving eyes, her food forgotten even in her mouth.

He was a boy, and didn't care for this kind of admiration—not from women; not from women who were old; especially not from women who were related to him. He wanted to deny all the goodness they attributed to him, and ask them what else could he have done? Knowing that much more than dumbly acting out the part of a father would be needed from him, he had to be convincing, too, and that would exactly measure his courage.

Each completion—drink, dinner, dessert—destroyed their memories and hushed them, and the talk would end in the middle of a word. When they had finished eating they stood, silently. When they had put on their coats they stood, silently. When they had all arranged themselves in Orson's car they gazed at Orson's busy, cramped face as he twisted his neck to back the car out into the street.

Sophie sat next to Murray and never said a word as they rode, protected, smooth, past the lights and dismal streets and finally across the long bridge into Manhattan. The evening would always in Murray's memory be strangely bearable, and he would remember most clearly the feeling that his face was made of cement, and that, oddly, because it was no prow or grill of a car or nose of a fuselage (a memory of model airplanes), his face just kept pushing along, pushing along from one place to another.

In Saul's apartment, after they sat down and then convulsively stood up again, came the question of money. Murray was then redoing by nervousness and habit his tour of Saul's paintings: Peter Blume, Abraham Rattner, George Grosz—wild people, but here to Saul's taste in their mildest moods. The apartment itself was old, high-ceilinged, and the doorknobs were not knobs at all but fancy molded brass that always made Murray think of old-fashioned bathroom faucets; it seemed unsafe for such an antique set of rooms, with such antique fixtures, to be 'way up on the tenth floor, as if he had found himself flying, in a nightmare, in the Victorian gondola of one of Jules Verne's airships.

He was being expected—not actually summoned—back to the family, and he felt their desire to get down to business. As he came back toward them Orson began to take handfuls of hundred-dollar bills from his pockets and to make little piles of them on the coffee table.

"Wallet," he said, tapping one pile. "Watch pocket." He solicitously, with delicacy that was almost love, straightened one bill that was out of line. "Right hand pants' pocket." Two more bills here. Saul and Mae nodded; this had all been agreed upon. Sophie looked mildly superior, somewhat bored. She wore her most plain, yet sophisticated black wool dress, and didn't look quite so young as usual.

"There!" Orson said, and they all watched Murray put the money in the proper places.

"A lot of money," Saul said. There were twelve hundred-dollar bills in all.

"Start at five hundred," Orson said, and pulled his pants pockets inside out with a snap. "There's more money there than I earn in a month, and I keep running!" He held the white linings of his pockets out, and his pants came up above his socks to show the white, hairless cylinders of his calves.

"*You want a receipt? Go ahead, Murray, give him a receipt!*" Sophie said this, in her most bitter, nasty voice—the imitation that, from the young, has none of the softening or tentativeness of

93

such words from an adult. It was shocking, naked as a declaration of true hate. Orson took a step and slapped her—not very hard—and her face at that moment was so stiff, so callow and sharp it seemed to Murray that Orson must have hurt his hand on it. It really seemed as though he had, because he began to sob. "*Har har har*," he cried, and ran out into the foyer. Because of his pockets—little white wings—he seemed to go hippity-hop. They heard him sobbing out by the coat closet.

"That was unkind," Saul said to Sophie. Mae went out to comfort Orson.

"Well, he didn't have to hit me," Sophie said.

"He didn't hit you. He could if he wanted knock you out the window." Saul looked at her steadily. "If I was your father I would hit harder. Like *this!*" And unbelievably, Saul took her arm, turned her around, and gave her a solid whack upon the buttock. A good, hard one. Murray could almost feel it himself, it was so quick and made such a flat sound against Sophie's behind. Now she began to cry herself, and leaned against her grandfather, one arm around his waist, one hand rubbing her buttock. Saul patted her on the back. "Don't hurt your father," he said. "Be a good girl and don't hurt your mother and father."

Then Saul brought them all back together again, and Orson told Murray to start low, while Mae worshiped Murray's nobility with her moist eyes. Sophie stood gravely at his side while they all said goodbye and good luck and we'll see you later.

In the taxi his feet danced upon the rubber mat; his palms sweat. Sophie was quiet in her corner, and he watched the people on the streets, all of whom seemed to be going at right angles to him, and whose destinations he envied. The first doctor had his offices in a dark brownstone with polished brass spears and knobs around the steps, and the windows in the door were so clean they seemed not to be there at all. His wife was his receptionist, and she came with a wee face like a bat and questioned them. Her face was dark gray, and her skinny arms grew darker toward the places where they connected to her body, as if she were sick in those places. When he told her that he had been referred by Mrs. Greene of Yonkers—the code words in this instance—her little black eyes began to see. He didn't bother to remember the words she said, being as he was

94

in such a fit of insecurity. Enough to remember that she truly believed that he and his whore were filthy, had sinned, were damned, would burn in hell, would join in excrement and blackness and hot wind the seventh circle and that their bloody fetus would scream curses at them for its bastardy and murder.

"How does it *feel?*" she whined triumphantly. "Do you feel hot *now?* Do you, girly? Do you feel like spreading your legs *now?*"

They left soon, and Murray never knew if he had failed a test or not. "Goodbye," he said in a polite, even friendly voice, "good night." He looked back once, and she was watching them through the spotless glass. Maybe it had been a test of his need; he should have begged a little, and asked to see the doctor, anyway. But he never told that to Sophie.

The next doctor's name was Stein, and he had his offices in the theatrical district. They had to wait with many others in a small, bright waiting room furnished with Swedish chairs. There were real, original oil paintings on the walls: one of them looked almost like a Pollock, one almost like a Miró. After the nurse took their name (just one, and they had decided upon Berman) and Murray had looked quickly at the paintings, he sat imprisoned in his chair and wouldn't look at Sophie or any of the people. He looked only at *Life* magazine, as if his head were in a vise, and never afterward could he remember one thing about the other people who sat there, except that they were all adults and all quiet.

One of the pictures in the magazine was of a couple who stood on the beach where their child had just drowned; he came upon the page unaware, and he looked at their faces as they looked at the sea and it seemed all at once that life was far too dangerous. He wanted to cry for the two stricken people, and he wanted to hide. In another copy of *Life* he came, similarly naked, exactly as unprepared, upon the picture of a sad, sick dog, and on the sad dog's shaved, bloody neck was sewn the amputated upper body, just the front half, of another, smaller dog—a mutt, a stunned, white-haired mutt with his paws awry and his long tongue hanging out. And Murray was deeply sick, deeper than nausea, as if he had been shown too much of a perverted sweetness, a heavy sweetness composed of his own brutal fascination and the unlimited sadism of the human race.

They waited for nearly an hour, and then the nurse called for Mr. and Mrs. Berman and they went into the doctor's office. The nurse took them in and then withdrew with what seemed to Murray to be a knowing discreetness. Dr. Stein, muscular and middle-aged, sat at his desk and looked them over. His face and balding head seemed to be nothing but various shades of red, all pale, as if he were nearly an albino. He asked them to sit down, and his light brown eyes, too, seemed washed-out and reddish. He wore a light green surgical smock, short-sleeved, and his big red-freckled arms glistened. While Murray decided how to begin, the doctor watched, and though he hadn't had much luck with the code words before, Murray decided to use them immediately—Dr. Stein, at least, was not a woman.

"We were referred by Dr. Diamond," he said.

"Which Dr. Diamond do you mean?" the doctor asked, raising his big arms. "There's a hell of a lot of Dr. Diamonds. New York's full of Dr. Diamonds."

"I don't know which one," Murray said, and Dr. Stein bugged his eyes at him. It seemed almost as if he had little muscles just for eye-bugging; his eyes slid out as if on stalks, while his reddish face stayed behind.

"Who referred you to Dr. Diamond? Who gave you his name?"

"I can't tell you, Doctor," Murray said, and was aware that he pretended more frustration than he actually felt. He pretended to be strangled. "I'd like to, but I can't! I promised not to."

"Ah," the doctor said, and his eyes went back in. He lowered his arms, finally, to the desk, and no longer looked as if he were about to catch a basketball. "I take it that the young lady is in trouble."

"Yes!" Murray said, relieved.

"My advice is to get married."

"We can't do that," Murray said quickly. It seemed to him that he had begun to fail again, that he was too calm. No, he was neither calm, nor calm looking, he was sure, but his symptoms were cold and incorrect, and would not please Dr. Stein.

"Why can't you? You look like a nice couple. You should see the freaks get married every day."

The doctor had now found an attitude; Murray knew it would be bluff and fatherly, and again he could predict failure.

"We can't, Doctor. Sophie's only fifteen. We intend to get married later (the lie had been prepared), but we just *can't* now."

The doctor nodded, and manufactured a weary sigh. "Look," he said, "Now don't I feel for you? But do you know what I have to lose?"

"Yes, I do," Murray said, pretending to be ashamed, but really sick with inadequacy. He knew this game by heart, having lost it so many times. The words were always familiar, the disrespect in his heart was always understood by his opponent and used against him: he always bought.

"Do you? Look! Sometimes . . . Listen! I'll tell you this sincerely!" The doctor became sincere. "Sometimes I do a favor for a friend, for a wife who doesn't want—maybe can't afford—another child. You hear that? I trust you. Come here. Look at this box."

Murray had to get up to look. Screwed to the side of the desk was a little black box with a red light glowing upon its side.

"Look. I've got a little past, you understand? Political. Probably you don't." Murray nodded avidly, disgustingly eager to show that he understood. "Well, I supported the wrong party. Aren't they after me? I've got to be careful. Look at the box. Take a look. Look at it."

And Murray looked. Lost, bored, deadly bored with his weakness, with his utter disrespect for the man he listened to and for himself, he looked. The box told, by lights and little buzzes, whether or not the phone was tapped; it also told, in some related way, whether or not the office was bugged.

A good box. A very expensive, complicated box. Did he see how it worked? Oh, very interesting! And all the time other words were forming themselves in Murray's mouth: *You ass, do you understand how I hate you? How I cannot plead, but can only nod and nod?*

Soon they left, and the doctor had had not only the last word, but all the words; if he needed any reason he could see with his reddish eyes, smell with his reddish nose, the disgust in Murray's heart.

Money hadn't even been mentioned, and Murray remembered it as they stood on the sidewalk waiting for a taxi to come by. He felt the square little lump in his watch pocket, and put his hand into the side pocket of his pants to feel the crisp, cloth-like paper there. Sophie hadn't said a word. She stayed as close to his side as she could without touching him, and when a taxi stopped he opened the door but did not help her in.

They had to cross Broadway, and as they waited for the traffic light the interior of the taxi was shoddy and bright. Sophie looked at him from her corner, her too mobile face plain, unprotected in the cheap, gay light, as quivery as if it had been skinned.

"I caused all this trouble. It's all my fault," she said.

"Oh, Sophie," he said, and she slid over to him and took his hand.

"Christ, Cousin," she said, crying a little, "what a mess!"

"It's hard to undo that sort of thing, isn't it?" he said rather coldly. She was such a big girl, and she now laid her head, her thick black hair up under his chin, on his chest. Automatically his hand went to her broad shoulder and began to pat—a sterile gesture of doubtful comfort. She sniffled. Her shoulder was as substantial as wood.

"I didn't even want to stop. That's the awful thing," she said, and it seemed that he could feel her ragged, unstable voice right on his sternum, as if she had licked him on the bare skin.

"I just went all the way. Three times," she said, "and I don't even *like* him very much. Sometimes I think I'm a sex fiend, Murray." She drew away and turned her face toward him. Her lips, puffy and wet, quivered, and her face again looked so naked as to be indecent —the bare young face attached to the long body that was too big, too hard for a girl's. He patted away at her shoulder, and as he did his wrist began to get tired from the continual, idiotic patting. He found himself removed from pity; the nearer she came to him, the farther his sympathy fled from her, and he cursed himself for his callow, selfish coldness. If only she weren't so plain, such a horse of a girl. If only, he thought, knowing this to be the cold, unjust truth of the world, he could want to have her himself—if he could feel, in her acquiescence, her passionate moans beneath the Irish boy, a rising of his own desire. But she could not occur to him that way, and therefore her mistake was without interest, without beauty.

Did she feel this? Soon she moved back to her corner, and all the way back to Saul Weitzner's apartment building she gazed out the quarter-window. When he happened to look at her, her face was stern; but he felt that she hadn't made any resolutions, nor had she found any sudden strength. Did she look bare-naked at the kind of life there was for her? He never knew how deeply she had been troubled, or how well she took it all, or how badly. When they returned Mae had readied a bed, hot-water bottles, clean cloths—all for nothing. But they all appreciated what he'd done.

Several weeks later Sophie wrote to him. They'd finally found a doctor in New Jersey, where the heat wasn't on, and she told him all about it—about how it hurt quite a bit, and how the doctor packed her with cotton gauze and kept her overnight. The letter was cheerful, almost gossipy—as if it were really nothing but a lark. She didn't like the doctor much, though; he was a shnook. There was nothing in the letter to suggest the big quiet girl he remembered looking out the taxi window, or the child's gazing face. At the end, however, she said that she would always remember:

I will always remember what you did for me, Murray, and love you always. You are my favorite.

xxxxxx

Sophie

She would remember. Perhaps she thought he'd done his best for her. From where he sat in his dormitory room he could see the common and the dusty, graceful elms, new leaves peacefully turning in the air. Suddenly, without premeditation, he beat his hand against his ear—the gesture immediately seemed too theatrical, and it hurt too much. No, there was an alternative, and it was worse: she really didn't mind that he had cheated her of love. She had put her awkward body in their hands, maybe, but kept like an ugly child to her cold and wounded self. Goodbye Herky; goodbye Murray. No one was too young to perceive indifference cynically, and her letter, with its six gay kisses at the end, was just to let him know that there were no hard feelings.

Thus his real adventures refused to help him believe in his daydream journey—just as the dead bird, now cold, beginning to stiffen upon the papery leaves, did not suggest at all the excitement of its headlong flight or the fine skill of his shot.

WHEN RICHARD and Shim came down from the mountain, Murray was out in the field behind the barn with his Mauser. They heard his first zeroing-in shot, and then a stillness followed as he walked up to his target. Then they could see him standing by the bank with his target, a coffee can, in his hand. He turned and looked at them. Richard was tired, and as he looked at his tall, graceful son he felt proud and yet desperately old, as if it were himself he saw there, the old fall umbers and golds surrounding himself as if they were the tints of age. The boy was as fresh and as alive as his most youthful memory of himself. He felt, too, in that tired moment, love as a kind of fear of loss, but he could not tell if it were his own son or his own youth he feared to lose.

Or had lost, both of them. His son was here, and could be touched (maybe) and spoken to. His youth he did not have, if one counted years, but he still had the most tangible symptom of it, a strong and obedient body. At his age it was precarious to keep whatever lilt was left in his sinews, and no more than a bad week could turn him into an old man. He had seen it happen to others; it would soon happen to him. It hadn't yet, by God! and yet he knew too much to think that the young whippersnappers couldn't outrun him. He had only so much time, and soon, if he were lucky enough to keep on living, he'd grow to a straight chair in a warm room, like old Zach.

Shim left him and went up to examine Murray's target. Murray set the can against the bank, and he and Shim paced back, with measuring strides, seventy-five yards; across the stubble field they marched as if to a slow drum. Richard stood by the wall and watched the two younger men. Murray lay down and adjusted his sling, then aimed and fired. The sound of the shot seemed to divide itself into two sounds: *ack-thuh.* The first crack of it, remaining sharp in the mind, seemed also the last sound, as if the more sonorous thunder of the echo had come first, and this gave Richard the odd feeling that he knew of the shot before the explosion had occurred. Beside the can a little hump of sand had risen. Murray adjusted his rear sight, then aimed again.

Ack-thuh! The can rolled down the bank with a flat, can sound: *tankle-clink.* That, evidently, was all the ammunition Murray was going to waste.

It would be a while before dinner, and Richard went to his room and lay down, then raised his legs, unlaced and took off his boots. His stockinged feet, slightly damp—humid warmth upon them— quickly cooled as he lay there, and he drew the spare blanket over him, feeling his exercised body cool out and then need the nice pressure of the hard wool. The blanket, Shim had told him, had once been a section of the long-drying felt of the Leah Paper Mill. Hard, beautiful wool, it had once run at great speed over the humming rollers. Now he rubbed the hemmed edge of it and let it keep him warm.

After dinner, according to Shim's custom, they would again examine the guns, then gather their equipment together and place each hunter's gear upon a chair in the kitchen. Tonight, full of game (he and Shim had each shot two birds), they would let Shim pamper his excitement, even help him, and have a drink—one, maybe two, no more. Zach would watch, perhaps regaining, perhaps enjoying, some excitement about what he could no longer do. Before his laryngectomy he used to tell stories of bear-paw snowshoes and of rifles with obsolete cartridge designations such as forty-four forty, or forty-five seventy—the first number caliber, in hundredths of inches; the second, grains of black powder—and the old, heavy bullets, in Richard's mind, flew slowly out of their ancient smoke and into the sides of great gray bucks. This always in the deep snow of an old winter.

Tomorrow—and he thought: How few first days there were in a lifetime—even one as long as old Zach's—of deer seasons! Thirty or forty, at the very most. Tomorrow there would probably be no snow at all, and he could imagine only, on bare ground, the buck he had startled in his headlights, a fat, tawny modern buck, plump and muscular. Not that he wouldn't gladly settle for a doe; he had hunted deer enough to know that one man was presented with few daylight glimpses of the animal.

How strange they were, how stupid sometimes, and how crafty! When they were wary a man was made to feel as clumsy, as slow as an addled monster out of its element, yet when they were stupid their gift of opportunities was so freely, so often given that it seemed to go beyond stupidity and become nothing but generosity —as if they asked for a bullet as a man might ask for food, or love. The white-tailed deer: he tried to make himself, who had been a near stranger to most people in his life, and who often had to approach others by way of a transference that was not quite natural —almost telepathic—tried to place his consciousness with the vivid animals now in the dark spruce, now in a geometrical slash of blow-down trees. Tall ears hearing constantly, with fantastic preception of depth and direction, the subtle meanings of rhythms, dark eyes seeing great light without the lessening filter of color perception, black noses smelling upon the always moving air time, distance, danger: he might himself have been a fair, great buck. Might have, if the energy given his loins had been by accident the more desperate, direct energy of the hooved deer. He would have been a buck to grow old and triumphant; he felt that his energy and his senses —translated, still mammal—would have allowed him much success as a deer.

But as a deer how gray, how old would he now be? No matter; the problems of his life—those problems he had not been able to solve—would never have arisen. A buck was far too grand, too much of an egoist to care for anything but the sheen of his own pelt, the roundness of his own haunches. A buck let his does test the safety of his path, and felt no guilt after the sacrifice; his life itself was his only worthy concern—his life and his dominance in the rut.

God, how simple! And then, for a long moment in which he did not, as he usually did, hold tight to his slippery version of himself as a civilized man, he felt himself to be a great buck in the forest. It was as if his body changed, the fulcrums of his joints grew deer-like, the flesh slid back along his lower limbs, his shoulders and his haunches turned massive above the delicate, hard cannon bones, his thick neck grew erect above the bunched muscles of his brisket. The illusion of this change was so strong he had to roll over onto his side, and he lay there impatient to rise and leap; he could even feel (half dreaming of the inevitable return to manhood) a thickening, a wrinkling of the dura of his skull, as if grand antlers grew down through it into bone.

The night is important, as is the season; it is cold, and in fall. The apples are not yet frostbitten and therefore not yet soft enough to crush against the toothless upper palate, but the moon is so bright it is almost irritating to the wide eyes with their light-enhancing internal mirrors; the deer's eyes gleam back at it. Each opening between the thick orchard trees is as bright as a little day, but beneath the branches it is quite dark, for the light is from a single source, and the clear air of the night, like empty space, does not seem to diffuse light, to soften shadow. But the buck's senses are one instrument, and when pure dark crosses a part of sense he does not care or know that his other senses still perceive; he has oriented his night and he knows with a pure perception beyond imagination where each source of odd sensory irritation springs. The only darkness of his mind, the only partial doubt, is a certain wedge which begins downwind (although the air hardly moves) and extends, widening, out toward the field beyond the brook until it becomes, to him, indefinite and beyond—beyond the range of his enemies' ability to kill him. He knows who makes each sound. He is beginning to feel his intoxication—the poison, of course, is any part of carelessness, any lessening at all of his great preoccupation with his sacred body. A cold night for mad heat; there is the buck he chased away, there are the does who keep a certain wary distance. He is about to become drunk, and it is as if he feels constrained, somehow predicting his madness, for he circles and checks again. This takes him downwind of a doe, and suddenly he leaps back toward her, his prancing strangely awkward, the energy of his hoofs prodigal and careless, so that the leaves fly, and small rocks crack together. He is brutal, and somehow gawky—aggressive, and it does not quite fit him, as if he were really gone mad. The doe is there, and his nostrils are full of her. There is a still moment not of consideration but of farewell, perhaps, to the last idea not compulsive.

You! Now! the eye, the breath declare.

He leaps at her just as she turns, and he clasps nothing but branches and brush, which sting him. He is gawky and stiff, full of rage: he would kill her with his hoofs or antlers if his madness did not strike him through his nose. He leaps again, and her sudden compliance means nothing but the fastness of his locking, scissoring forelegs and the deep, ungraceful constricture of his back. She shudders and is deep and open to him, and he shoves, slips, pierces her, and his clasping foreknees are rigid in her nervous flanks as she leans into his short, monstrous stroke. . . .

Richard rolled off the bed. Caught in the hard wool of the blanket, he fell heavily to his knees. Outraged at himself for the wild dream, he tore the blanket from around his legs and threw it across the bed. He trembled, frightened by his precarious mind; he had nearly had an orgasm.

Yet he trembled, too, out of danger. Not the danger of his imagination, but a deeper danger that might or might not have been inspired by the dream (and was it a nightdream or a daydream?): as the buck rutted in the dangerous moonlight were his enemies attracted by his random sounds? He remembered that the most handsome buck is still, to some, mere meat: sustenance. His dignified, excellent defense—and there was no rut now left in Richard, only wariness—is perhaps against this image of himself as a meal. Or is such dignity in harmony with that idea? What he felt was danger, and he still felt it, as if someone were looking, like a hunter, at the mirrors of his eyes.

Although he would have locked the bathroom door anyway, he felt that by carefully turning the lock he was ensuring himself of a slightly unnatural privacy, and it felt good. He took a fairly long bath, shaved, then put on his expensive slacks and cotton flannel shirt. In a way that reminded him of the insight of puppy love—that pure and naked jittering of the nerves—he knew that Opal would also be taking care how she looked. He knew that this meant nothing like a contract, but she would be doing it partly for him, and they would both know it. As he went downstairs he felt strong and clean.

It was one of his eccentricities, he had always thought, that he had never had sexual intercourse with any woman he didn't in some way love. Even if he hadn't liked the girl too well, when it came to the time—to the final welcome she made him, when she put her arms around him and at the same time did not hold back at all—especially when she opened to him the soft, wonderfully smooth insides of her thighs, and when in all that lovely softness his hard sex penetrated—how could he feel anything but love for such generosity? And perhaps that was the reason he did not have an orgasm the one time he tried a whore, during the war. What generosity was there when the gift was so directly purchased? "What's the matter with me?" the whore had asked, in such a polite, unwhorelike voice; she was one of those people who take themselves seriously, who want to be good at what they do. She then offered to do anything his quirks or perversions demanded, but he quickly professed inadequacy, and said that he had drunk too much. He couldn't say that he hadn't felt something like love then—or maybe what he felt was pity instead of gratitude. He knew that a certain idea had been thoroughly and vociferously discredited: the idea that the woman, in that exchange, did nothing but give.

But now, after dinner, he watched Opal, and suddenly he had to sneeze, and did. He wondered if this happened to everyone when in the imagination he saw himself doing this or that. He wondered if Shim knew why he had sneezed, but discounted this: one sneezed for many reasons. Opal walked to the sink, and Richard in his mind slid between her legs. *You ass!* he thought, is your mind between your legs? But the self-accusing voice seemed to come from a long way away. She seemed naked to him, and he could have licked her buttocks, and put his tongue on her smooth dark flesh anywhere. *For Christ's sake!*—and on a full stomach, too. This last thought he tried as an antidote, and had to smile: he was sure that if he could have seen the smile in a mirror it would have looked goatish. Murray noticed the smile—whatever it looked like—and just barely lifted an eyebrow. Shim was talking, and since the shooting of the clay pigeons that morning Richard had found himself and Murray exchanging little warnings and smiles. He wondered if Shim noticed this.

They had eaten well: this time Opal had split the thick breasts of the partridge, braised them, and then put them into a very hot oven for a few minutes. The meat, golden on the outside, as white as paper on the inside, hadn't lost its moisture. Now, on each plate, there were only the delicate little halves of skeletons, such graceful little structures it didn't seem possible they could have supported so much flesh. With the birds they had had the usual country food—from boiled potatoes to bread-and-butter pickles, the flavors most bland and subtle: home-canned beet greens against home-canned dandelion greens, for one, and the difference he could hardly remember now—perhaps one of slight degrees of bitterness, perhaps one of color, the different shades of ancient green suggesting past summers, moist heat in the rich earth, one the tight skin of a lawn, the other the lush tumescence of a garden. There were sweet cider with just a mild hint of acetic acid in it; yellow cheese which crumbled and was yet somehow buttery; green olives, celery, macaroni and cheese, salt and pepper.

Now he tried not to think of Opal's private places and imagined lovely moans. He had better not. He had other things he had to do, and the first was to join in the ceremony of preparation for the hunt. As Opal cleared away the dishes, Shim began to show his equipment. The first item was a Randall knife for which he had paid twenty-five dollars.

"Ain't it *wicked?*" he asked, drawing the bright blade from its tanned dark sheath. It was wicked, and light in the blade, Richard found when he was allowed to hold it; the blade made itself to feel light, and dangerous, even though the balance was precisely at the base of the hilt. The blade curved perversely, like a kukri. "Course I carry Zach's folding knife, too." This Shim pulled out of his pocket, and opened. The stag handle was worn to the white by hands, and the short, straight blade had been sharpened narrow.

"*Hup!* Gutted. *Huch!* Many a deer!" Zach said proudly. "*Huch!* I let him. *Hoach!* Use it now!"

"You was a hunter," Shim said, and his father, out of embarrassment and pride, smiled fiercely.

Richard wondered if Zach had ever had doubts about his son—had ever wanted more assurance than such compliments gave him. Perhaps it was too late in Zach's life to ask him. He looked over at Murray, and couldn't tell if Murray had compared fathers and sons. Murray looked down at the stag-handled knife, which he now held, and his face was serious and calm; he didn't seem to be thinking about the knife.

And then Richard thought, Aren't we all good people here? Don't we all do what we do very well? Why should I doubt my son? He looked at Murray, at the steady, strong boy Murray was. What right had he to bitch about too little information? The boy had always done better than they had expected of him, always pleased and surprised his parents (a doubt here; he no longer presumed to think for Rachel). His son was a grown man—he watched the strong, square hands as they caressed the knife—and as another grown man Richard wondered if he had the right to ask prying questions.

But he remembered too much. Not too much, maybe, but he must, as any father must, be burdened with all the scenes of all those twenty years of his twenty-year-old son. One came to him now: when the little creature came home from the hospital—that same afternoon—he held the warm, delicate little body against his chest and was surprised at the tenderness he felt, surprised at his reaction to such soft helplessness. Why so sensual, so immediate? He knew, for instance, that there was a direct nerve reaction between a woman's teat and her womb when a baby suckled, but he had been unprepared to find himself, a man, getting an erection. He hadn't thought of the analogy, just then, and wondered about himself. Wondered, but did not really worry. He had always been in full control of odd symptoms. He knew he was a man—knew in the rather scientific sense that proceeds from symptoms, yes, but does not leap to generalizations.

Shim spoke to Murray, who still held Zach's worn old knife, and now weighed it in one hand, the Randall knife in the other.

"Which one you like best, Murray?" Shim asked in his meaningful voice; whenever Shim spoke there seemed to be some ironic implication. Murray looked up and smiled, and his generous face seemed modest.

"One is beautiful and new," he said, "and the other is handsome and old." He smiled at his parallelism.

Shim reared back in his chair and roared. "Murray, you say the God-*damnedest* things!" He laughed and laughed, then rubbed his chin with his fist, an imitation of a blow, and they could hear the scrape of whiskers. "Like Zach," he said. As though he were sitting for his picture, the old man didn't move, but he heard. "That old bone-handle jackknife, now. It ain't too pretty, but it's so goddam straight and plain, why, it *is* sort of handsome," Shim said.

"*Hoach!* Stuck! *Huch!* Many a deer!" Zach said.

"Zach, he lost this knife once," Shim said. As Zach grinned, the little diced squares of skin below his ears crowded together. Richard had heard this story years before, from Zach himself.

"He did!" Shim said. He got up from his chair and stepped back, the knife open in his hand. "Didn't you, Pa?" Zach quickly nodded, his washed eyes alert, the thin cartilage of his nose shining like pearl.

"*Huch!*" he said, and then decided not to speak. Nodding instead, he let the air out in a plain belch.

"Happened like this," Shim said. He stood back from the table and crouched a little, being a hunter in the woods. "Zach had his old forty-five seventy. Wait a minute!" and he went into the living room, then came back, blowing dust from a long, brown lever-action Winchester. "This here's what he had. Well! This was Christ-all years ago, you know, but anyways Zach was going along nice and easy, keeping his eyes open as usual. First day of the season, about two foot of fresh snow—no crust. Quiet. Just sluffing along easy, see?" Shim sluffed along a few steps. Then he stopped moving altogether, and his yellow eyes were stern and watchful. "There he was," Shim said, still not moving at all, staring fiercely at the door. "There he was, a nice fat buck, six points." He began to whisper. "Not more than two rod off. Buck didn't see Zach at all. Upwind, nice soft snow, just behind some little bitty hardwood saplings. Just make him out. Ayuh! Six points." Shim brought the rifle up slowly, and cocked it. The two clicks were very loud. "Buck heard him cock his piece!" Shim yelled, startling everybody. "Buck jumped straight up in the air five feet! Zach, he aimed and pulled the trigger!" Shim pulled the trigger: *click.* "Click! God-dam firing pin frozen! Son of a bitch! Click again! Buck jumps straight up in the air and comes down ass-end-to! Click! Zach, he figures maybe it's a dud cartridge, so he jacks in a new one!" Shim worked the action as he danced to the side, still peering toward the door. "Buck's up in the air again! Zach, he takes a bead on him and when he comes down, *bang!* Buck drops out of sight!"

Zach was a big man, and in that year—1926—he was six feet tall and weighed 190 pounds. This Richard remembered from Zach's account of that day. He had heard the story from others, too; it was famous in Leah. What had happened was this: the buck, when Zach came up to it, was down, and looked to be dead. Zach put down his rifle and was about to stick the buck in the sticking place just above the brisket, when the buck came to life. It merely had a broken hind leg and had been in what was, most likely, shock. Zach grabbed the antlers and decided he wasn't going to let the buck go. Even with one broken leg the buck could have run right out of the country. When telling about it, Zach had said, "He soon took that knife away from me."

Zach and the buck, who weighed as much as Zach, wrestled all morning. The buck would soon have finished Zach except that when he went to rear up in order to stab with his front hoofs, Zach could wrestle him over against his bad leg, and down they'd both go. This way they progressed, a yard or so at a time. Some-where along the way Zach's jacket and shirt were torn right off him, but he wouldn't let go. When they came to a brook Zach tried to drown the buck, but he couldn't hold the head under water long enough. He tried to wedge the buck in the notch of a tree, but got caught himself and nearly snapped an ankle. He tried to break the buck's neck, but couldn't twist hard enough. All morning the two of them thrashed through the woods, face to face, snorting and glaring at each other. The buck bit his own tongue, and his blood and Zach's blood got all over both of them. Zach wouldn't let go, though, and finally they came to the plowed road. Then somebody came along in a T-model Ford, as Zach told it, and stunned the buck with a tire iron—stunned him long enough so Zach could let go and they could stick the big neck vein with a pocket knife.

Zach was in bed for a couple of days after that, healing up and watching his bruises turn green and yellow. But he was in good shape in those days, and that same season he got another deer (a doe), and an elk out of a herd that passed across the mountain. These two were illegal, of course; that was a good year for venison. He found his rifle easily enough, and next spring, when the snow went out, he went back and cast around all morning until he found his knife.

While Shim acted all this out, using a chair for the buck, Richard could not help glancing at Murray. He knew that Shim would notice any lack of attention, and that Murray would notice it too, but as he watched Murray's face he suddenly remembered that his son had come to the mountain unwillingly, and the amusement on his face as he watched Shim's performance might not be real. Where did Murray want to be? What did he want to be doing?

"Why'd Zach hold on like that?" Shim said. " 'Cause there's one hell of a difference between a deer track and a deer. That's what a lot of city people can't git through their heads—that you don't just go out and aim and shoot." It was apparent that in this case Shim didn't consider Richard and Murray city people. "If I got in the same position Zach did, by God, wouldn't I be all over that buck?"

Zach sucked air: "*Huch!* Didn't git. *Hough!* My deer. *Huch!* Every damn. *Hoach!* Year."

"Legal, that is," Shim said, and this pleased Zach very much. He smiled and rocked back and forth from the waist.

"*Huch!* Not even. *Huch!* Then. *Hough!* Sometimes!"

Zach had taken many deer from the mountain, most of them during the legal season and in daylight, but many by torch and flashlight. There had been hard times, and venison had come in handy on the rocky hill farm. His washed-out old eyes were now set deeply in his freckled lids, and he looked up into a corner as if he were thinking upon the days of his vigor. There seemed no regret in him that those days had passed, and Richard wondered if the old did pine with any strength of emotion for days that were past and gone.

Now they were all silent for a moment; except for the chink of dishes as Opal washed them, and the metallic tick of the hot-water tank, there was no sound, and it seemed to Richard that they all thought of the deer who moved on the side of the mountain— so far away, yet so possible, it always seemed on the night before deer season began, to find and have.

Finally Shim jumped up from his chair—the one that had a moment before been a buck deer—and went to get his rifle. Murray got his, too, and they carefully put both down upon the table.

"Don't those krauts make guns!" Shim said. "Ugly as sin!"

Murray looked at him with interest. "The way a gun ought to be," he said.

"Right! You take a Luger pistol, for instance. It looks more *like* a pistol. So ugly it's pretty. You know what I mean?"

And so they inspected the guns and the gear—Richard's included —and had another drink. Shim marveled at each weapon, worked the bolts many times, and finally sat back with his own Arisaka in his arms, his hand playing smoothly with the silky mechanism of its breech. Outside, it rained softly; it was too warm for snow, but Shim said, "Oh, I like it wet and quiet. Quiet, that's how I like it. I seen more deer on rainy days than any other kind. Git the weather report," he said to Opal. She slid down from the high stool she had been sitting on and turned on the small kitchen radio. In a moment out came music and the incredibly sleazy, whorish voice of a Negro woman singing a love song: "Oh, baby, baby! Oh, baby, baby! Oh, baby, baby! Oh, baby, baby! Oh, baby, baby, doan I love you! Oh . . ."

"Agh!" Shim shouted, pretending to retch. "We got five minutes till news time. Turn it off before I puke!"

Opal, with an indifferent shrug, switched it off.

" 'Oh, baby, baby, baby, baby!' " Shim imitated the voice. "Night before deer season! 'Oh, baby, baby!' It ain't *right!*"

PART TWO

The skin and shell of things,
Though fair,
Are not
Thy wish nor prayer,
But got
By mere despair
Of wings.

—Henry Vaughan

‌‌‌

‌‌‌‌‌‌‌‌‌‌‌‌‌‌‌‌‌‌‌‌‌‌‌‌‌‌‌‌‌‌‌‌‌‌‌‌‌‌‌ 14

RICHARD KNEW he had been asleep, or was still asleep: he opened his
eyes (or seemed to) and there was the room, all bright but somehow just out of focus, and Murray was standing at the foot of his
bed staring fiercely down at him. Not moving, just staring at him,
and Murray's face was stern and sad, it seemed, too. The horrible
thing about it all was that he knew immediately from Murray's
expression that no response on his part was expected—as though
he were either unconscious or dead. Richard became terribly afraid,
and sat up to find the room dark except for a faint, hazy glow that
was the window. The fear remained, and as he reached for the
lamp beside his bed he dented the paper shade with his fingers and
nearly knocked it over. He was still afraid that Murray *would* be
there at the foot of his bed, but the yellow light came on, finally,
in his fingers, and no one was there. He had dreamed that he was
standing again in the field and Murray was zeroing in his rifle; but
he had known that was merely a dream, because it was obviously a
duplicate experience. He knew that he had been there before. The
shot: *ack-thuh,* and the feeling that he had heard the shot before it
had happened, and Murray walking up to the target—of course he
had been there before. And then to wake from what he knew to be

115

a dream into what was, presumably, reality, and to find that he hadn't quite made it back. . . .

It had been Murray's face, clear and straight, but with an expression upon it he had never seen there before—the expression of a man looking at death. He shuddered, and shuddered again, then reached down and squeezed his thighs as hard as he could. Their vibrations came back up through his arms: it was like holding onto a spinning drier with an unbalanced load—the energy of the tremors didn't seem to come from him at all. "OK, OK," he said in a soft, secretive voice. "Come off it right now." He got out of bed, shakily, and went to the window. It was three o'clock, by his wrist watch, and though the night outside was not pitch black, it still misted. The moon was up, above thin but damp clouds, and he could almost make it out. The trees were wet and still, and on the branches near his window tiny highlights winked.

He went back and lay down on the bed, and had a sudden urge for a cigarette. He didn't have any, so that settled that; he wasn't about to start smoking again anyway. The initial fear he had taken with him from the dream was fading away, now, and he found it possible to remember Murray's expression without having the face itself appear in front of him. What an expression! He had seen it on the faces of many men, and no doubt had worn it himself. Strange that one always disapproved of the dead—or maybe it was of the death they so obviously, so drably wore. He suddenly wondered how many men he had killed in the war. Impossible to tell. Impossible. One rarely aimed at a man in that war, but at the earth where men hid—it was more like spraying insects. But he had killed men—aimed straight at them and fired, and his bullets went right through them and broke their veins and crushed their lights out, so that they no longer had the strength to stand so delicately balanced upon their two legs, and had to fall down forever.

Someone could have looked sternly down upon Richard Grimald, too. It could have happened easily, any time. And of course it would happen. Only temporarily did one manage to forget that. And then he thought of Rachel, because he could not bear to think of his own death without Rachel. Who would mourn? Not mourn, so much as, perhaps, suffer it. Yes, suffer it, and therefore keep that death, in a way, alive. The one who died did not die, but was dead, and felt nothing, and was nothing. What stupidity! he had to think. What a mess of stupid, disorganized guff that was! He was afraid, lonely in the face of his death, and he wanted his wife back, here, now, long and warm beside him. He wanted to smell her, to feel her weight upon the springs, to breathe her breath.

"My wife," he murmured. She should be right here, and she was not, and, therefore, something was wrong—as simple as that. And all at once it seemed terribly simple; the one word *wrong* solved it all. That word would stand up in court! *Wrong*. Simply that, and everyone would have to understand immediately. The judge's gavel would fall, the jury would nod, the clerk would stenotype (the bailiff would bail?), the psychiatrists would relate (whatever that meant), and the whole silly mess would be over with.

"Rachel," he said softly; his hands gently curved themselves, and his fingertips slid along the cold sheet. For a moment he felt like crying, but the image of himself crying—the big man with the black mustache crying?—superimposed itself upon his eyes. "God damn it!" he whispered.

He decided to take some aspirin; he would have to get up in a couple of hours, and maybe the aspirin would help him get back to sleep. God knew how, but he would try it anyway. He took two aspirin out of his bottle and turned out the lamp before he went next door to the lavender bathroom. He didn't turn on the light, but felt for the plastic tumbler above the bowl, rinsed it once, and washed the aspirin down. When he came out he glanced down the hall, and his fear suddenly returned; someone stood at the hall window. At least it looked as if someone stood there against the dim light. He knew that he couldn't go back into his room without finding out for certain. Why had he turned out his light? Had he been afraid to be caught silhouetted against it? He walked down the hall toward the window. It was somebody, because it moved—turned toward him: now, with fear still left in him, he saw that it was Opal. She was kneeling on the bench below the window, and she had turned, silently, halfway around. In the darkness he could see nothing about her face, only the outline of her cheek and the bow of her glasses.

She whispered to him, "Can't you sleep?" and because she whispered, because it was so startlingly conspiratorial, he shivered violently and almost had to sneeze.

"What's the matter?" he whispered back, and she moved closer to him in order to whisper again.

"It's Shim, I think." She tapped her fingernail lightly against the windowpane. "I think he's up on the mountain. I think I heard a shot."

"I dreamed I heard a shot."

"No dream. I wasn't asleep. Look." She pointed out into the night, and in the dim light from the clouds he could see the line of her bare arm. "I think I saw a light up near the top of the ski tow. It's so stupid! He *knows* Spooner is after him." She shivered herself.

"You're cold," he said, and couldn't keep from putting his hand on her shoulder. Her nightgown was filmy beneath his hand, and her warmth came through it. He smelled her dark hair. "He's taking a chance," he whispered, glad that they had to whisper—his voice at that moment might have been unsteady. She didn't draw away.

"Spooner is the one who's taking a chance," she said, and he knew that she pretended to ignore his hand. She trembled. "I don't think Shim would let himself get caught. I don't think there's anything Shim wouldn't do," she said, and shivered again.

She smelled warm, lovely; she smelled of bed, and he wanted to pick her up in his arms and put his face against her. "You think he would do something drastic?" He didn't believe it; he was aware of his dishonesty in saying such a thing.

"I don't know," he said. His hand moved down her arm, onto bare skin. It was excruciating. He thought wildly, should I do this? I should damned well *not* do this. Will she let me do this? Yes, she will.

The hand slid from her arm to her waist. So narrow! So uncertain! And with relief that the decision had now certainly been passed, he turned her around and pulled her to him, hard against his rumpled, suddenly unsubstantial pajamas, and kissed her. When she first felt him against her she jumped nervously, then let him press her against the whole length of him, and with a little, flutter-

118

ing spasm of the lips, opened her mouth. Her arms, in a compulsive motion—she may have been imitating the usual, dramatic gesture—came up and around his neck, and as he lifted her up, his hands upon her dark, warm flesh, hips and buttocks round and warm, her soft lips nervous against his lips, he felt what he knew immediately to be lust. There was pepper in his nose, his ears rang, and he had in his mind, not quite complete or *seen*, the image of a bar of white iron imbedded somehow in flesh, and slowly the bar began to bend; slowly and surely, the white bar bent.

She had been struggling to get loose, and he realized that he must let her go; his strength was so much greater than hers, and yet he wondered why he hadn't immediately noticed her desire to get away from him. She shuddered—no doubt about that, it was revulsion—and he was shocked by it. His feeling had been all desire (lust, he'd thought a moment before), with no reservations whatsoever. He had to have her, and because he was a careful man he let her go, knowing that the time hadn't come yet. But he saw himself begin to plan; he would let the sensuous present lie in wait, and appear to be an understanding man.

She moved back, and so successfully was he able to postpone his desire for her he was amused: she was actually panting. Panting like a dog. He was amused, he supposed, by her ambivalence toward him as a man—now that he had none at all toward her as a woman. He could feel her breath, in little gusts, and smell it—the stale breath of cigarettes, the exciting breath of her own mixed-up desire.

"I never felt like that before," she whispered. She wouldn't run away. Evidently she had to talk about it.

"I know how I felt," he whispered back. Now he felt that he was in control of himself. Once a problem had a desired end, he was usually able to solve it. He reached out and placed his hand, gently, on her neck below her ear. She didn't draw away.

"Can I come up close and talk in your ear," she whispered, "and not have you pull me against you?"

"Yes."

As she came up to him, he bent down, and she cupped her small hands around his ear. "I thought Shim was like you," she said. "At first I thought Shim would be like you."

He had to tremble, and wished he hadn't. The little mouth in his ear was too warm, too near to his senses.

"But he wasn't?"

"He's not gentle. Why does he feel that he can't be gentle?"

"Shim is a very odd boy."

"Yes. I'm a very odd girl, too," she said, and he thought: Oh, are you? We'll see. We'll see about that.

"Well, I am," she said. "I don't know what's wrong with me, but I am. It isn't all Shim."

Her little mouth touched his ear. He moved his hand up her arm, up along the forearm, past the elbow. Each little increase in its design, each little convexity of tendon or muscle termination increasing his pleasure in it. It was a beautiful arm: he thought again how surprising a woman could be who did not at first glance conform to the general idea of beauty—how she might, taken as she was, in a perspective relevant only to her, be the most beautiful creature in the world. Rachel was, even at first glance, beautiful, full of sex. Opal had to be touched, and then, as if her beauty had to have a conductor, as if it were not so much visual as electric, she became whole and perfect. His hand grasped her arm just below her shoulder; the firm sheath of flesh in back gave way to the silk of her armpit. Remembering his promise, and his strategy, he slid his hand back to her wrist, then back to her hand, which turned and now lay in his.

"I know what you want to do," she said, and for a second his heartbeat rang in his ears.

"You don't know how much," he said.

"We can't," she said, and he thought: We! Yes.

"No, I guess not," he lied carefully.

"Shim might come back," she said, and he heard his heart again. "No, I don't mean that—I don't mean it that way," she added quickly. "I'm no cheating bitch. I'm not."

"Of course not," he said, and turned and kissed her on the forehead. He put his hand on her breast, and the nipple was distended and hard. "Of course not." He took his hand quickly away.

With a sudden, almost desperate motion she put her hand beneath his pajama top, lightly against his side, then withdrew it so quickly it seemed as if the reaction had been more involuntary than cerebral—as if the motion had been controlled by the nerves of the spine. Then she turned and ran away from him; her door closed softly.

He was conscious of his own breathing, and he scraped his hands harshly down his torso. Even as he did this—this desperate motion much like that of a drunk who tries to rub his face sober—he was proud that she had pressed against the body of a hard, lean man. Before he went back to bed he looked carefully and for a long time up toward the ski tow, but saw no light and heard no shot. For some reason he went quickly to sleep.

<<<<<<<<<<<<<<<<<<<<<<<<<<<<<<<<<<<<<<<<<< 15

IT SEEMED to Murray that he woke up just before he heard the shot. It was so far away—such a soft sound, really—he didn't think that it, by itself, could have awakened him. And he wasn't wakeful because it was the first day of deer season. That had kept him awake all night, once, when he was sixteen and his father had taken him out of school for a few days just to come up here and hunt. That was the first season he'd had his Mauser. Strange how excitement could fade away—just not be there any more—and all he could remember it by was a little fact like a sleepless night, or a counting of the hours he once spent working on a rifle stock. He couldn't remember at all the quality of that excitement; all that was left were the little facts, like old invoices.

But who could have been shooting on the mountain in the middle of the night? Most likely Shim, but it might have been anyone from Cascom or Leah out with jacklight and shotgun. It would be awfully dangerous for Shim, with Spooner after him the way he was, even though Shim was the kind of man who looked for danger—was always ready for sarcasm, argument, always stared straight into trouble or embarrassment with an interested, almost avid expression on his face. All that energy for it, all the time!

He went to his window and felt the night air. It was still moist and drippy outside; in the woods it would be quiet going. Maybe he would get a deer with his ugly, beautiful Nazi rifle. *Slick, slack,* the bolt would go, smooth as the joints in your arm, and then . . . all that blood, all that meat. How different were the adventures he wanted! But what were they? He went back to bed and lay on his back. As he stretched, his legs felt strong and supple.

"Somewhere there is my love," he whispered, aware of the corniness of the idea, yet ready to defend it. Why couldn't the world, even for a time, be lovely and full of fairy tales? Were the old movies all lies? He had to find out, and the answer was not here on the side of Cascom Mountain. Yesterday he had seen a B-47 fly over—so slow it seemed, so high he could hardly hear it— just see the glint of it and the vapor trail that curved back around the world. And then suddenly he realized that in that speck of metal was a hydrogen bomb, and the men who flew the plane could, if they took the notion, put it together and blow up the world. Just ordinary men, the kind who blew their brains out every day. How long could the world last? While there was tender, lovely flesh left in the world, and somewhere a girl with kindness and passion— just the one to be killed first, to be riven and destroyed by the first stupid, murderous explosion—while there was the possibility that she existed, while he had time to find her, he must go and look.

"I'm in love," he whispered, and had to smile. But it was sad, just the same. Give me time, he thought, give me some time. Leave my world alone for a while, please.

He was in love with the idea of love—that is (let's figure it out, Mr. Grimald), is love an idea? Or an emotion? Can love exist without its object? Oh, his love was plenty subjective, and thus it had an object: a lovely girl. She should have smooth and loving arms, be soft yet strong. She should be brave, yet hurt for any pain or sorrow.

"Oh, my God! I love you!" he whispered. And yet she had no face, no voice, no color.

The girl in the dream had been blonde, but that blondness was like a blank canvas. It was what she was, what they wordlessly knew about each other, that mattered. She could be an Oriental, a Negro —just so she was vivid and lovely.

And then, of course, he could get on with his life, and use his talents for himself and for the world. Would there be time? His father thought him wasteful, that his leave of absence from college was a waste of time. How could he tell his father that time was short, and that he knew how short it was? He had to go looking. He wanted to pack his things right now, and go.

It would be morning, perhaps—a hotel morning in a gray city that every morning seemed collectively to have a hangover, and he would walk, looking, looking, along a street of quiet lofts, and find a small, triangular park where the winter trees would move, brittle and disconsolate, and an old newspaper, pages and pages of gray print, would fly apart in the aimless wind and then scrape the cement before it melted against the iron fence. All cold and bare, the sun far away and yellow, shining dimly on a row of ash cans, the benches too dirty to sit on—why look there? Why? Out of ugliness, to him, came this eternal paradox: among the ugliness man made of himself, made of the places he lived in, there would always be found the sweet youth, the perceptive, selective innocence, the candid, level gaze of beauty that was always, strangely, another product of mankind. Honesty, generosity, compassion, beauty to the marrow, to the last dark center.

He reached above his head and took hold of the cold brass bars of the bedstead, then pulled them together so that they bowed slightly—not so hard that they would not return—just testing them, his strength, his control. Someone walked down the hall, past his door. It was three-thirty in the morning, and he must go to sleep.

When Shim woke him up it was five o'clock. He looked up at Shim's face in the bright lamplight, and Shim grinned down at him.

"You going to shoot a deer or not? It's deer season, boy! You awake?"

He nodded, and Shim left the room. "Yahoo!" Shim yelled in the hall. "Come on, you hunters, grab your socks!" Shim was gleeful; he'd actually been trembling.

When he came downstairs Murray was surprised to find Opal up, cooking breakfast. She was nervous; the plates rattled a little too much in her hands. He remembered the shot on the mountain; perhaps it *had* been Shim. That was reason enough for any amount of nervousness. He looked carefully at Shim, who was sharpening his Randall knife. Sharpening it? With precise fingers Shim moved it in circles on the fine side of his boxed oilstone. He'd sharpened it last night. He wore a green chino shirt and soft green wool hunting pants, both fresh.

His father came down, and Murray was amused to see him make the same inference. Then he was interested to see his father and Opal exchange glances. And hers was, even as they both convicted Shim of jacking deer at night, somehow hot. Yes, hot, buzzy, confused. He didn't see her look directly at his father again.

Old Zach came in and washed his face at the sink, his little bag dangling, then tucked his napkin under it and sat up to the table, ready.

"We got to eat well," Shim said. "Need a lot of energy to drag all them deer out of the woods."

"*Hough!* Heard. *Hough!* A shot up. *Huff!* On the mountain," Zach said. They all looked at the black windows. The kitchen light was bright, and seemed unnatural; soon it would begin to grow light outside.

"Do tell," Shim said. "Them dang poachers out again!" He did look tired around the eyes. Murray didn't think anyone else had seen a fine rim of blood around the cuticle of one of Shim's fingernails. "What you going to shoot, Murray? A buck, or a good eatin' doe?"

"Whatever kind I see, I guess."

"Best kind for eatin'! Just don't take no sound-shots!"

As Opal set Murray's ham and eggs down in front of him, the soft inside of her arm actually slid smooth and warm along the side of his neck. He was rather shocked, but didn't show it, he was sure. She had done it deliberately, and it was the last thing he would have expected her to do. She liked him—acted rather motherly toward him and all that—but he never expected her to touch him. That wasn't like Miss Midget at all.

And again, after they had buckled and slung their gear, as he

124

followed Shim out the door, she put her hand on his waist and said, "Good luck, Murray." His father followed after into the cool, damp air, and then the steplight went out and they waited a moment for their eyes to adjust to the darkness.

<<<<<<<<<<<<<<<<<<<<<<<<<<<<<<<<<<<<<<<<<< 16

RICHARD LOVED his own excitement. Dawn was coming; overhead scudded insubstantial clouds, and stars came out here and there, were silently brushed out, then came on again. As they waited for their eyes to get used to the darkness he felt his rifle's action, and hefted it by its stock's thin pistol grip. Ammunition, a sharp, clean knife, a clip to fix his deertag to a deer's ear (if he could catch such an ear!), a length of nylon rope—he was equipped lightly. His boots were pliable and silent, his pants and jacket soft red wool that would not scratch against the brush. It would be a day of silence, a slow day for still-hunting, for watching the wind, for close looking.

He was elated for another reason. The look she gave him when she touched Murray's neck! Was he old? He was a man, and could do anything. He wanted now to slip into the woods alone, to stalk. Oh, she was ready now—scared a little, trembling a little, craving the touch of him. There would be time: he would hunt, and do well—given luck, of course—but in the dark woods he would move as though he belonged there, quick, his wits sharp, his eyes clear, his weapon deadly.

He was full of glee: and then she had, for only him to see, again touched Murray as she wished him good luck. Then she turned and stared up into *his* face; dark, serious, her lips open a little bit. She had made up her mind, all right. Or lost it! And that little deception—being demonstrative in such a . . . what? Comradely way? Motherly way? toward Murray. Women did not have to learn love's stratagems. She would now arrange to receive him, he knew. And wherever, whenever it was, he would be ready.

They began to walk toward the ski tow. They had made a plan for such a silent day: at the base of the tow Murray would go south, parallel to the slope, and take a stand near the open field upon which Shim had caught young Spooner in the light of the flare. Richard and Shim would climb to the top of the first ridge—all this done slowly, for the deer could be anywhere, then take parallel routes back down toward Murray. This, they had calculated, would take until ten o'clock—four hours to travel less than two miles. Murray would have plenty of time to find a good stand. On such a quiet day, knowing that they couldn't be tracked on the damp and springy ground, the deer might not run very far. Of course, too, they might stand ten feet away and let a hunter go blindly by.

Shim once said that he could smell deer, but Shim said a lot of things. You didn't have to smell a deer to shoot out his shining eyes at night, when he was hypnotized by a jacklight. Where had Shim stashed his kill, though? He still hadn't got all the blood out of his fingernails this morning.

As they walked, single file, their boots made small noises, softer than the ground wind. The real wind was higher, for the misty clouds flew silently overhead, very fast; their silence and speed excited him, and seemed to predict great action. The beginning day seemed weird and momentous—but it was always like that on the first day of deer season, no matter what the weather. Murray left them—no one spoke—and as the sky lightened he followed Shim up the long tow slope. Shim walked steadily, not too fast—they didn't want to sweat themselves out, and it wasn't just for comfort: deer had sharp noses, and the wind on the mountain turned and was fitful in the morning; best not to stink too much. The odds were large enough already. As they went around a deep patch of ground juniper he reached down and gathered several of the berries, by touch—it was still too dark along the ground to see them, and bit into one. Bitter, harsh as gin. He spat it out again, and followed.

Shim was gone, off into the woods to the left, and Richard climbed on until he reached a certain tall spruce whose needles sighed, whose trunk was straight. The trees around it had been cut down, but it still grew tall and narrow as if it were deeply surrounded. He moved into the dead lower branches in order to merge his silhouette with the tree's, and as the day came on, the sunrise white and clear, blue growing across the sky out of a deeper, darker ultramarine, he stood quietly and let himself cool out.

All that morning he moved slowly, then stood with his outline carefully broken so that whatever habitual movements he happened to make with his hands, his head or his shoulders would not be too dramatic against a lighter or darker background. The deer could not see the red of his clothes, and he had to keep remembering this. Shim wore green, but that was because he didn't want to be seen by other hunters, not because of the game.

He faced the wind as much as possible, and examined each new vista carefully, section by section, before he brought his body fully into it. His rifle was always ready, held hunter-fashion in the crook of his left arm or, if he used his sling, barrel-down over the back of his left shoulder where it could be swung up and over into aiming position in one smooth movement. He saw fresh sign, but none so fresh it excited him. There were a few moments when his pulse picked up and his arms grew hard. Once a partridge, sneaking beneath a bent alder in a swampy place, looked in the deceptive distance as if it had deer's legs. Once a squirrel snapped a twig that, from the sound, must have been as thick as his body. Once the sun flashed against the gnarled roots of a blown down pine, and for a lovely moment the bony wood was the antlers of a buck.

What did it matter that a deer did not appear before him? One might at any moment, and each new moment brought him as near a possible, unpredictable chance at fate as would a new birth and a new life.

He met Murray at a little after ten o'clock. Murray had a good stand among some tall beeches where he could see quite far along the edge of the field and in certain directions up long, chance corridors of trees. Richard would have passed him by, but Murray gave a short whistle and there he was, not far away. They were both glad, for the moment, to relax somewhat and to move not as hunters.

"Nothing?" Richard said.

Murray shook his head.

"No really fresh sign at all," Richard said.

"Shim came by about twenty minutes ago. He's circling around. Said he jumped a skipper but didn't shoot."

"I would have."

"So would I. I wouldn't mind, even if it was small. Not so hard to drag out, anyway."

"Good eating. I'd like some of that tenderloin tonight," Richard said.

"Shim wouldn't settle for a skipper," Murray said.

"Hurt his pride to use his tag on one."

"Wouldn't hurt mine."

And so, almost ritually, they made the hunters' talk. They didn't look directly at each other, but back into the trees: it was as though they were hunters who had met by chance in the woods, and neither knew anything about the other except, by his red clothes and rifle, that he was a hunter too.

"A rabbit came by about an hour ago," Murray said. "Had me all nerved up for a while, till I saw what it was. Sounded like a whole herd of deer."

"A squirrel did the same to me. Sounded as big as a horse."

"Getting colder—maybe freeze tonight."

"Might snow."

"Hope so. Then we'll find where they are."

"Was that skipper alone, did he say?"

"Far as I could tell."

They were silent, listening. The leaves had begun to dry out, and now they heard loud rustlings and crunchings from up the hill. It turned out to be nothing but a red squirrel, who ran up a tree, much closer than he had sounded in the leaves, and screamed and chattered at them for a moment. Murray threw a stick against the tree trunk and he shut up.

"Going to be noisy this afternoon," Richard said.

"Shim said he saw bear sign," Murray said.

128

"Try to see a bear, though."

"Did you ever see one in the woods?"

"Once—far away across a field. He was turning over rocks looking for grubs. All I had was a shotgun and birdshot."

"You never see them when you've got the right gun."

"Shim told me they got forty-five off the mountain—Cascom and Leah sides both—last deer season."

"Most with dogs, I bet," Murray said.

"Deer hunters get a lot of them, though."

"You think it was Shim out jacking last night?" Murray said.

"You heard the shot?" Richard was startled by the question, but then he remembered that Zach had mentioned the shot at breakfast.

"I think I did," Murray said.

Then he might have heard them by the hall window—but they had spoken very softly, and the window was a good distance from Murray's door. "You didn't sleep too well, I guess," he said, and now watched Murray's face carefully.

"Just woke up for a while. I guess the shot woke me up. You think it was Shim?"

No, Murray hadn't heard anything else. But he would have to be careful, very careful. "I wouldn't doubt it. Meat for the winter?" They both shook their heads tolerantly.

Richard found himself getting impatient to hunt again. "Which way did Shim go?"

"Said he was going to make a big circle around to the right, then end up back here again."

"I'll go around the field to the left, then."

"Good luck."

"Same to you."

And again he was off into the woods, hunting. He could see the field off to his right, and slowly, slowly, he moved along about twenty yards from its edge. Small balsam were growing up among ash and pin-cherry saplings here, some in little islands perfect for hiding deer. A fine place for their day beds. He would be oh, so quiet and careful here—so sharp with his eyes, and if the deer were bedded here, and leaped up . . . His hands felt expert and savage upon his rifle, and when he stopped he was completely still

129

—all of him immobile except his eyes, and he was aware even of their deliberate movements.

<hr> 17

MURRAY WATCHED his father move off into the trees. He had looked happier; he supposed that the unhappiness he had detected in his father could, at least for a while, be forgotten. Now his father was a hunter, and could concentrate upon that. He hated to worry a man who was already worried, but his father had always seemed so capable, had taken charge of things and solved them so often, he didn't doubt that somehow he would bring his mother back again. There seemed to be no reason for their separation. He didn't think either one of them was unfaithful. He guessed they were both still young enough for that—seriously—then smiled at his own first childish thought. His father was still a handsome man. He hummed the lullaby:

> Yore daddy is rich
> And yore mammy's good lookin'.
> So hush, little baby,
> Don't you cry.

Just old. Pretty old, both of them. In their forties. And he did resent a little their troubles with love. He was the young one who should have full rights to that exciting problem. Old people ought to steady down and let the young ones have their adventures. One generation at a time, please! So, he thought, we make our parents, even though their blood still runs red, into institutions—sort of corporate entities which should be run by highly responsible committees rather than by glands and hearts.

130

He loved them both, though, and it was not possible to love a corporation that much. He wanted them both to be happy, and he was sure (or was he again their child?) that in order to be happy they must be together.

Something moved just at the periphery of his vision. He heard nothing, but something had moved. He waited for at least thirty seconds, then slowly turned his head. There, by a bunch of basswood brush, half hidden behind one of the beeches, was something green. Shim. The eyes, disembodied by a skein of branches, looked steadily at him, but Shim evidently didn't think he had been seen. Murray casually looked on by. Shim liked to play games, even though such a game, with a jumpy hunter, might be very dangerous. Murray sat still, now acting hunter himself, and let Shim try to come closer. Then he became impatient with it all; he felt that he had outgrown this business, and hadn't the time for it. So he put his rifle down, placed his cap carefully on a mossy rock next to the tree he had been leaning against, put his head on his cap and nonchalantly stood on his head.

Shim whooped. "You seen me, by God!" and he came walking up. "How long you seen me?"

"Just now," Murray said as he got back on his feet.

"I'm pretty sneaky, you know! You got to watch out for me."

"You are, all right," Murray said.

"I'm going to sneak me a deer, too. You watch. Git that big buck your pa saw on the road."

Shim's orange hair seemed thinner today, his face paler; his whole head was sweaty and unhealthy-looking. His rangy arms and shoulders were restless under his chino shirt. "You know what I done to young Spooner," he said fiercely, narrowing his eyes. Then his face turned sly, and he said: "You go out with girls? You had much to do with the women, Murray?"

"Some."

"What I want to do—sort of a little project, you might say, is grab a hunk of Spooner's wife. Oooo, man! What a nice little split-tail he got for himself!"

Murray was shocked by the word. Split-tail! A square-tail was a trout; a pin-tail was a duck. But a split-tail! For the moment, at least, it seemed to be the filthiest word he had ever heard in his life, and he wondered why. By Shim's expression, and his waiting, he was aware of the shock it had caused.

"Nicest little split-tail you ever did see," Shim said, watching.

Yes, it managed, more than any other word he could think of, to dehumanize. Split-tail. To dehumanize and yet keep the violated object somehow delicate and frail, so that the violation was all the more brutal. He was a little shocked, to, because Shim had been married for only six months.

"I'm figuring out how I'm going to git me a nice juicy hunk of that stuff, boy."

"You ought to get friendly with Spooner then, shouldn't you?"

"You think so, do you?" Shim said quickly. "You think I ought to git real palsy-walsy with him? Real buddy-buddy?"

Murray was somewhat resentful that Shim had perceived his shock, so he prepared to demonstrate his worldliness. At the same time he was rather ashamed of himself. "You got to get into the house before you get into her pants," he said.

Shim laughed. "Oh, Murray, you're a regular philosopher, you are! I guess I better go apologize to Spooner!" He looked sly again. "Oh, sure! Got to git into the house before I git into her pants!" He punched Murray on the arm and said, "Ain't we devils, though?

> "*Dartmouth's in town again,*
> *Run, girls, run!*"

he sang in a high, squeaky little voice. Then he was all serious again, and suggested that he take the stand for a while—it was a good one—and Murray still-hunt. Murray would circle to the right and maybe, between the two of them moving and him watching, they might jump and see a deer. "I think that buck's hiding out around here. I seen his sign."

As he left Shim, while he was still in Shim's sight, he consciously hunted. It was getting colder, and he was a little stiff at first. When he was safely out of Shim's sight he relaxed, and then found himself merely walking along, snapping twigs and scuffing leaves. After a while, some hunting instinct left in him, he decided he'd better sit again so that if his father did push a deer out he'd at least have a chance to see it. He found a place at the edge of

132

some hemlocks where he could see down a barely recognizable tote road, broke off a few lower branches of one of the hemlocks, and sat down on the soft needles with his back against it. Maybe if it snowed he would get some of his interest back, but he could not summon much of it now.

For the first time since he'd come to the mountain he wondered how long he would have to stay in order to fulfill his contract with his father. They hadn't spoken yet; he was sure that in this week his father would speak seriously with him. But what could he say in answer to his father's questions? Didn't they already know each other as well as most fathers and sons? Not as equals. He didn't think, really, that his father wanted that kind of a relationship. They had it, of course, in certain things—like that hunting conversation, where they had acted almost as if they were distant acquaintances. They would never be buddy-buddy (Shim's old-fashioned phrase), though. Obviously his father was putting off the time when they must speak to each other. Now he seemed to be using the hunting, after having used it once to get him up here, again as procrastination.

His father was an honorable man—that he never doubted. All men procrastinated, but his father always kept his word. An old-fashioned virtue, of course. Rather corny? Rather Mickey Mouse? Rather square? All right, but for his father's honesty he had nothing but gratitude—deep gratitude that could never be worn away. Bone deep, lifetime long, and with all the inevitable barriers what else could a father give a son? When his father spoke, he spoke out of the steady knowledge of all he had seen, all he knew really to be true, and if he were wrong he could at least explain, honorably, his train of logic; and Murray usually found his syllogisms, if not always his major premises, correct.

Tears came to his eyes, and the branches above him turned prismatic. How silly, but a man should have such a father, and honor him.

About his own honor? He had tried not to think about it too much—what it meant. What could be excused by youth? What could be excused by hurry, a sense of mission? What could be excused by youth's feeling, sometimes, of immortality, of the tremendous length of the years? One always had a past which contained certain experiences in which, it seemed forever afterward, one's honor had suffered. It depended upon the mood in which they were recalled. Now, after having appraised his father's honesty, the things he himself had done just last June did not please him, nor did they seem merely neutral—not even after five months in which much had happened. One measure—he hadn't thought of this until now—was that he hadn't mentioned what he'd done in June to Shelton when they came back to school. It was as if he had chosen to leave June out of his summer altogether. *Now* he thought of it. Did he dare? He smiled nervously from his ambush in the brittle woods, but he remembered the ancient record he played over and over while swatting mosquitoes in the old barn of a recreation hall: *Long Ago and Far Away*. And the silver, thick-shanked needles he had to change, and how he had to hold the old Victrola with one hand and crank it with the other; how he rubbed 6.12 Insect Repellent on his arms and dreamed of Christine's hair, which would be black and aromatic—smelling of the lake, and of her narrow hands coming up over his shoulders and sliding back down over his clavicles. He shivered, and the silly old tune took on that strange nostalgic power that only the banal can really command, because the banal never re-creates itself, but only brings back, pure and simple, whatever was there.

The summer job arranged by the Athletic Department would not begin until July, and Charlie Gilman, the backfield coach, had steered him onto a job for the month of June—building a beach at a summer camp on Lake Cascom. Because the camp didn't have a loader, all the sand had to be shoveled into the camp's old Model-A truck. "Better than going back to the city and getting flabby," Charlie said. "Don't swim too much—wrong muscles—anyway, you won't have time. Just shovel your tailbone off." But, like many jobs, it didn't turn out to be so hard after all. The amount of beach they wanted was small, and it took him just five days to haul the sand. After that he did odd things—scythed brush, painted, repaired the float and dock, caulked rowboats. The camp was called Winnicom, and was run by an old couple named Wilson; it would open later, in July, and whole families would come for most of the summer, families that had come there for years. It was hardly commercial, very cheap, and while the Wilsons had hired him for the whole month, they chose to be grateful for each repair he made. Ordinarily the people who came back each year to their favorite cabin and favorite rowboat did most of their own repairs. Mr. Wilson was a retired professor—in fact he had a men's dormitory named after him at the state university.

"No longer am I a mere man," he said to Murray, "I am an edifice." They were both standing thigh-deep in the cold water, rolling fieldstones into a breakwater; Winnicom was on the rocky, pine and birch side of the lake—the northwest side—where pine roots coiled into the water, beaches would never stay, and it was cool and dark in the mornings. Mr. Wilson pulled one of his long, ropy shanks out of the water, put his foot on the breakwater, and leaned his elbows on his knee. Already he was tanned. He looked, like many lean old men, not only tanned by the sun, but as if he had been tanned by a tannery: wrinkled but pliable, preserved. His head was smooth all over, except for a few very long wisps of bone-white hair and the harrowed places around his brown eyes.

"Charlie Gilman says you're an excellent football player. He's my nephew, by the way. Not a very *bright* boy, but honest as the day is long."

"I guess so," Murray said. The old man's fingers, wet and brown, looked like old rawhide.

"The usual modesty, I suppose. I can see you're bright—not like a football player. Excuse my prejudice, but I've tried to teach generations of football players how to distinguish between the eighteenth century and that other century that began with eighteen hundred. I always wondered how Charlie could remember all those complicated football plays."

"It's hard sometimes," Murray said, "especially when somebody's just hit you on the head."

"Ridiculous pastime."

"Once our quarterback couldn't remember anything but his high-school plays, so we played for ten minutes that way."

"But Charlie said you were an English major."

"I am."

"Well, I'll tell you something, then. I played four years of football at Bowdoin." He laughed, and waded back to shore for another stone.

135

Mrs. Wilson called them in for lunch. She, like her husband, was lean, withered, and Yankee-looking. She was very easygoing, especially about her housework, and was usually rather disorganizedly preparing the next meal. When not doing that she hunted mushrooms, her mushroom book in hand, and she would scrupulously try each new kind (this day it was a strange hue of coral mushroom) a meal or two in advance before she served them to Murray and her husband. She also liked to cook such things as porcupine and woodchuck, which she stalked in the nearby woods and fields with an old singleshot .22 with a folding stock—something called a Marble Game Getter. The Wilsons nearly always read during meals, which they ate on the big screened porch of the main cabin, and next to each of their places was a wooden bookholder. When Murray expressed approval of this custom, Mr. Wilson made him a bookholder too. They all kept their places with table knives.

This noon they had macaroni and cheese, which was rather conventional food, for them, but Mrs. Wilson swore that fresh-water clams, if she could find a book about them (was Murray going to the Baker Library by any chance in the near future?), looked awfully meaty. That evening they were going to have the legs of forty frogs she had gigged at night along the shore. Her hair was wispy and excited looking; her glasses were always dotted with spray of one kind or another, smudges and loose eyelashes; Murray wondered if she had ever heard that glasses could be cleaned. All through lunch she read a book about the hunting wasp. "Not something to eat," she said seriously.

Because the Wilsons were so casual about the work he did, instead of being diffident he found himself disapproving of their casual attitude toward maintenance; he changed things without asking, began projects he knew they would approve of with nothing but vague wonder. He moved the children's play area—swings, teeter-totters, and sandbox—away from the parking area. He knocked down the big outdoor grill and built it again so that it faced the prevailing wind and the cook wouldn't have to breathe smoke all the time. He hauled gravel for the parking area and filled in the potholes. He sanded and repainted the swing seats (after having received a large sliver from one of them). He found and removed the huge submerged rock that had shredded the bottoms of all the rowboats. Sometimes Mr. Wilson helped him, and when he did the old man worked right along with him, and in a wonderfully tactful, tacit way made it clear that he was there as helper only, and that Murray would give the orders.

Murray's main project was to limb the dead lower branches in a pine lot right behind the row of guest cabins; then, instead of a brittle jungle that was dangerous to your eyes if you walked into it, Winnicom would have a little park there, and a longer view. It might also help cut down the mosquitoes, which were terrible in the early part of the summer.

He enjoyed the work, but much as he liked the Wilsons he did not always enjoy the long evenings. He didn't have a car then, and one day he borrowed the Wilsons' old Buick and was gone all day looking at secondhand cars in the little towns within twenty miles of the lake. In Leah he found a Volkswagen that was several years old but seemed to be in good shape. He needed five hundred dollars more than he had, wired to his father in New York, and the money came the next day. It took him three days to get the car registered and insured—he had then been at Winnicom only two weeks—and that night he went in to Leah to the hog wrassle.

The women looked like women, and he danced with a hard young girl who looked sixteen but who informed him that she was married and had two kids. "What're you, a college boy?" she asked him. The band was mostly accordion, and when a jumpy old man leaped to the raised platform, clicked his heels and began in a high, musical voice to call a reel, everybody went out for a beer. Murray went out, too, past the squashed-faced, aggressive lady who had, as he had entered, stamped his wrist with fluorescent ink. He didn't go back.

He remembered some of the people he had known in Leah from his winter in high school there, but all the friends he might have wanted to see were gone into the service or to summer jobs somewhere else, where there was more money. There was one girl he had seen off and on since then, but not since the previous fall—Gretchen Harris. When he called, her mother sounded shocked, even angry, and said that Gretchen was married. He didn't really want to see Gretchen anyway, he realized as soon as he had picked the telephone off its rack in the telephone booth. That wasn't what he wanted—what he'd always got from Gretchen. They had always disliked each other, she what she had called his "superiority" and he her avid little brain. She called him "Mr. Superiority" and he called her "C.P.A." They argued and fought; she resisted; she gave in but never gave in; he also called her "The Cake-Haver," for in the face of what her literal little mind must have recognized as a fact, she still claimed chastity. Many facts. Many, many facts. Ah, well. In a forgiving, beneficent mood, now that Gretchen was no more, he hoped that she had married the kind of slob who drove the kind of car she wanted.

He could drive over to Hanover to a poker game he knew of, but he didn't want that either. He wanted nothing imperfect, nothing to be a compromise on this summer night. Whatever it was he did must be nothing ersatz, nothing vicarious. So he drove back to Winnicom, went to his cabin and changed into his trunks, then swam through the soft black water toward the float. The water was cold—but real, he thought; he let it slide over him, dived to the rocky bottom, the weedy, forbidden, shivery place where the oily weeds reached up for him with a touch that was almost tentative (*tentacle*, he thought, relishing some horror— that was real, too), and the weeds caressed his naked, tender skin. He turned and slid up toward the air, where starlight was the only light. One last long streamer touched the hollow of his foot— the last kiss from below—and he kicked hard until he reached the float and rolled onto the harsh dry wood.

One of the drums bonged softly. What wind there was came down the dark mountain beyond the lake and crossed a mile of water before it touched him; it was cold. But real. The float creaked. The drums, slapped gently by the waves, hummed and bonged up through the resonant wood. The Milky Way swung (not from the movement of the float, but from its own haphazard design, the random, accidental course of the universe) precariously across the sky. Orion's belt, the Big Dipper, and straight over Cascom Mountain the North Star: that was where the wind came from. He wished she were here to shiver with him, to shiver in his arms, not from the cold but from a shared and lovely awe, part fear, for their dangerous hold upon the overturning world.

The raft was real—it hummed to itself as it rode on the dark water. The sisal mat beneath his shoulders scratched painfully—almost a substitute for heat, but not her sweet, tender heat—whoever she was.

The lights from the Wilsons' cabin shone, warm on the tops of the little waves. Around the lake few lights burned because it was too early in the season, and the dark lake seemed more primitive than it really was. The water itself was always deep and black at night.

A screened door slapped against its frame. He could hear the buzz of the spring, and someone came walking down the path to the dock, then stepped onto the boards and came walking out to the end of it.

"Murray, is that you? Are you alone?" A shy voice— Mr. Wilson's.

"Yes," Murray said.

"We just wondered . . . when you're through swimming—isn't it *cold?*—would you stop in for a minute, have a coffee or a beer?"

"I'd like to," Murray called, and he had a surge of affection for the old man. *His* hold upon the world was even more precarious; he was nearly seventy years old. But he'd held on all those years, and presumably hadn't bumped too many other people off. They were very *happy* people, he was sure, and it seemed to him, as he considered the Wilsons, that such happiness had to be deserved. Or had he seen, or heard of, a happy boor, or a happy sadist or miser? One would have to discount a lot of propaganda, he supposed. He had certainly seen unhappiness in nice people; that was common enough.

The wind had dried him off, and he didn't look forward to the water again, but when he dived in it was surprisingly warm compared to the cold air, and he swam slowly, almost luxuriously in to shore. His chest scraped on the new sand, and as he stood up into the cold breeze he felt very strong and clean.

The Wilsons had a hot little fire of pine slabs going in their fireplace, and he sat down on the rug in front of it, conscious of their age and his muscular, healthy youth. They examined him, he felt, and found him quite a specimen. Rarely did such narcissism come unaccompanied by a little guilt, but now they seemed to examine him in just that fashion. Mr. Wilson got him a beer, and Mrs. Wilson found a huge Turkish towel and carefully draped it over his shoulders. "You're so *healthy*, Murray," she said, then sat in her deep wicker chair and looked at him admiringly. On the table next to her chair was an incredibly snarled ball of fish line, and she took it, adjusted her hazy glasses (as a surprise, a few days before, he had cleaned them for her, but she never noticed) and began to pick away at it with her hard, slightly arthritic fingers. She pulled out a long loop, looked vaguely around in the air, then hung it over one of the curved metal pieces on her bridge lamp. He was sure she would forget where she put it, and expected that when she next got up the lamp would go over. He made a note to grab the lamp when she got up. But he was wrong; soon she followed the line, a perplexed expression on her face, up and over the bridge lamp. "How on earth!" Then she remembered that she had put it there.

Mr. Wilson smoked his pipe, a straight meerschaum with an old-fashioned running horse carved along the stem—old-fashioned in that the front legs and back legs were fully extended at the same time. His dark fingers caressed the horse's shiny rump. After a while, with the same shyness in his voice, he said, "Murray, we want to ask you something."

Murray hoped he knew the answer, or could give it. Because of the Wilsons he wanted to do well in any examination they might give him.

"In a way, it's a favor," Mr. Wilson said, "but I don't suppose it really should be. . . ."

"Now, get to the point," Mrs. Wilson said.

"Well, it's a little plot, in which you're involved—but you don't have to be. Oh, it's all quite tentative. Forgive us old busybodies!"

"Get to the point," Mrs. Wilson said, but she wouldn't look up from her untangling.

"Well, let me! Now: we've got a granddaughter. . . ."

"We've got five granddaughters and two grandsons."

"Please, Mary! Now you won't let *me* get to the point."

Mrs. Wilson did look up. "It's not really this bad, Murray."

He could only look and listen.

140

"We've got a granddaughter about your age, Murray," Mr. Wilson said, "and we're thinking of asking her up here for a visit. Usually she doesn't come until July. But she's been ill and we think it would do her good—but we don't want her to be lonesome! She's a very good-looking girl."

"Good-looking! Why she's as *pretty!* She's as pretty as a picture," Mrs. Wilson said.

"Christine's her name, Murray. She's had polio—left her just a little bit awkward in her walk. Well, let's say she limps a little bit."

"The tiniest little bit!"

"Well, one of her calves is smaller than the other. . . ."

Mrs. Wilson broke in: "Murray, would you, if we asked her here, be kind to her? She's never had much to do with boys. Just be kind to her?"

"I'll try," he said immediately. Yet he remembered with some fear another time when he'd been asked for help, and had none to give, when his cousin Sophie had been in trouble.

"Her picture. Show him her picture—the one from last summer," Mr. Wilson said.

Mrs. Wilson got to her feet and the lamp went over; she'd looped some more fish line over it. She also had some tangled around her feet. While Murray untangled her, Mr. Wilson went upstairs for the picture. Murray felt as though he were being sold something—that feeling and a half-pleasant, half-fearful curiosity. It did seem a little crass, somehow, to be shown a picture of the merchandise. By the time he'd untangled the fish line from the hooks of Mrs. Wilson's quail-hunting boots, Mr. Wilson was back with a framed picture—one of the kind with a little triangular foot on the back so that it could be stood up on a bureau. Cautiously, he looked at it.

A figure standing at the bow of a rowboat: slim, in a dark, one-piece bathing suit. Narrow waist—yes, and the leg with the thin calf was the one placed up on the gunwale; the gesture looked deliberate.

He always wondered why he thus catalogued the figure of the girl while the face was there, laughing at him. He didn't yet look directly at the face, a pale disc surrounded by black. Long, slightly protrusive collarbones, immature-looking breasts—hard to tell. Some slender grace in the waist, the way the hips were canted, her arms akimbo, pale hands pressing upon the shiny cloth. And the one calf deliberately in profile. The knee looked bigger than it should have because of the nearly straight line from thigh to Achilles' tendon.

The face laughed, but he didn't feel like laughing back. A smudge for each large eye, but a wide mouth with even lips and teeth. Sadness about the eyes, maybe. The black hair looked soft, and whisked her shoulders as she turned toward the camera.

He didn't know what to say. She had struck him. She seemed possibly the most beautiful girl he had ever seen; perhaps it was that the expression on her face exactly called out to his sadness now. He handed the picture back to Mr. Wilson, and while the two old people looked at him, suspense in their faces, he was afraid. He was close to childhood, closer than he had thought, childhood where wishes are possible but where, forever and ever, a wish carries with it its own ironic penalty. The child knows all about that, and soon figures out that it is better not to make a wish at all.

The old faces still looked at him, were still ready for disappointment.

"I was afraid she'd be fat," he said.

"Fat!" Mrs. Wilson was so relieved. "Heavens, Murray, nobody in our family's *fat!*"

"She's very skinny," Mr. Wilson said. "We're always trying to put some meat on her."

"Skinny!" Mrs. Wilson said.

"Well, slender, you might say."

"She looks very nice," Murray said. "She looks like a very attractive girl."

"She's a lovely girl," Mr. Wilson said, and in his voice there was some kind of strain. "We love her so much," he added quickly, and he turned and carried the picture out of the room.

Mrs. Wilson didn't look up for a few seconds, then she looked brightly at Murray and said, "We have some other pictures, and some of her letters—would you like to see them?" Her voice was strained, too, yet determinedly bright. He said yes, and when she got up the lamp went over again. "Oh, hell!" she said. "My grandson is responsible for this!" And quite angrily she took a pair of scissors out of her apron and snipped the fish line apart in several places, then wadded it up and threw it into the embers of the fire. She apologized: "I don't know why I bothered with it; it's only a hand line worth about twenty-five cents."

Mr. Wilson didn't come downstairs again, but Mrs. Wilson went upstairs and brought down a thick manila envelope. "You can take these along with you if you're interested, Murray," she said, and he thanked her and went back to his cabin. He didn't open the envelope until he was in bed, then dumped everything out of it onto his blanket and went first to the photographs, expecting to see something about the girl that might break the strange mood her picture had put him in. In a way he looked for relief from such a strong feeling; she couldn't be all that lovely. Photographs were great liars. And of course she could be stupid and insensitive, or a blabbermouth or something like that, or have a fantastic ego. People who had been sick could be impossible.

But the snapshots he found among the letters did not dispel his first infatuation at all. Here were her large dark eyes, serious this time, beneath the harsh line of a bathing cap, and they looked right at him, intelligent and wide open. No self-consciousness in that face; it just observed. Her nose was a little flattish, maybe, but whatever variations there were upon the conventional idea of beauty seemed, in context, just right. And of course they would, because intelligence and humor shone out of that face, he was sure, and not only because of that, but because he was almost in love with Christine already. He could tell he was, because whatever blemishes he found on her came into his consciousness already half excused. That, for instance, was definitely a pimple on her forehead. See? It didn't appear in this one where the sun made a plane of her forehead and darkened the hollows of her eyes. Her breasts *were* small. In this one she chose to hide her bad calf and recline self-consciously, like a starlet, on the dock, and even the act was graceful. She was so spare, so slender. The visible leg was perfect; it seemed a monstrous way to put it: "The visible leg." She was full of grace, and her presence in each photograph belied such dissection. Yes, her foot turned in a little, but (here it came,

143

love's rationalization) it seemed quite endearing, like the awkward helter-skelterness of a very young girl.

Well, he would read her letters. His hands were shaking just a little bit, and there was a slight, unnatural feeling in the back of his throat—a kind of negative pressure, if there were such a thing. Too much would depend upon her words, because a word could be so revealing and hard to excuse.

How old was she? He glanced through the letters quickly, noting that all the dates were within the last year—her grandmother must, if she had saved them, have kept out any earlier letters. In those that were handwritten the writing was round but well formed, and very clear. The margins and the lines were straight.

NEWTON, MASS.
January 7th

MY DEAREST (AND ONLY) GRANDPARENTS,

So you want a great-great grandson, do you? And because I am now eighteen I should run (limping) into the marriage business! Your little verse was very funny, and I have one for you, but on a different subject, I'm afraid. It's just another of my animal collection, and of course the moral doesn't apply to you.

THE MOA

The moa, in a prosperous era,
Traded his wings for a big viscera,
Drumsticks nearly five feet tall,
And a gizzard as big as a basketball.
The dingo, eating moa raw,
Might contemplate this circular saw:
Talents are few, and talons are many,
So keep the first if you have any
(there might still be an outer bird
if the inner bird had heard this word).

I'm not sure that dingoes ever *ate* moas, to tell you the truth (Grandmother sure would have, though!). They may even come from different subcontinents. And of course dingoes may have claws, but not talons. So you see what an indifferent scholar I am?

I love you,
CHRIS

144

PROFESSOR AND MRS. HUBERT WILSON:

In response to your request for a recent photograph of Miss Christine Wilson, our publicity department yawned, rolled over and fractured its third cervical vertebrae (now don't get worried—just a joke); however, we did manage to come up with this highly expendable Polaroid shot of Miss Wilson, in which she appears next to her sister's leading man, Mr. Icky Collins (he thinks his name is Charles Joseph Collins; Sue calls him Icky and I call him Guano Joe. . . .

The suction in his throat increased. So bright, so charming, so silly! He read the letters; most were answers to questions he didn't know, or talked about people he had never heard of. He was jealous of this other life of hers, and frequently had to remind himself that he didn't know very much about her at all, whether or not she went to school, even how tall she was (this he tried to figure out by comparing her to the rowboats in the pictures, and wished he had Shelton's protractor and compass). And she might not even like him.

BOSTON, MASS.
April 10th

DEAREST GRANDMOTHER AND GRANDFATHER,

Well, here I am again, in the hospital. I am absolutely certain (neither snow, nor rain, etc.) that the W. family faster-than-sound grapevine has informed you of all the details, so I won't go into my symptoms.

I include my latest poem. Sometimes I like it, sometimes I don't. You ask for copies of all of them, and Daddy volunteers to have them mimeographed at the office (you'd *know* that!) but honestly, I read them over and none are right. Some are silly, all are pompous, some are childish: "Dusk is my velvet curtain/Swishing across the stage." Agh! Swishing Dusk? Sounds like a character out of Tennessee Williams. And then there was my Dylan Thomas period, which is best forgotten. Everything was *green* then, except grass, which was *golden*, or *forked*, or something like that!

Thank you for the lovely book on George Herbert and Henry Vaughan. There is a line of Herbert's I think is so beautiful: "Groans are quick, and full of wings." I keep thinking about it, maybe because I hear them all the time here—unexpectedly from a door I'm passing, and the room that was all white and barren-looking suddenly becomes all full of a real person and real pain.

The other day I went back to my old alma mater, the children's ward, for a visit. Miss Pease, the head nurse, is still there; we had coffee and she got mad at me for being back in hosp. again. All the pretty young nurses and students have changed, and more have come in their places, just as pretty (Grandfather!).

The children have changed, too. Please don't be unhappy if I get morbid, but I want to explain about the poem. Two little boys, about five or six years old, were shooting each other with toy guns (looked just like real guns, too) and having a wonderful time taking turns shooting or being shot. They maybe even enjoyed the being shot part more than the other! They were both very, very sick, especially one of them, but I won't go into that. But the shot one would fall back into bed so relaxed and so happy! And a little girl was watching and asking them to shoot her, too, and they did, even if she couldn't fall down just right. She had cancer, and was in such pain—you could tell by her eyes. I'm sorry. But they played and played, and I remembered playing the same game on the lawn at home with Sue and David. We used to call it, "Bang, you're dead!"

BANG, YOU'RE DEAD
by Christine Wilson

In the bush there jumps a wren
Nervous about the shot children
Who gaily clutch their hearts and fall
Upon the soft grass by the wall.

"Bang, bang!" they call, in happiness;
The killed are happy as the quick
To fall to rest with such lightness.

The summer grass is cool and new,
The summer sky is warm, is blue;
The wren may jump and disapprove,
But the gray clouds ever move,

And children wake unto a day
When grass has weathered to the quick:
It is a game the children play.

I don't particularly like the gray clouds—sounds rather ordinary, don't you think? I'm working on that line. I hope the poem isn't too morbid for you. I try not to be, really. Then, I think, Grandfather will say (not you, Grandmother!) that I've been pretty cruel to dig a poem out of those poor sick children. But what can we do? Sit around and weep and weep for all of them—all the sick children? When I get like that I don't *do* anything, and I get irritable. Yesterday I was very rude to Mother. She didn't do anything, particularly; she just looked so stupid and helpless standing around my bed. I told her to sit down, for Christ's sake. Would you tell her I didn't mean it? If *I* do she'll create one of her love scenes, and then I'll get mad at her again. Poor old Ma. She insists that what I have is undulant fever, because she had it at my age!

Well, maybe I am getting morbid. I would love to see you both and exchange wisecracks or something.

Love to you dear old fuddyduddys,
CHRIS

In another letter, dated back in February, she had written, ". . . so I don't just sit around waiting for what Sue insists upon calling a 'dream boy.' But, yes, I have visions and daydreams just like anyone else. . . ."

How would I do? he thought. I'll be man enough for you, Christine. We can exchange wisecracks, too. And I know a few other things besides "the gray clouds" I'd question in your poem. What about the wall, there in the fourth line? Isn't that just there for the rhyme? "But"—he spoke out loud, now, but softly—"I like the line, and the rhyme, 'To fall to rest with such lightness.' Oh, what a light and lovely feminine rhyme that is, Christine!"

The bare pine boards, the open studding of the cabin made his aloneness too obvious—they were so bare and functional! And he was only talking to himself. Moths fluttered softly against the screens, their little eyes gleaming green and orange.

He would have to be very careful with her when they first met, and not reveal himself too much. He wouldn't let her know that he had read her letters, of course. She certainly wouldn't like to know that they would meet on unequal terms. And the leg, how would she want him to act about the leg? And then he thought, Too much of this planning business is stupid; he would do what he would do. He might not even like her. What if she had a shrill, hard voice, and never shut up? But she wouldn't. She would know (she knew so much!) what she seemed like to other people. She would know she was pretty, but not that she was beautiful. And this, really, was his most perfect secret and power, and he felt very lucky, supremely lucky, to have it: she just happened—psychological, aesthetic, whatever causes had made him react to this particular girl—to be beautiful to him, probably to him alone. She would be too bright for most boys, and would probably not bother to hide it—perhaps in defense of her awkward leg.

"Not too bright for me, though," he said out loud, and recognized in his voice a kind of threat. "This one is *mine*," he said, gloating this time, "so keep your cotton-pickin' hands off, Guano Joe and Tom Terrific and whoever!" The idea that she might settle for someone less than he frightened him, and he had a pang of jealousy. And then, gloating some more, "No, she's coming here!" *Vanity, vanity*, he thought; all right, so what? She goan love me, Ah goan *have* her!

But with tenderness, strength, whatever she wants. And then he thought, My goodness gracious sakes alive! Let's face it, Murray Grimald, you *have* done rather well with girls; you *are* tall, dark, and handsome, not to mention intelligent, funny, brave, sensitive, well coordinated (modest?). Not only that, but you have a real date-bait type car, a dashing Volkswagen with a cracked muffler and some ancient puke etched into the upholstery.

She was eighteen (some time in December or January), and in spite of a certain brash worldliness, which probably covered up for the tender skin all intelligent people had (a tenderness that approached cowardice but never had a chance to get there), she would be really naïve; a virgin, no doubt, but a virgin neither out of fear nor out of avarice. How wonderful, he thought, to come to love knowing so much, perceiving so much about the world, yet inexperienced in it, unhandled and unpawed by it.

And only *his* gentle, almost worshipful? no, *appreciative*, but in some strong, even selfish way, *deserving* hands should touch and caress her.

"Christine, Christine," he whispered, and the moths at the screen fluttered their talcum wings and gleamed their eyes. He put the photographs and letters back in their envelope, and turned

148

off the light. As he went to sleep, curiously vivid visions appeared—the girl in the photographs moved, and touched him; he and Chris out in a rowboat on the dark lake, Orion turning in the sky; he and Chris, her slender arm just touching his, lying on the float in the late afternoon sun, the drums gently bonging; he and Chris in his Volkswagen, driving down a road in a green and rolling land, a road that led them far away, far away to a new country; he and Chris in bed together, her narrow hands sliding coolly up his ribs, and her . . . no, that one would not continue. That one was to be deserved, and must be waited for with piety and modesty.

In the morning, before he had remembered Christine, he awoke with a strange sense of joy, as if whatever he would do that very day would no longer be a part of his long wait for real life; as if his vicarious childhood were over. And as he rubbed his eyes he did remember Christine, and that she was coming. At breakfast he lied, and said he hadn't finished looking at her letters. But he felt that they saw his excitement. Why hide it from them? All he could think of to say was, "She sounds like a wonderful person."

Oh, you don't know, he thought, that she is practically mine already.

Mrs. Wilson poured his coffee, and with the percolator still in one hand, ran her other hand down his biceps. "You're so strong, Murray! No wonder you can work so hard."

And he did work hard that day, pruning the pine grove behind the cabins and piling the brittle dead branches. He foresaw a time when he would (though somehow dishonorably, because they would still be paying him) want to spend much time with Christine, and he wanted to finish the job first. She might come with him and they could talk as he worked, but that might get rather boring for her. Of course he would have to figure out something to do so that she wouldn't suspect that he was a kind of paid companion. And he couldn't go to the Wilsons and ask them not to pay him; his job should not be given such businesslike status, and it would make the Wilsons unhappy to think of it that way—unhappy, at least, to know that he thought of it that way. He worked hard all morning, and in the afternoon Mr. Wilson came and helped him.

"We called, and we think she can come," Mr. Wilson said. Something about his voice worried Murray, and he tried not to show it.

"Think she can?" he said as he threw an armful of branches on the pile. He said it casually and immediately started back, adding over her shoulder, "Is she still sick?"

"Well, she's not very strong," Mr. Wilson said. "Not like you, Murray." That sounded a little happier, a little hopeful, for some reason.

That night after supper Murray went to his cabin and looked at all of her pictures again. He became nervous and impatient, and walked along the shore for a while, slipping along over the mounds of roots, between the pines whose needle-covered hummocks jutted out over the water. On his way back he went into the barn that was the camp's recreation hall. It wasn't wired for electricity, and he lighted an oil lamp in the huge room beneath the notched beams and hand-formed purlins. The loft was high above and silent; an old shelf-paper sign drooped between its thumbtacks: HAPPY BIRTHDAY, DEAR HARRY! and the small, original barn windows reflected the amber lamplight. Idly he wound up the old Victrola, set it low, and put on the first record he found in its warped cabinet. It was an old song, "Long Ago and Far Away," and as it played (a smooth old band from the days of World War II, he thought, and a sweet-voiced woman who stayed on the note from beginning to end), the song, in the weird way old and maudlin songs do, became forever afterward the touchstone, the crazily magic, nonsensical cause for complete memory of his love for a girl he had never met.

Every day he worked hard at the stand of pine, and little by little between the trees a small park grew of soft little humps all covered with long, tan needles. But Christine didn't come, and as the days passed the Wilsons seemed to grow very cool toward him. At lunch one day late in the month Mr. Wilson looked at his hamburger steak and said evenly, "If you're through with that envelope of pictures and letters we'd like it back." Mr. Wilson never came to help him with the work any more, and rarely even read at meals, just looked at his food, ate it, and went upstairs.

"What's the matter?" Murray asked Mrs. Wilson.

"Why, nothing's the matter," she said, trying to look bright about it; not managing. Once, from his cabin, he heard them shouting at each other, but couldn't understand the words. He grew afraid to ask about Christine, and his worry about the immediate relationship between himself and the Wilsons tended to make Christine's power over him lessen—at least during the day. At night he often went to the barn and played "Long Ago and Far Away" softly on the old Victrola, sad in the high old room. He dreamed about her once—they stood together on a ridge and watched a line of clouds so brilliant it hurt his eyes. The clouds all looked like camels far away over Cascom Mountain, and in back of the ponderous and dignified clouds the sky was black, like a curious negative, for the clouds should have been dark, and then he looked at his lovely Christine and her hair was blinding white.

At times he found in himself a silly remnant of his Jewish paranoia: was it because they had found out that he was half-Jew that they had grown cold and hard in his presence, these Wilsons, these Anglo-Saxons he liked so much?

Then the day came when he had to leave for his construction job. When he was ready to go the Wilsons came out to his car. "Goodbye," they said. He looked at them, knowing the worry his face reflected, and Mrs. Wilson came running up to the car, her Bass boots crunching on the new gravel, and she tried to put her face inside so that she could kiss him, but the window wasn't open wide enough, and her bony cheek was creased white by the edge of the glass before he could open the window all the way. She reached in and squeezed his arm as hard as she could and kissed him on the cheek. The old man had turned back, and then she did, too—stepped back away from the car so that he could go— and stood with her skinny arm, the lumps of her elbow bluish, raised to wave goodbye.

He was very upset, and felt like crying. His throat hurt. He didn't want to leave them that way (and yet his hands and feet worked competently enough, and the little car climbed smoothly up the long driveway toward the main road), and not only did he want his parting with the Wilsons to be affectionate and understandable, he felt deeply sorrowful, almost self-pitying, as if he had been cheated of Christine and her soft arms and steady eyes. But he *had* to go. All right, they would see. He would scheme a little, and he would meet her somehow.

It was good to see some of the team again, those good-natured goosing numbheads, and he was in much better shape than they were. That summer they worked jackhammers, dismantling the concrete foundations of an old National Guard armory, then built forms for pouring another foundation. He was tired at the end of each of those long summer days, but healthy and deeply tanned, his hands hard as rocks. Occasionally they went into the little town and had a few beers; occasionally they played rather unimaginative poker with the permanent construction crew, but mostly they ate, worked, and slept.

Back at school in September he cornered Charlie Gilman in the field house, one rainy day, and asked him about the Wilsons and about Christine. Charlie, the ex-athlete, his thick waist always tightly belted, half turned away as though he had something he really had to do at exactly that moment. Murray side-stepped with him, though, and faced him. Why the guilt? He *had* been chosen, hadn't he!

"Why, they're all right, I guess," Charlie said.

"What about the girl, Christine—the one who had polio? They said she was going to come up last June."

In Charlie's baggy, burnished face there was a great deal of pain. How do you get to put things together all of a sudden? Murray wondered as he watched Charlie trying to put just a sentence together; there was some terrible thing Charlie tried to say, and he should have seen it long ago.

So when Charlie finally managed to say that Christine had leukemia—the polio she'd had long ago, as a kid—and in July went into a coma—they'd thought she might have six months left at least; but in July she went into a coma and she died—a sweet kid, Murray, but that's the way the ball bounces—when Charlie finally said it and then hurried off, Murray knew what he should have known, or guessed, were he not so goddam lousy egotistical about the stupid lousy egotistical charm he planned to use on her. Christine was dead in the summer. Dead. And whatever sensual dreams he'd had, whatever exuberance he'd had about his worthiness, now turned rotten, sinful. Blood no longer moved through the chambers of her heart; her game leg now pitifully lay like a stick, out straight, the foot turned slightly inward.

He went back to his room in the dorm. School hadn't started yet, and Shelton wasn't back, so he sat in the unoccupied-looking room and stared out the window at the wet old leaves left from the summer that was over. He *had* been chosen, hadn't he? Charlie Gilman had picked him out for them on order, Christine's "dream boy" she said she never waited for, the one whose qualities would most likely appeal to her. "A real intellectual type," he could hear Charlie saying to them as they busybodied themselves for their beloved granddaughter. Charlie had hit some mark or other. *Use me!* he thought, *for Christ's sake use me! But will you use me sometime to help?* Must I go merrily on past the bodies of babies and children, all the sick children, and always come out a stupid failure?

Ah, but the poor old people; how they had watched his strength and done almost superstitious homage to his gross and obvious fine health. Leukemia, cancer, and they could not understand it. Half the time we study to kill and half the time we make signs and incantations out of terrible, god-awful love. Perhaps they wanted more from him than his talents could ever warrant: a transfusion for their beloved of his life and energy. How the old lady had squeezed his muscle! And if they wanted him to, he would have been so glad to try.

When he moved his head quickly to the side, trying to shake it loose from such memories, a sharp stick poked him in the cheek hard enough to draw some blood. He put his finger to the spot and then examined the little red smear. "Keep right on reminding me," he said to the stick, to the tree, to, he guessed, nature in general. "Keep on telling me I'm alive but only sitting on my dead ass."

He had to be going and doing. He pretended to speak to his father: "I say, O.M., Old Indian, Old Stone-Age Man with all your bloody honor . . ." His voice turned suddenly bitter, near to crying. "Explain to me just what I am doing here." In his lap he held a machine out of one end of which could come, at great velocity, a most ingeniously and subtly perfected complex of metals; first a cap of bronze, which also functioned as a plunger. Behind this cap was a wee air pocket, and behind this air pocket was a certain amount of lead alloy, surrounded by a graduated jacket of copper. A most wonderful invention, worthy of man's ceaseless aspirations, his unflagging inventiveness, his inspired and never-ending search for perfect happiness. This bullet was meant to strike just one material—in fact it wouldn't work very well at all unless it struck one certain material, and that was living animal tissue; when it struck living animal tissue, at perhaps twenty-five hundred feet per second, it did its work beautifully and spectacularly, for living animal tissue, being approximately 70 per cent water, was nearly incompressible, and the hydraulic effect alone was truly fantastic.

That was the way to think! Never mind the rest—the strange dignity of life, the fear, the tears: flesh was 70 per cent H_2O, right? That was something you could get your teeth into, now, wasn't it, Old Scientist, Old Know-How?

"Not you, really, O.M.," he said apologetically, "because I'm a man too, I hope, and I'm part hunter too. But why don't you yell at me, sometimes, out of frustration and anger that is really love? I've seen Mother when she wanted to blubber and scream and cry, but, Pukka Sahib, that wasn't done in our house."

And then he thought: I am not being fair at all, and it isn't just because I love the man that I think so. He is what he is, I suppose, and what he is, is a man. For better or worse a real, red-blooded goddam man, a credit to the tribe. But . . ."

He had been hearing a sound like a long breath; a familiar sound, one that anywhere but in the deep woods might not have been noticed, and now he looked straight up into the clear blue sky. Three tiny vapor trails grew in silence far ahead of the sound of breath, and the sun glinted just once, needle-like, from the silver crosses with their slanted bars as the planes bore toward the southeast in formation, the vapor trails curving around after, like the thinnest strands of cobweb.

He raised his rifle and pointed it at the tiny silver airplanes. "Bang, you're dead," he said, and laughed bitterly.

WHEN RICHARD had completed his circle around the open field he passed by Shim, who had moved thirty yards away from Murray's original stand. Shim didn't signal to him, preferring no doubt to play the deerstalker, so Richard pretended that he didn't see him. Fat chance of that, he gloated; today in the woods he was as sharp with his eyes as Shim, that woods animal, ever was. And he could outstalk Shim rather easily in another situation, too; in that game he was much more adept, all right. He smiled, and shivered with pleasure. Maybe tonight something would happen.

It was getting late, now, and the sun would soon go behind Cascom Mountain. It was getting colder, too, and the leaves underfoot were brittle, and had little frost lights on them here and there. All the way back to the house, even though he couldn't help making a lot of noise, he never relaxed, but kept looking and expecting. There would be at least three-quarters of an hour more of light, and it would be a good time to pick a spot, especially on the first day of the season when the deer had not yet become almost completely nocturnal, and sit out the light altogether. He had been hunting with all of his attention ever since daybreak, and no deer had appeared; but there was another kind of game (he smiled, and shivered again), and at least he knew where he could catch a glimpse of it.

Before he went into the kitchen he flicked the glittering cartridges out of his rifle, then picked them up and carefully wiped them off before he put them in the cartridge case on his belt. Zach sat in his chair and watched his portable television which, as usual, he had set up on the kitchen table, his straight old head incongruous before the wide brass rabbit's ears. He and Richard nodded to each other, and Richard put his empty rifle, bolt open, in the corner and went upstairs. His legs were tired, but still felt very strong. His whole body felt nicely tough, and woodsy, as if, even though tired, it could go hunting again and do quite as well in the woods as it had all day.

He took a shower, deciding that he would plead an old man's tiredness if, by odd chance, Shim or Murray returned before dark. What a lie that would be! His wife could leave him, his son could go hipster or whatever the hell Murray meant by quitting school, but by God he was still a man in his prime, and one thing he knew was that Rachel hadn't left him because of a lack of a certain kind of attention. In the mirror his long face seemed quite young—well, not *too* young, but still somehow full, still in contention, not decreased at all in the firmness of its cheeks or the positive and possible look of its eyes. Light blue, they were, and could not look soft; that was a cool, contentious blue in the pale iris; the eyebrows and mustache were pure and original black, too, and the teeth sharp and white. He shaved carefully, then brushed his teeth before he stepped out into the hall with a towel wrapped around his waist and his hunting clothes over his arm.

And got a delicious shock—a tingling in his nose and in his loins—because Opal stood there waiting for him. He stopped and looked down at her. She wore neat dungarees, and her shirt, styled like a man's, was light blue, crisp and jaunty, graceful in a squarish, boyish sort of way. He had to keep himself from sneezing, and he could have taken her right there, before she spoke, but like a hunter he wanted to be sure.

"It *was* Shim last night," she said, trying not to be embarrassed by his nakedness, not able to find a place to look. Then finally, blushing, she looked him in the eyes, and hers were brown, shy and nervous.

"Did he jack a deer?"

She nodded. "I know where he keeps them. Do you want to see?"

"Yes," he said, "I want to see." And she blushed harder, her dark skin turning the color of a rose; a dark rose, he thought. He put his hand on her arm, ostensibly to let her know he would go on by and get dressed, but of course it was a caress, and she moved slowly, as though she were dreaming, just out of his way.

156

He dressed quickly. His hands were shaking, and he thought, This is hunting, when the game lusts after the hunter! He had a vague but powerful memory of a child's tale about a hunter: yes, and in it all the game—the deer, the foxes, the rabbits—all came to the hunter because of a spell, or a granted wish in the dark forest of childhood memory. But how had that story ended? He could not remember, but he remembered when, as a child, he had read it. Strange: it was in hunting season, on his uncle's farm in Iowa, shortly after his father died, and he remembered all the bright pheasants piled in the front hall, their iridescent green and golden feathers, their berry-bright red eye patches gleaming in the light that came from the big Iowa sky through old-fashioned patterned-glass door panels.

Opal waited in the hall, and he followed her down the steep back stairs. She was so short he could have touched her head easily with his foot on the way down, and as he followed her he wanted to pick her up, to pet her, to take off her clothes. The Portable Woman, he thought exultantly, The Sex-homunculus, travel-size; the distilled, reduced, essential female appetite! She made him think of his new, expensive, accurate wrist watch—small, thin, beautiful—but Opal was thin only in those nice places where a woman should be thin.

Zach didn't bother to turn toward them as they went by. "We're going to get some cider," she said to Zach, and Richard knew that this was the first and most important of many lies. How smooth and easy it was for lovers! He and Rachel had so easily evaded her family, too, no matter whose house they were in, when he had first gone to work for Saul.

He followed her down the cellar stairs into the cool, earth-smelling damp air. Potato peels, he thought, and was chilled, pleasantly, after the kitchen, which was kept hot for Zach's old blood. Above them the voices of television were faintly raucous.

"Look here," Opal said. She pulled a string, and in the dim light from a small bulb she led him to the one cellar window. On the frame at the bottom there were little bits of brown blood, and brown and white hairs here and there. "He's careless," she said. "Spooner might get a warrant, and he'd find those hairs."

"But where's the deer?" he asked, and put his hands on her

shoulders. She let him pull her against him. He took off her glasses and put them in his pocket, then picked her up to kiss her on her trembling mouth.

"Let me show you," she said, without quite enough breath to vocalize the last word.

"Yes, show me," he whispered, and kissed her on the neck, feeling out the smooth, hollow places he had been thinking about. She signaled to get down, and as he put her down he thought how there was that purely tactile language, too, she would not have to learn, but as a woman instinctively know, and the words were *Kiss me, wait a second, caress me there, put me down, I don't mean it*, and the words would become longer and more complicated, too.

"He's got a refrigerator in here," she said. "I'll bet you can't find it."

He looked around, impatient of the refrigerator; he wanted warm game. Well, there was the furnace, its octopi arms reaching up into the floor above; there were the cider barrels (they had better remember to fill a jug); there were the odd shelves, here and there, of unpainted, darkened pine, full of Mason jars; there was about half a cord of stove wood. . . .

"Where is it?" he asked, keeping impatience out of his voice.

She went to one of the cool-air intake vents of the furnace, where the vent came down the wall and turned at the floor before it came across to the bottom of the furnace. The vent pipe was at least three feet wide, but very shallow, made of galvanized sheet iron. At the wall, she reached down and turned something that was in the shadow, then pulled on the whole upright section of the vent pipe. It swung open—heavily, ponderously, and there was a bright room on the other side of it, gaudy-bright under white fluorescent light that flickered as it came on, and he was afraid that someone was there. A red carcass hung in the small room, a carcass so red, so bright it almost hurt his eyes, so bright a blood red it looked artificial.

"The light goes on when you open the door," Opal said, "but you can turn it on from the inside, too." They stepped inside, and the small room was somehow full of murder, not like a butcher shop, perhaps because it was so deliberately hidden; it was full of death. The bodies of three small deer hung from hooks in the fiberboard ceiling, each hook cruelly through the tendons of one front leg near the hoof. Two were skinned, bright and headless, but the other was still in its skin and had its head on; it was a doe, the eyes glazed open and gummy in the cold. One eye had been punctured by a buckshot, and was wrinkled and black; it looked like a piece of skin from an ancient Negro.

"My God, he *is* an outlaw," Richard said, but he thought of Shim only as a cuckold, and the false door and the secret place seemed a child's game, even if a deadly one.

"He is," Opal said, and she shivered. "I told you last night I was more worried for Spooner than I was about Shim."

"Do you worry about Shim?" he asked, and they both knew what he meant.

"I worry about him."

"Bluebeard's cellar," he said, and she didn't smile.

"He likes to kill them," she said.

"So do I. What do you think I came up here for?"

She merely shivered again, and he crowded her against the wall to kiss her. At first she closed her eyes, but then, perversely, it seemed to him, began to fight him, and her eyes were open and full of horror. He was down on one knee trying to undo her clothes, and she pushed him so hard he lost his balance, and his face pressed into the side of a bare carcass—into the naked, icy meat, which swung slowly away and then came back as if to kiss him again.

"Are you crazy?" she asked, horrified. "My God! You want to do that here?"

"I want to do it," he said. He wiped the cold touch of the meat from his face.

"Do you love me?" she asked.

"Yes, I love you," he said, trying to recoup this minor loss. He would have to take care until the time was right; that might have been disastrous. Sense against sensuality. "I'm sorry, but I lost my head," he said, smiling to indicate that he was a fool for love, and knew it. "But I want you so much, Opal. Can I have you?"

"I love you," she said, "but please don't hurt me. Let me take my own time." As she spoke her teeth clicked together, partly from the cold. He wanted her so much he wondered if he might actually

159

be in love with her. What was the difference? Had there ever been a difference?

They went out of the refrigerator room into the cellar and filled a gallon jug with cider, then he kissed her again, her arms tight around his neck. "We could never dance together," she said. "It would break your back." That wasn't the dance he had in mind. Then she whispered, and his nose itched as the words hissed in his ear: "Shim said he was going to kill another deer tonight."

Then she would come to him, of course, when Shim was safely off to his night of hunting on the mountain. He gave her back her glasses—gently, diplomatically placing them on her little nose, behind her little ears with deliberately careful fingers, and then he picked up the cider and followed her up the cellar stairs.

At supper Shim was haggard; he had hardly bothered to wash, and treated his plates roughly, pushing them away as soon as he had eaten enough, clapping his silverware down into the grease and roughly wiping his unshaven bristles so hard his paper napkin shredded apart.

"Pooped out," he said, and looked around with a suspicious grin on his face. Then he got up and went into the living room, and they heard him flop on a sofa.

There had been little discussion of the day's hunt; Shim had jumped only the one skipper—nearly a fawn. They had quickly decided that tomorrow they would hunt the same area, reasoning that other hunters might push the deer across from the Leah side of Cascom Mountain, or perhaps the Cascom hunters might push them up toward the mountain from the lower valleys. It would be a night with a bright half-moon, and the deer would range around. Murray said he wouldn't be late, but he would like to try out the Arnolt-Bristol again. He didn't seem very much interested in the hunting, and for a moment Richard felt guilty about that, but he was so glad Murray didn't stick around! He had other things on his mind tonight.

Mind? he thought, and grinned at Opal, who was clearing away the dishes. She frowned and shook her head: *Be careful.* Zach got out his television again, and the sports car buzzed off down the road toward Cascom. He sat with Zach for a while, but didn't watch the blue screen; he watched Opal's beautiful little rump, and waited, and waited. He thought he couldn't stand it, then remembered the mail he'd been given just before dinner, and took it up to his room to read it.

But he couldn't seem to bother with it. The envelopes wouldn't open right. One was from Saul, on company stationery, and the others looked business—uninteresting. Forgive me, Saul, he thought, and threw the letters on the bedside table. Nervously he walked down the hall to the window and watched the slice of a moon move through wispy clouds. The great round mountain seemed to tilt, slowly, ominously, its roll-center the very center of the earth. He shrugged his shoulders impatiently. When would Shim go out again?

Maybe he was in love, he wanted her so badly. *Opal*, he thought, *hurry up, I want you:* an incantation in E.S.P.—*Shim, go murder a deer. Go get yours on the mountain, because I want your wife.* Time refused to pass; if he'd had voodoo paraphernalia he'd have used it.

He picked out Saul's letter and tore part of it along with the envelope. Saul was thinking of retiring. Yes, yes, he always did. Yes. With a shiver of impatience he tried to concentrate on the words Saul had typed himself:

What a business! It makes us money, it is not too hard to keep going, but I never liked it. It never seemed to me a work to give a man a good feeling inside. We are so different, Richard. You are a good man and I love you for it, and I trust you with everything in the world, but I must go out all the time, an ugly old Jew with a terrific accent and try to change everybody before it is too late. A lot of good it does! Now all our bombers are on alert, I heard it on the radio. I don't know what, but while I have the time some crazy thing makes me have to work on the whole world all the time. Do you understand? It is for me my duty.

You know I haven't any money? I gave it all away! How stupid. But I must retire, and we will make fair arrangements. My heart is not good. I am as you know overweight for perhaps fifty years.

Sometimes I hate, Richard! Right now how I would like to shake your hand and reassure you. That does not make sense, but what I mean is I know you are worried and unhappy. But sometimes I as

161

I say I hate the whole *dirty* human race for their filthy stains and sweat and deodorants in their armpits (business!) and why they always kill each other and enjoy so much hurting each other. I could yell I am not one of them! And then I smell my own stinks and find myself full of hate also. And then I remember such fine and loving people. Your son Murray, a pearl! Rachel, my daughter, something is wrong, she is a good girl. Will you wait a while and be patient? She does not see how you love her, I think. . . .

Yes, yes, Saul and his messiah complex! No. Of all the people he could not understand, Saul was by far the best, the kindest. . . . More words came to him, all of them strangely meaningless: *compassion, humanity, mercy, love, justice*—Saul's favorite words, his favorite abstractions. Patience, Saul had said, but that word meant nothing either. What time was it now? Seven-thirty. It had been dark since four-thirty.

And then there was a gentle tap at his door, a little, tentative, soft tap-tap-tap, as if by a fingernail, and to Richard it was as loud as guns, grenades, carbines. Swiftly, in his stockinged feet, he went to the door, ready to find her, looking down for her nervous, excited face. But he found there green chino, and jerked his head up to find Shim's hideous grinning orange cat face straight in front of him. He lost his breath, but Shim spoke first.

"Where's Murray?"

"Driving my car." Quickly he was able to cope again; it had not been fear, but there had been plenty of adrenalin forced into his blood, and he had been ready for anything violent.

"Shit. He never is around."

"What's the matter?"

"Had something I thought he might want to see, but it can wait," Shim said. "I'm always waitin', it seems." Shim grinned again, and left. He, too, was in his stockings, and made no noise at all except for a squeak and a click as he shut the bathroom door.

Richard sat on the bed and tensed his muscles, then stretched the extra energy out of them. Shim didn't understand Murray very well if he thought Murray would go jacking deer with him. Or did he? Who the hell understood anybody but himself? He didn't understand Opal, for instance; he just understood something about her at the moment—that she would come to him, that he had to wait.

But she didn't come. Shim had finished in the bathroom and gone back downstairs long ago, and she didn't come. Finally he put on his loafers and went down to the kitchen. Zach sat watching television, his rapt old head motionless, emotionless as laughter swarmed around the box like busy but invisible insects. He went into the living room to find Opal in the flickering semidark in front of a small fire, sitting 'way back in the corner of the big divan, her arms around her knees.

The firelight gleamed palely on her face, and her black hair was like shadow. She knew he was there, but didn't look up at him.

"Where's Shim?" he said.

"Gone killing," she said. "Why don't you go, too?"

He sat down at the other end of the divan and watched her. Something had gone wrong, all right.

"Are you afraid of me?" he asked.

She didn't answer.

"Are you?"

"I'm afraid you're a liar," she said.

"So are you, but what difference does that make?"

"I told you I wasn't a cheating bitch."

"We aren't responsible for those words." He thought that was pretty good.

"I am," she said. "Oh, God, I don't know!"

"All I know is what I feel," he said, thinking hard; but wasn't that true?

She turned her face toward him, and as the fire picked out the delicate line of her neck he had what he could only identify as a spasm in his lower back. God! She was lovely.

"I don't know about you," she said. "Sometimes I think you are kind and gentle—such a loving person. I thought I saw it when you talked about your wife, and about Murray the other night, and I began to go all crazy and soft about you. Then you seem so selfish. . . ."

"I'm selfish about you," he said, hardly listening, figuring out

163

how long it would take, what he had to do. Kind and gentle, loving—how often those words were in the air. Cruel and hard?—those, too.

Everyone wanted to make him what he knew he wasn't. He was an animal, and a good one, and this, even as they looked out of their own animal eyes, was what they all seemed to resent. And wasn't Opal an animal? Didn't she really want only an excuse she could call irresistible before she had the animal pleasure she craved? She wanted to couple with him, to have him because he was a fine lean animal and was ready for her, but first she had to be a lawyer, and argue her moral case, and inevitably lose it in that kangaroo court where the judge and the jury were also humping, craving animals. *Come on*, he wanted to say to her, *get it over with*. If he lied to her it was not really a lie, because it was what she wanted, and what she would eventually convince herself of anyway. And if he lied to her it was because survival and desire were all that bothered animals.

High on the dark walls of the room all the gray bucks' eyes gleamed, and as the firelight flickered up by the wagon-wheel lights and moldings they seemed to nod their great heads, with dignity and strength, telling him yes, yes. If he were a buck and she a doe in her present heat, he would leap through the little trees, hook her with his forelegs, and mount . . . but she wasn't a doe, and part of his natural equipment as a man was a clear masculine voice.

He moved toward her, but not too close, and put a deliberately gentle hand on her cheek. Still clasping her knees, she let him turn her head toward him, and he could just see in her face desperation, mistrust, sadness. Her hair was soft over the back of his hand, and her earlobe, cool as a pearl, was at the tips of his fingers.

"I do love you," he said. "That's why I seem so impatient—maybe even selfish. I love you so much I can't stand it, Opal." Her eyes grew soft, moist. "I want you so much," he said, and let a certain amount of pathetic desire enter his voice; she should give him what he so pitifully needed. She put her hand on his cheek.

"You do mean it," she said. "I think you do mean it!" and impulsively jumped toward him, their heads nearly colliding, and kissed him quickly on the mouth.

"I love you. I love you," he said, keeping his hands off her.

164

"Wait for me," she whispered, getting to her feet. Then she added, with a great deal of embarrassment—a kind of confusion, he thought, of tone: why must such brutally definite arrangements have to be made in the name of true love?—"I'll come to your room." And she walked quickly to the front stairs.

Now. He went carefully to the kitchen; Zach still watched television, and the volume was satisfactorily high. One last scouting trip before madness, madness! He was mad already. The Arnolt-Bristol was not back. Before he went upstairs he quietly opened Shim's gun locker and saw that his automatic shotgun was not there. Then he went to his room and lay on his bed to wait. He heard her in the bathroom, heard her with fantastically perceptive ears go to her room, then after a long time come down the hall, step, step, step, cautiously to his door. He opened it for her and she slipped in and into his arms as he softly closed the door and they moved toward the bed.

"Will you be gentle with me?" she asked in a small voice full of breath. "Please be easy and gentle with me at first. I'm scared."

He hadn't been with any woman but his tall Rachel since the war. No other, and this one was so different, so small, this one.

"Please don't hurt me. Please be gentle," she pleaded. He would be. While it was necessary he would be.

"Shim never . . ." she began to say, but then she ran out of breath, and her need, ambivalent as it may have been, made all conditions unnecessary.

For him the room did not exist, or any conditions either. Once she cried like a cat—not all pain. He heard his own voice, or a voice in his head, he couldn't tell: *Here's one, you bitch, Rachel! Watch, see this animal! Ungh! Ungh!*

Once Opal moaned, "Oh, God! I love you!"

Love, that funny syllable! There was only a triumphant pressure in his head, his back. His strength was hydraulic, cleaving, and there began to grow, to wax between his bones something sweet: yes, sweet, shameful, an egg, a rupture made of pain and inhuman pleasure that would invincibly burst and destroy itself deep in her, and it grew and did.

Then it was over, and her brown eyes, wet, raped, full of love, ate him.

165

She moaned, her eyes wide open, and pulled his head down to kiss his face and rub her cheeks on his mustache. She wouldn't let him go, and he felt desperately that he could stand right up and walk, and this hot little homunculus would still be attached to his body; he would have to put his pants and shirt on over it. But he knew better than to struggle—he would have to talk his way out and away from her. Now his senses were so cold and practical, and the very touch of her was irritating, even, in places, painful.

She watched him with her naked eyes, black hairs wet on her cheeks, and shook her head, sighing at the wonder of it.

What's so wonderful? he thought. The white porcelain bowl and pitcher gleamed antiseptically on the stand beside the bed. He felt himself shrinking within her, and it seemed a joint without meaning, like inept plumbing. Suddenly he was, not afraid, but coldly aware of his life. Shim: who knew where he was at this moment? And where was Murray? His life was that he had a son, and a character that he carefully presented to the world and to himself, and a wife, Rachel, née Weitzner, in whose thighs he could lie without embarrassment, legally, sanctioned by law and the world, and no one could shame him with undignified complications.

"I love you," she foolishly said. "Do you love me? Do you love me?"

"Yes," he said diplomatically; he couldn't make himself repeat the words about love.

"Then why do you want to get up?" she said, kissing his chest. "I don't want you ever to get up."

He was not pleased by this recklessness in her. Now he might, possibly, be a little light in tone—puncture any high (low?) seriousness there was in this steaming bed. He might say that he had to go to the bathroom, using some silly euphemism; but that wouldn't fit him, and he didn't want to show weakness, age— and why lie when such weakness would be upon him like a bullet, anyway, before too many years passed? Clearly he saw his flesh beginning, in this refusal to use any excuse, to lose its sadness, and she began, slowly to become again a wonder, an appetite he

166

must satisfy. Look at her: he rose up on his arms and saw her hard little breasts, the pink buds of the young and childless, the smooth round of her belly where he grew like a centaur out of her hips, and her shoulders that curved toward him. She was a wonder, and he would, he wanted again.

And then they realized that they had heard the Arnolt-Bristol come into the parking area, and now someone was coming up the stairs. Now he was all strategy and worry, and she, too, had lost her recklessness. Whoever it was, probably Murray, went into the bathroom, and quickly she gathered her clothes and put on her robe, then fled back to her room.

There was relief in him when she made her door unseen, but it was not over. Her odor was on him, and her moist heat was again exciting. Love or not, he wanted it again.

But he was no longer mad. He didn't enjoy the first twinges of returning responsibility, the guilty little shiver he had right now. He was safe again, at least, and he'd had Opal. What was he thinking of, his score? A kind of point system? Let's see, if tomorrow he shot that eight-point buck he'd seen on the road, would that give him in all nine points altogether, here on the mountain? Or ten?

He put on his pajamas and bathrobe to wait for the bathroom, lay back on the bed and watched the shadow of what must have been the last moth of the year. The moth flopped about on his lamp, and the shadow on the ceiling looked like a great book, opening and closing. There went Murray out of the bathroom, and he supposed Opal would be next. A knock on his door—Murray. He could only let him in.

"I saw your light on, O.M.," Murray said. (He would have to worry, perhaps, about that light, Richard thought.) "That's some car you've got there."

"How did it go?"

"Fine."

"Did you keep the r.p.m.s up?"

"I tried to keep it above two thousand," Murray said.

"How high did you go?"

"I got it up around six thousand once, in third. That's all."

"Would you like to have a car like it, Murray?"

"No, I don't think so. Not now, anyway, O.M. I just want my old junk. It goes." Then Murray tried to break away from talk of cars, and Richard could see his hesitancy. "I just want something rather anonymous at the moment, O.M. I just want to go—just want it to go."

"On your trip?"

Murray smiled at him. "Weren't we going to have a talk sometime? I mean about the trip?"

To Richard, Murray looked like a grown man. He's as big as I am, he thought, but why should that surprise me? "I've always been able to trust you, Murray," he said, "but can you see why I was a little worried—with the army waiting and all that?"

"Oh, I can see why you were worried. I don't blame you, O.M., but I don't know if I can explain why I want to go." Now, in the boy's face, he saw a kind of pity, and it was disconcerting to be the object of pity!

"I couldn't understand it?" he said.

"I don't know," Murray said, sadly, and that was even more disconcerting.

"Is it something you're ashamed of?"

"No, I don't think so. I don't think I ought to be ashamed of it, O.M." Murray looked thoughtfully at the bed.

Richard began to get a little irritated by the guessing game they seemed to be playing. For one thing, he wanted to get to the bathroom and wash up; he'd heard Opal leave it.

"Well, what *is* it?" he said, then smiled, trying ineffectually, he knew, to take the edge of irritation off the question.

"Do you have time to listen?" Murray said.

"Yes, it's only . . ." he looked for his wrist watch, and found it in the twisted blankets, "ten-thirty. Why shouldn't I have time?"

"I don't know, O.M. You looked kind of impatient."

"What is it, then?"

Murray was embarrassed, as if he needed help—questions to answer, perhaps—but Richard could not think of the questions.

"Did you ever have the feeling that the world was going to end, O.M.?" Murray said, shamefaced for a second. When he saw that Richard was not going to smile, he became serious again.

"Do you know what I mean? That we won't be around much longer?"

"Maybe I felt that way about myself once, in the war," Richard said. "In fact more than once."

"Yes," Murray said, becoming excited now, "but hell, I wouldn't mind that so much. I'd just as soon take my own chance like that. . . . I don't mean it wasn't rough and all that—it must have been terrible—but didn't you feel all the time that we would win? That whether or not you died, we were still going to have the world?"

"What difference would it make to me if I were dead?"

"But you see, you might not be," Murray said, "but if the whole human race was dead you couldn't gamble on yourself any longer. There wouldn't be any odds at all."

Another of Saul's abstractions, Richard thought: The Human Race. "And you think the human race is a goner?" he said, smiling, but Murray didn't smile back.

"Yes, I think it might kill itself."

"You poor kid!"

"I don't think it's so funny, O.M.," Murray said, looking at him with harsh and level judgment.

"Well, all right," he said, "maybe they might try. Maybe you're right, there, but you know why they won't succeed, Murray? Because the human race is too goddam tough to kill." After making this statement he felt a little proud of the human race, and braced a bit, just to be worthy of such toughness.

"You're tough, all right, O.M.," Murray said, and Richard could not quite find any irony in his son's expression. But suddenly he did feel that he was being made a fool of, and he tried to control his anger; maybe the boy was right, and the vain anger he felt was the death-characteristic itself. Now he must think of something to say that was self-deprecating, because he must not be laughed at. Vanity, vanity, he thought, but that is the way we animals are. And then he thought, *tough*; the word had changed meanings since his time, and now didn't it mean something else to a college kid? What was it? No longer strong and hard, but something like a mess, or something difficult in a less complimentary way. Was that what Murray had meant? He knew immediately, with a rather painful sense of loss, as though a long line had broken somewhere miles and miles out, and the break could never be found and fixed, that he could not ask.

Murray was still trying to explain, and if there had been a moment in which to clear the air, it had passed.

"Maybe they won't kill everybody, O.M., but I'm afraid—I mean I'm really scared—that they'll kill . . . I know this sounds stupid and romantic! I'm afraid they'll kill the one I'm looking for. Isn't that stupid?"

"You're looking for somebody?"

"Yes, I'm looking and looking," Murray said; then he smiled, and added, "I'm not really crazy, O.M., am I?"

"I've always taken what I've had," Richard said.

"I suppose you have, O.M."

Again, was there irony? He tried to explain: "What I mean is, why do you want to cover so much ground? Where are you going, to do all this looking? What do you want, a girl? You've always had plenty of girl friends, Murray. You want to go on some silly *quest*, like a knight of the round table?"

"On my trusty Volkswagen," Murray said, laughing.

"But what's the hurry? You're only twenty years old, Murray. Why don't you finish college first? Listen, you'll be surprised how things happen. You'll meet her, all right."

"The hurry is that I don't think they'll give me the time, that's all. You know I don't go for this 'you were meant for me' stuff, and you know I'm not silly enough to think that marriages are made in heaven and all that crap, O.M., but even you allow that we might start blowing each other up any time now. Sometimes I don't even dare read the papers or listen to the radio. And I've got so much I want to do!" Murray did seem almost desperate, and Richard wondered if, possibly, it was the impending divorce that helped to make Murray afraid for the world—if Murray thought now that all contracts could be broken as easily as the one between his own mother and father.

Wait a minute! He had been so nervous before that he hadn't thought—he swung his legs over and picked up his mail. There it was, a long envelope with a familiar set of names on it. He'd vaguely thought that it was a bill. *Troy, Sherman and Kaplan,*

170

Attorneys at Law. Rachel's lawyers, recommended by her buttinsky
sister Ruth, of course. He opened the letter and saw one word
before he put it back on the table, face down. The word was
divorcement. Well, it would not be impending much longer. Time?
Maybe his son was right, and no one ever gave anyone else enough
time. What could he do now? He'd known it was coming, but
that strange legal word seemed to prove it for good and all. What
could he do? He felt a little sick. Go screw Opal? At the thought
a little thrill hit him somewhere in his spine—a little tremor.
By God, he was still a young man, wasn't he? Maybe he could go
seduce Rachel! Oh, you ass, he thought, you blithering ass! He
wanted his wife again, but he couldn't ever have her again. No
amount of pride in his manhood, not even the most sanguine,
jumped-up optimism could hide the fact: knowing her, knowing
himself, it was impossible. He had let her drift too far down that
murky stream they called analysis, where the kind-looking fish
nibbled away at parts of you called motives, or emotions, where
there was neither privacy nor responsibility. Now she was gone into
that alien place the air of which he couldn't even breathe, and
all the time he had stood proudly by, waiting for what he considered to be his by right, by talent and by law. What the hell
was I doing? he asked himself, Is there some principle of human
relationships, some little formula, that nobody ever told me about?

"What's the matter, O.M.?" Murray asked, his voice full of
worry and kindness.

How could he answer his son? He might despair, throw all
his worries and inadequacies down at Murray's feet and take whatever comfort Murray had to offer. Yes, there was a great weariness
in him, and he was an old man, and here was his only son who
had turned out, God knew how, to be a big, generous, and forgiving man, a man with whom he might be so completely honest that
neither dignity nor pride would matter at all any more.

"Murray," he said, but at that moment there was a tap-tap
on the door, and he thought, *Why, the little fool! The silly bitch!
Doesn't she know!* Murray opened the door, and Richard was
tremendously relieved to see that it was only Shim.

A strange-looking Shim. He wore, over his wrinkled, baggy hunting clothes, a once-white butcher's apron, now smeared with the

pale juices of meat; in places the cloth was pink, in places it was grimy, where dirt had rubbed into grease. The hilt of his Randall knife, as greasy as his hands and forearms, protruded rakishly from its leather sheath, which he wore belted over the apron. He leaned against the doorframe, and his face was pale, orange-pink, as if it had received its own ration of gore. His eyes were glittery, yet not quite in focus; he looked stunned. Richard thought of a soldier—say a Tartar warrior after a victory that had turned into slaughter, and the act had become, though still pleasurable, intoxicating, even cloying. Then Shim raised a tumbler of cider—one reason for the stunned eyes—and drank. A drop of cider hung, pierced by reddish bristles, on the tip of his chin.

"What, you hunters?" he said, "to beddy-bye so bloody early?" And he leaned 'way back to laugh silently, his red mouth wide open. He beckoned to them with a greasy finger. "Come on, I'll show you a shecret. Come on, come on, won't take a shecond! My goodness! I can't hardly talk straight!"

He turned, and they couldn't refuse; Shim never took refusal into his considerations. Richard put on his loafers and followed after Murray. Shim, he was almost certain, purposely exaggerated his drunkenness. He wavered from side to side on the stairwell, and balanced himself in a hippy, rather effeminate way, as if he were trying to slink.

The kitchen was empty, Zach having put away his television and gone to bed. Shim went under the sink for the gallon jug of cider (did Shim know who had carried it upstairs?) and though he poured the three glasses unsteadily, he didn't quite spill any. He was not really drunk, and Richard warned himself to be careful; he hadn't the slightest idea how Shim would react to a certain bit of knowledge, except that Shim enjoyed violence. The warning, however, was to himself: he must consider the situation dangerous, for he found it hard to do so. Wasn't Shim, for all his crazy, ominous posturings, a cuckold, and probably impotent? Yes, but what had that to do with violence of another sort? He had better not relax at all in front of the man. Shim's ironies, the constant expression he wore of secret, shameful knowledge—who knew what dirty things he knew? Again Richard was reminded of a cat, because a cat seemed so stupid, and yet it seemed also to know so very much. How did a cat get its information? There were ways, he supposed, that an ordinary man could not understand, circuits he could not perceive, and a cat had to act out of suspicion, remember; he couldn't afford to wait for proof.

Shim presented them with huge tumblers of the pale cider, then beckoned them on, grinning, grinning his filthy grin, down into the cellar. The light was on, and when they had descended into the cool, unmoving air, Shim turned in the light that was at the same time glaring and inadequate, and put his finger along his nose. "Shecret, you hunters. Oh, ain't I a shneak!"

So Shim was going to show them his Bluebeard's closet, and try to shock them. Richard stood in the cellar next to his son, both audience, and Shim did a weird dance, waving his arms like a magician before he would reveal the secret door. Richard suddenly remembered, with much wonder now that the moment had safely passed, that he had been about to pour out his insecurities, his perplexities upon Murray! What a terrible slough he must have been in at that moment! Or had he, really, been about to tell Murray that he was so unhappy—no, probably not. How could he, when he didn't feel that way at all any more? It was impossible to remember the sadness he must have felt, the self-pity he must have been about to indulge in.

Finally Shim pulled at the false vent pipe, and it turned into an insulated door and slowly swung open onto the violently white and red room, white where the fluorescent light glared on the white walls, rich, gaudy red on the meat. Shim had been busy—he must have been here all evening, from the work he'd done. The two does that had been skinned were now all butchered, and most of the meat had been sealed in plastic for the freezer that took up one end of the room. And he had thought, just because Shim's shotgun hadn't been upstairs in its usual place, that Shim was on the mountain. That kind of carelessness, he supposed, came directly out of the rut. He *must* be more careful.

The third doe's skin had been peeled down below the ribcage, and the effect of those rags and flaps of loose skin hanging below the bright meat was one of half-nakedness, as though it were somewhat indecent for the doe to be half-clothed. And then he saw the slit up her belly to her brisket, and in the dark crack there gleamed the ivory insides of ribs.

All at once Shim seemed quite sober. "I ain't a pig, you understand, but I do like my deer meat. I don't cut down the herd much! You believe it? Look!" He swung the half-skinned doe around, spread her legs, and jammed a stick of wood between her hocks to hold her open. Out came the Randall knife, and he made two expert slits from her rectum upward, then neatly peeled out her whole sexual apparatus.

"Look here," he said. "I always leave these parts in until I git to where I can see better." He laughed at his night work. "So's I can tell. Now this doe should have been bred this year. See here." He held up the long tube, silver-white and pink, with the ovaries and womb on the end of it, neatly slit it part way with his knife, and ran it inside out with expert, show-off fingers. "Look, she's a lousy virgin! So damn many does around, why, the poor buck, he can't get *to* all of 'em. This here's what we call a 'boarder.' She eats the food but she don't produce." His finger came out of the tube with a sucking sound. "So you see, dear judge, I really done the state a favor!" He bent back and giggled, then took a sip of cider. "Drink up!" he said, frowning at them.

Murray seemed interested, but somewhat detached; his expression was inscrutable, but he paid attention. In himself Richard detected surprising pleasure. He liked the neatness of the scene of an hour before. While he was upstairs with this man's wife (why should his having cuckolded Shim make him feel so friendly toward him now?), this carnivore was down here in the cellar dismembering with unnatural glee his female victims. It should, probably, have struck him with at least some horror, but it did not. It absolutely did not; he enjoyed the idea very much, but why, in God's name, he would never know.

Was Opal up in her bed thinking about him? He had to suppress a grin; he felt very strong (the cider? He'd finished his) and somehow in *charge*; wasn't he the man, among them all?

"Hard work, you know?" Shim said. "This critter's too cold to skin easy, and I damn near pulled my fingernails off." He swung the doe around. "But have a look at that pretty little backstrap!

Tender? Man, I could eat that raw! That's what I was thinking about before—how about I cut us three nice pieces out of this one's back, we take 'em up and just *sear* 'em under the electric broiler? Ain't as good as charcoal, but *tender?*" He licked his red lips with a red tongue.

Richard was hungry. He also had been at some tiring work. Again he suppressed a grin. It, too, made you hungry. *This* illicit tenderloin also looked good to him. He had to swallow some saliva. "Sounds fine," he said.

"Murray?" Shim asked.

"After that supper we had?" Murray was acting, now, and Richard felt somewhat betrayed—a strange sense of loss, very slight but there, that Murray did not want to join them at their meal.

"Man," Shim said disapprovingly, "this stuff is just like candy. Melts in your mouth."

"You go ahead," Murray said. "I'm pretty tired, as a matter of fact. I think I'll just hit the sack."

Shim shrugged his shoulders, and it seemed to Richard that he sneered just as he turned away—a little sneer that just barely disarranged his lips for a moment. Then out snicked the Randall knife, and with a few neat incisions Shim separated the tenderloin from the groove along one side of the doe's spine. Dark red, rich without fat, a roll of meat came loose that was about two inches in diameter. "I could eat it like a banana," Shim said, held it up to his mouth and pretended to do so, his teeth clicking on air.

He led them out of the secret room and then carefully shut the door. "You got your glasses?" he asked. He certainly pretended to be drunk no longer, but trotted right up the cellar stairs, the meat in one hand and his glass in the other.

Murray stopped in the middle of the stairs and turned, diffidently, toward Richard. "O.M.," he said, "what I did want to talk about before . . ."

"What, Murray?" Richard said. He looked up at his son, at his son's youthful face that was so much like his own and yet so difficult to read. In the kitchen Shim was banging around with the broiler pan.

"I wanted to ask about leaving—when I can go."

"When you can go?" Was he keeping Murray here? Was it like

that? Of course. It was like that, but he had envisioned a time of comradeship and hunting; now he was merely keeping his son to a promise. "When do you want to go?"

"I'd like to leave tomorrow morning," Murray said, sympathy, even some pain in his voice. Also much determination.

"Tomorrow morning," Richard said vaguely. He could hardly justify a plea for Murray's staying. What had he done but pursue his own game? Suddenly he was desperate. This all must stop, and his life must resume some of its former meaning and order. He was a father, and at least for a while yet, a husband. He loved his wife and son, he really did. Why must everything around him that was his, that not only was *his*, but was so perfect for him, so delightful to him, leave him? Mine, he thought. And now my son, leaving me for some quest I can't join in on, can't even understand. For a moment he felt like a man whose arms had been cut off at the elbows.

"Please, Murray," he heard himself say, "please stay one day more. We'll hunt together tomorrow. How about it? Will you?" Then he watched Murray's determination change through what he must believe to be love. Of course; hadn't he counted on Murray's generosity? Hadn't that quality in Murray always won out? He and Rachel both had depended on it far more than either of them ever deserved. His son's hand reached down and tapped him on the shoulder.

"OK, O.M.," Murray said. "One more day. Maybe we'll score tomorrow."

They went on upstairs into the kitchen, where Shim was slicing the backstrap. "Sure you won't change your mind, Murray?" Shim said without looking up.

Murray didn't answer. He had gone to the window, and he looked out into the dark.

"I think it's snowing," he said. Richard and Shim both went to the door, and the three of them went outside into air colder than it had yet been that year.

"Cold!" Shim said. Yes, it was snowing, those grainy little balls not much bigger than Number Nine shot that always seemed to come first, before the first real flakes of the year came down. Their *tic-tic-tic* was audible on the ground, especially on the odd dry leaves scattered in little drifts near the doorway, and were cool little dots and dashes on their ears and hands. The moon should have been above the roofpeak of the barn, Richard estimated, but the barn stood square and high, black against blackness, and the little snow closed the sky in and down, so that it seemed to hover just a few yards overhead.

Each year the first snow brought back his childhood, and it had always seemed that in that season, on that very day all through his life, he had been expectant and happy. The light from the door behind them, and from the windows, threw their shadows out, where they cut strange holes in the air, and the snow disappeared where their shadows loomed—really, it was more as if their shadows pierced a warp of tiny white threads, and then the threads began again just before they hit the ground and turned miraculously into the tiny bouncing grains. He held out his hand, and the grains bounced and quickly, as they hit again, melted on his palm; it was such a delicate, tender feeling they gave him that it didn't seem they could have been made of ice.

"If this keeps up!" Shim said. "Well, one thing: no more night work for me—but I got enough meat anyway." In the snow it would be too easy for Spooner to follow the trail of a jacked and dragged deer right back to Shim's cellar window.

"Maybe we'll find them tomorrow," Richard said. He was still full of remembered joy; other years and other expectations mixed themselves in with the new snow, and he believed that they would find the deer, even though he knew that it wasn't that easy. It was easy enough to find tracks, but the deer were also aware that they left tracks, and they moved farther and kept a more distant watch upon the hunters. If they bedded, their trails would lead downwind, so that they could smell a hunter long before he appeared, or the trail would loop past their point of vision, so that they might lie in their beds a few yards away and see who came plodding after them; or by many intricate jumps and side steps and doublings back they could make their cuneiform patterns frustrating and unreadable.

The snow was a clean wind in his nose—a kind of frosty nonsmell that somehow had character to it. He felt immediately younger—younger even than the men who stood beside him, and he looked toward them with an unspoken, youthful challenge: who would get a deer?

Shim went back inside to prepare the steaks, and for a while Richard stood next to Murray as they watched the snow, which began to turn, now, into slightly flatter, slower-falling crystals. He put his hand on Murray's shoulder, the snow there cool against his palm, and said, "Tomorrow we'll see a deer."

Murray turned and smiled at him, his hair frosted with glittering flakes—even his eyebrows decorated with lights. "You mean one with his skin on, O.M.?"

"Yes, with his skin on, and maybe a good rack, too. How about it?"

"It makes me think of other times we hunted," Murray said. He sounded very old—nostalgic, maybe, but happy in the memory. "Remember when I got my Mauser, and you made them let me keep it at school?"

"Yes, that season."

"That was a nice doe. I sure was proud of it," Murray said.

"So was I!"

"That was the year you shot the bobcat," Murray said.

"Yup, that was the same year." What had happened to the years when his son was his—those few short seasons when he had first really wanted the boy to be with him because he was old enough to be trusted, and when the boy had wanted nothing more in the world than to be with his father? Three or four seasons out of their lifetimes, that was all, and now that those seasons were over no amount of love could bring back anything but absurd imitations of them.

"I wish," he said, and then stopped.

"What, O.M.?" Murray said.

"Oh, I don't know, Murray. I wish it was that deer season again." A silly thing to say.

"I didn't sleep a wink all that night, I was so excited," Murray said.

"God, was I glad when you shot that big doe! Wasn't she a beauty?"

"She was to me, I'll tell you!" Murray said.

"Maybe tomorrow . . ." Richard began to say, and he was still full of delightful, irrational hope. But then Shim called them in.

Murray changed his mind, and they all sat at the table, hunters all, Richard thought, in their good strong clothes (all except his), all sharp of eye and tooth! But they didn't have to be sharp of tooth for this steak. Blood rare, it flaked apart at the touch of a fork; the kind of meat you were not conscious of swallowing. It diminished in the mouth, and yet gave the impression of firmness; close-grained, it was just touched with the tallowy, dark flavor of venison.

It was late, and they finished quickly, then took one more hunters' look at the snow. Smooth white, now, and silent, the flakes had begun to cover everything; it was still cold, and whether or not it continued to snow, it would be a perfect day tomorrow. They smiled at the weather and said good night, each having cast a glance at his rifle and gear. Richard plucked his stag-handled knife from its sheath on his cartridged belt and hoped like a kid that it would gut his own big deer before the next day was over. It was sharp, but he stropped it twice on his oiled rifle sling, and then it cut a paper kitchen towel like a razor blade, *snip*, from top to bottom.

Shim nodded in appreciation. "You keep a sharp knife," he said.

They all went to bed, then. Before he got into bed he stood still, feeling as happy as if this time were years ago, feeling too that he and Murray had, if not recaptured their past closeness, at least recognized together, with words and the touch of hands, that it had once existed. Perhaps it would again. Just as it had separated them, time might bring them together again.

He took the twisted blankets and sheets and pulled them back. It was then that he saw, bright as a wound on the snow-white sheet, a spot of blood.

PART THREE

Guess, friend, what I am and how I am wrought,
Monster of sea, or of land, or of elsewhere?
Know me, and use me, and I may thee defend,
And if I be thine enemy, I may thy life end.

—Sir Thomas Wyatt

SHIM WAS in the hall, yelling them up: "Grab your socks, you hunters! Bacon's on, eggs next! Get the hell up!"

Richard's eyes were wide open at once. Outside, it was still cold; the frosty air had filled his room. It had come in through the three-inch opening below the sash, and now he felt it against his eyes. It was as if this new air were so pure it could not mix with the odors of house and people, and had totally replaced the old. He went to the window, and the floor numbed his feet; it was like walking on thin sandals made of flesh. Outside, there was the soft, muffled darkness of new snow, and he wondered how the snow could make him so happy. When light came, it would seem to come out of the snow itself, the whole world would light softly from within, as the moon seemed to do, and the black trees would hover above a whiteness too delicate to support them.

The cold air made his pajamas feel as thin as gauze, and as he took a breath his nostrils felt as though they had been seared clean; he had a vision of them as smooth, glassy pipes leading straight to his warm lungs. He shut the window and began to dress quickly. Long wool underwear, extra socks. Shoepacs, now, instead of leather boots; these were rubber over the foot, with twelve-inch leather tops to breathe out moisture and keep the felt innersoles and stockings dry.

These were the clothes he liked best, the strong, plain clothes that without decoration or apology did what clothes should have done, kept out the harsh weather and still let the man be out in the weather, part of the real world. Yes, he thought as he straightened out the tough sailcloth pockets of his hunting pants, he was an outdoor man; but what a peculiar word to use for infinite space —outdoors—when, really, the tiny places man closed in with doors were so scattered and insignificant compared to the world of trees.

Shim looked a little more rested, now that his activities of the night had been curtailed. Murray was already down, and that looked like a good sign; he'd always been the first one to get up when they'd hunted together before. Maybe the snow had given him back some of his old excitement. He sat near the window squeezing powdered graphite from a plastic cylinder onto the turned bolt of his Mauser. It would be cold this morning, and oil would have turned gummy on the freezing metal. Richard looked over his own gear, and again was joyful at the precision and spareness of it all. His Westley Richards rifle in 300 magnum—the honest English strength of the long bolt, the careful matching of stock and action—he could follow the magazine plate's edge all the way around, and the metal fit the wood as if the walnut had grown around the steel. And the Lyman receiver sight he'd had fitted to the rifle—though it was American-made it went perfectly with the rest of the mechanism; it had been conceived in the same hunting spirit, and for that clean, craftsman's world he felt great kinship.

The smell of bacon and eggs, and of the old kitchen which had never managed to lose, and never would, the peculiar farm smell of old potatoes and turnips, of years of much good food prepared and eaten in it—those odors had entered the walls and moldings and would never come out—these meant guns and hunting to him, too. After his father and mother died he'd spent all his time away from school at his uncle's farm in Iowa, and there too the kitchen had been the jumping-off place for excitement: down to the blinds on the Iowa River at Lone Tree, when an ice shelf extended out a foot from shore, and the huge sky might suddenly be full of the whistle and wind of mallard wings; or the gentle flush of quail in a fallow pasture, and his first double with a shotgun, when he was sixteen; or a long walk through the yellow stalks of corn still too moist to harvest, the mud heavy on his boots, everything drab and mucky—and then a cock pheasant, gawky and slow but out of the earth itself, it would seem, all his unbelievable color, green and red and polished golds and umbers fresh and clean, would fly straightaway and at the shot fall spinning, totally disorganized, and there he would be against the black mud, a treasure trove. From warm, aromatic kitchens, before dawn, the times of his life that he remembered best for their pure excitement and uncomplicated resolutions had begun.

He went to the door and opened it. Again out in the dark he felt the presence of the snow, and he hadn't needed the white straightedge along the doorsill to tell him of it. Sounds were different, smells were different, and his senses, enlivened by nostalgia, told him all about the coming day.

Their plans, of course, had changed. They would all go up to the ridge until they found tracks, then plan some concerted effort. On snow it was more important that they hunt together; while one might push the deer on, the others would try to get around ahead, and try to guess their patterns of escape.

They ate quickly. Because of the snow and a clear sky, now full of stars, light would come very quickly once dawn began. They decided not to have a second cup of coffee. Murray finished first, and made them some cheese and salami sandwiches, and then they buckled on their gear, making the last happy decisions about where to wear knives, ammunition, where to put the lengths of rope they hopefully carried in case they got a deer. Richard decided not to take his cartridge belt—a matter of superstition, for once on a similar day he had left it home by mistake and got a deer. He hung his knife on his regular belt and put his small cartridge case, which held just an extra six of the pretty, deadly things, in his jacket pocket. Such changes often were the result of superstition, and though he smiled at himself and didn't tell Shim or Murray why he had done it, it was a gesture toward past happiness and success.

Neither Zach nor Opal had appeared, and he was glad of it—

Opal because of the embarrassment inherent in a change of desire, both because only hunters should be up before dawn, helping each other's enthusiasm, buckling on weapons, making the standard remarks that were suddenly in the early morning fresh and exciting again.

"Who's going to git that big buck?" Shim said. He was ready, his Arisaka over his arm, bolt open. He put on his green cap and adjusted the visor.

"The one I saw on the road," Richard said. "Wouldn't I like to get a shot at him!" And he could see the huge animal leaping across the white, and the gold bead of his rifle's front sight following.

"How about a bear? How'd you like that?" Murray asked.

"Git a young one, boy. I love that bear bacon!" Shim said.

They were ready, and as they left the kitchen they held their empty rifles, it seemed to Richard, carefully, lovingly—or maybe that impression came from the profound respect they all had for them. There was another bit of superstition: even an empty rifle must never be pointed at a man, as though there *were* some magic in the weapon, and even out of an empty chamber the ghost of a bullet might come, and kill.

They stepped off the sill into the snow, about eight inches of it. Richard almost expected to feel the coldness of it through his boots and stockings; of course he didn't, but he was made aware of the warmth and snugness of his feet. With his toes he felt the rough grain of his stockings, and as he stepped away from the door and Shim turned off the light, he walked upon the earth made unfamiliar again. The snow was light, and though it was there—he could hear it sift past his boots—the ground he could not see was not quite so firm as it should have been; in between came this invisible, diaphanous stuff, and the earth had lost some of its substantiality. Later, as the light came, it seemed to him that the snow was more a kind of atmospheric layer, one of invisibility rather than of substance, and yet just before it bore his full weight it did make itself felt, even heard; there was a faint sound as it was crushed, like that of a nail being pulled out of wood—half squeak, half the noise of prying.

They climbed west, away from the sunrise yet up into it, for the light came down across the mountain and met them on the first ridge. There were many tracks, all fresh and powdery, all leading up toward the round knob of Cascom, out of the hardwood and up into the spruce and hemlock. Richard volunteered to push the deer while Shim and Murray climbed around to the ridge between Cascom and Gilman mountains, where the deer might cross over onto the western slope that led back down toward Leah. There would be many hunters out on such a perfect day, and there was a chance that other deer might come over from that side. It was a high ridge, for this country—about 2,500 feet, and if a deer were shot up there it would be a long drag out, but all the tracks seemed to lead up and up.

"Give us three-quarters of an hour," Shim said, "and we'll be set in a couple of good places I know where they cross over, then you follow the tracks."

Already they had heard shots from the distant valleys. "Scratch one porcupine!" Shim would say each time they heard a shot, or "Got that mammoth jackrabbit!" His contempt for other hunters was always evident; he hated to meet one in the woods, and this was one reason for his delight in the deer having gone high. They would see few other hunters as far up as the ridge.

Richard watched them go, faster now that they had a certain destination, then dusted off a stump and sat down with his back to a large hemlock. The wind sifted a sparkling mist of tiny, turning particles past his face, and the touch of them was cool and welcome. He was warm, and the air was very cold. Even in direct sunlight there was no sign of melting, and the snow slipped dryly off his boots. There were many tracks—the snow must have stopped quite early in the morning. Here a mouse had plunged along a blowdown branch, grooving its white sleeve. A jackrabbit had passed this tree, leaving its long, paired exclamation marks softly pressed, as if something as porous as new bread had been shaped and lightly pushed against the snow. He had seen earlier the deep channel a porcupine had doggedly bored—blind, it must have been in the deep fluff—to a pile of brush. The partridge were still sleeping beneath the snow, as far as he could tell; once he had almost stepped on one, when the snow one day was deeper but just as

187

dry, and the bird had burst up between his legs in an explosion of snow and whicking wings, startling him so that he shook for five minutes afterward.

He sat very still. It was the best time in the cold woods to sit as still as he wanted to, because the climb had warmed his body through. That warmth would soon seep away into the air, but for a time he was wonderfully comfortable, conscious of the cooling process only as pleasure. Later the balance would change, if he sat long enough, to shuddering cold, and he would have to move again.

Below him, through a chance break in the trees, he could see the gentler hills convoluting off to the east and over the other side of the earth—all of them dark with forest, marked here and there, but very seldom, with the white patches of fields or lakes. The fields were so small, so insignificant from here they seemed heroic efforts against the wilderness, and he was glad to see them that way. He wanted nothing but to be where he was, small among the trees, a hunter who must be forced to realize how wild the trees and mountains were, and how the odds were always with the real natives of the place. He wanted nothing but the meaning of the hunt, and to hell with civilization and all of its excruciating, impenetrable judgments, compromises, emotional storms and dialectical confusions. Here it was a matter of hand and eye, and the issue was the only clean and satisfying one, for there could be no argument: life or death. It was up to him to keep it so, definite and quick, and he knew his eyes were excellent, and that he was a good rifle shot. Not only that, but a man who had shot men did not get buck fever.

He raised his rifle and fitted it snug against his shoulder, the stock cold against his cheek, then took the safety off and looked down across the action, down the slim barrel at one of the little black triangles on the trunk of a white birch. A squeeze of his right hand, and in the chamber of the rifle, a few inches away from his eye, thousands of pounds of pressure would grow, and the bright bullet would begin its twist through the bore, which it would leave at a velocity of 2,920 feet per second. Over the distance of one hundred yards it would rise and fall just 0.6 of an inch. It would then be traveling at a velocity of 2,670 feet per second, and it would deliver to its doomed target 2,850 foot-pounds of energy. This at the signal of his hunter's reflex, all this dependable, irrevocable power, all his to use. He put the safety back on and lowered the rifle, running his gloved hand down the side of it past forearm, receiver, and stock. The sling was stiff from the cold, but no matter how cold it was, the machine would function exactly when he asked it to, and what fire and heat it would then create for him!

The heat of his body was fast leaving him, now, and as the first shiver came upon him it was the return to the reality of the woods; it was cold, and he was, after all, a tender-skinned man. He had a while to wait, but soon he would have to move. His toes were just at the point where they felt cool, and soon they would begin to numb. Already his fingertips were just a little insensitive about the inner texture of his gloves. He rebuttoned his red wool jacket—he should have done that as soon as he'd sat down, but that strange euphoric warmth had tricked him. As the cold penetrated—now it seemed the positive quantity—his clothes seemed thinner and thinner upon his body, and even though he counted the layers of good wool that covered his back he could hardly believe that they were there: thick woolen underwear made in two layers so that it would trap insulating air and not mat down, then a fine wool shirt, new and fresh, then a wool sweater made of yarn as thick as twine, long-sleeved, and finally his insulated wool jacket. And yet the cold pierced through all these layers and made them seem as insubstantial as a cotton T-shirt. He had always wondered how the deer could stand the cold. Granted, their faster metabolism and their coats of thick hair, each one of which was hollow for insulation, but their delicate legs! How could blood continue to flow through a foot upon which there didn't seem to be a lick of flesh, only the brittle bone and silver tendon?

All these were thoughts against the cold, the usual device, for he knew that a man was also an incredible animal, and could stand three times as much as he thought he could. Chances were that the deer, and other animals too, got good and God-damned cold in the hostile winter, and they shivered and stood it or else they died, and summer found their curiously flattened hair and bones.

He sat a while longer, as still as he could, for he was hunting, but finally the heel of his left foot refused to respond at all; it might have been the very heel of his boot. As he stood up he shivered violently. Unpleasant, but he knew that it was the body's way to shake new blood along beneath the skin, and he was aware of his body's health and wisdom in such matters.

The shiver passed—he had waited for it; the important thing was that his only movements so far had been a simple leaning forward in order to put his weight evenly upon his feet, then a straightening of his body. To the three deer that at that moment appeared before him either no motion had been perceived, because of odd arrangements of the hemlock's branches, or else, in the completely unpredictable way of the hunted, the motions Richard had made had somehow not suggested danger. He did not move; neither did they. They stood twenty yards away, and he thanked God, even as he avidly examined them, that his weight was evenly and comfortably upon both feet, and that the ground that he stood on was level. One was a skipper, about sixty pounds; one was a little buck with nubbins for horns; and the other was from that point until a few seconds later all he looked at. It might have been the buck he'd seen on the road. No, probably it was not that large. This one had the thick buck's neck, like a gigantic biceps, it seemed, all pure muscle, and perfect antlers—yellow, gleaming, they left his gray skull on thick pedestals, then turned forward above the brow tines, perfectly symmetrical and thick, and on each curve there were three tines. He moved his head as if he were deliberately showing Richard the majesty and perfection of his armor. From his black nostrils breath shot out in narrow streams like those of dragons in storybooks. His eyes were black, but delicately lashed. His brisket was bushy and edged with dark. For a whitetail he wasn't awfully big, but the word that came to Richard was *strong*: he was a regular weightlifter of a buck, and would weigh more than his actual size at first suggested.

While Richard watched, and he would never know how long it actually was, the choices he made were the magic ones of a man chosen by the gods, and even as he made them he could hardly believe that he had them to make. Never before, in all his years of hunting, had this happened to him. His shots had always been at deer who had seen or sensed him, and were running. Now, where would he place his bullet? Where in order to stop most perfectly this perfect animal? His deliberation was not buck fever. He was ready, and he trusted his hunter's instinct not to wait too long. Even though nothing but cold air separated him from their constantly active, vibrant senses, they were not aware of him. Though they constantly tested the wind, looked with one deep eye and then another at various objects around him, they never examined him with anything but cursory attention—then on would go their eyes, their ears would sensitively twist toward something else. His breath, because of his coldness after having sat so long, was not so obvious as theirs; somehow they never noticed it at all.

But where, through the body of that miraculous animal, would he direct the energy contained in his rifle? He *must* have the buck, he knew. Not to have him now, when fate had so offered him, would be a dark and unthinkable loss. The neck, where it arched like a tree? Where was the spine, precisely, in that clutch of round muscle? The shoulders? His bullet should break both shoulders, and if it did the buck would fall—unless the bullet were deflected, and at this angle (the buck at the moment was quartered toward him) he could not be sure. No, he must run him through the chest, where the heart beat, and the great arteries served the lungs. He would have few parts of a second in which to raise his rifle and fire, but he would do it as near as possible upon the buck's exhalation of breath. At this range the rifle must aim itself by its correct fit and proper drop; he would see the gold square of the front sight, and it must in one motion, with no correction, arrive straight between his eye and the buck's great ribcage.

Now! Up it came, the safety off instinctively on the way: *there,* the gold, and a tremulous blur of brown, and the rifle pushed him back with a force that seemed stern; not shocking but authoritative, powerful, and as the weight of the barrel and of his arms brought it back down his right hand slid up and back and forward and the chamber was again full of a bright cartridge. His eyes were clear again, and the buck had leaped (this seen in the slight blur of recoil) above the snow once, then again past two large trees (his flag down, but not the others', who leaped with huge white pillow-like flags flying and were still leaping off, turning, back around him and up the mountain). He knew that he had hit. That knowledge was immediate; only a miss could be mistaken. But he wanted the buck, and could not wait for full evidence. Yes, he knew exactly where the bullet had entered, and what fatal damage it had done, but again he placed the gold square upon the leaping buck, and fired. This time he heard the shot, and the buck went down. He had placed his shot as nearly as he could—the range had increased in perhaps three seconds to forty yards—toward the ribcage again. He hadn't led the deer; like most naturally good shots he aimed where he wanted to hit, and his swing and compensating reflexes did all his calculations for him. Again his rifle was loaded, and he began to walk carefully toward the spot where the buck had gone down out of sight. He must not trip on brush or witch hobble hidden beneath the snow. Slowly now; he had to step over a fallen birch. He must watch. There was a brown flank that blended into purest white. No, it was another fallen tree. But on the snow, widely flung, was blood, many scattered roses and rubies on the clean snow, blood as valuable to Richard now as the finest jewels, for these bright marks were, until he found the deer itself, the only part of the wild animal he had stopped, and could touch.

There. With his last jump, as his wrecked heart had stopped, the buck had dived toward a tangle of brush. Thinking still, of course, with his simple jewel of a mind, he had tried to conceal himself, but just at that moment he had run out of life.

Richard stood above the deer in the triumph of his luck and his good shots, and it seemed to him that the wild strength and heat of the brawny deer had come over into his own body. He did a little dance of delight, his rifle over his head; now he was warm again, all right. The deer was dead, and he had no need to touch its open eye to know. Its tongue hung red from the side of its mouth, and from this side of the deer Richard could see the two large exit holes made by the expanded bullets.

His first shot had been a gift. His second had been magnificent; now he was extremely happy that he had shot again, even though it had been unnecessary. It hadn't destroyed any meat and it had justified this gift to him—shown that his skill deserved it.

But he had some duty left to the deer, and also to Shim and Murray and their plan. Quickly he opened the bolt, pushed the loaded cartridge down into the magazine and found a firm place to lean the rifle so that it would be out of his way. He took his ten feet of rope from his jacket pocket, made a loop around one of the hind hoofs, then pullied the rope around a branch in order to open the white belly to him. His knife, honed the night before on his sling, was sharp and bright, a standard, carbon steel blade with a blood groove and a bone handle. This he slid from its deep sheath and with it slit and gutted the deer. He had done this ceremony eight times before, and though he had to wet his hands in blood, intestinal fluids, sometimes in the green mess of the stomach when he had shot too far back along the deer's side, always it was a joyful act, always it was done in triumph and with great respect for the beautiful animal he worked upon. Out upon the snow he slid the tripas of the deer, the small intestine still working as it would, slower and slower until its contractions were stopped forever by the cold. He saved the liver and kidneys—a plastic-lined pocket in the back of his jacket received them, and they warmed the base of his spine; heavy, liquid-feeling, they pressed warmly upon him and pulled down the shoulders of his jacket. The heart was torn, black with the contusions caused by hydraulic rupture, and he did not save its shreds of valves and meat. With nothing but these rags of heart the buck had run at least thirty yards—no wonder he must treat this flesh with respect! The blood he had loosed from tubes and veins rolled out and stained the white crotch, from which he had cut the genitalia, before it made the blotting snow bright crimson at his feet. The lungs in handfuls—they too were wrecked, and now his face entered the steaming cavity where the ribs rose up, silver-ivory, Gothic columns in a dark cathedral. The life, the heat, the humid center of the graceful deer that was now no longer of the wilderness (and yet still was, really, just as Richard knew that he himself was)—his naked, bloody hands could touch, and now all this was his.

When he had finished he washed his hands and wrists in the numbing snow, which helped coagulate the sticky blood so that it rubbed off in pieces; then with partially numbed fingers he took his license holder apart and tore off the deertag. With the pencil stub he carried for this purpose he filled in the township and date: *Leah, N.H., November 2*, then pinned the little tag on the buck's long ear.

He stood up, and the ache in his back was not unpleasant. Nothing was; he knew himself to be mortal and subject to weariness, but he also knew that this ache would disappear as soon as he began to move. He must try, at least for a while, to push the other two deer up toward the next ridge where Shim and Murray waited. Again he charged his rifle with a cartridge: on a day of so much luck he might see a bear or a wildcat, and wouldn't that be a record! He felt that if he did see one or the other he couldn't miss, not on this day.

Quickly he followed the two tracks, and after a half-mile or so, during which time they headed exactly toward the place he thought Shim had meant, he heard a faint shot from high above him— faint and yet sharp: *pow!* And then two more, coming almost together. No one else could have been so high at this hour. It must have been Shim and Murray, and each must have had a shot; the two last ones had come too close together to have been from one bolt-action rifle. Wonderful! My God! he thought, I hope Murray scored! He laughed out loud, and turned back toward his own kill. He would have a long drag ahead of him, but that sweat would be all triumphant, and while he horsed the buck down through the woods he could contemplate Murray's possible triumph, too. Maybe they would all bring in their deer, and it would be a great day. Out with the bourbon and glasses! and he and his son would be sharpshooters, hunters together again.

 20

Shim climbed fast, and Murray followed him at a distance he tried to keep at ten yards. Shim, he felt pretty sure, was making a contest out of it, showing this young punk how fifteen years didn't matter if you were a woodsman. It was tiring enough; the ground was invisible, and sometimes it wasn't where you expected it to be, but a disconcerting two inches higher or lower, or had a perverse slant to it that necessitated a wearing shift of all muscles and joints in order to maintain balance. But on they climbed, in and out of hummocks, bending flat beneath branches, shifting their rifles from one hand to another for balance or in order to push a prodding branch out of the way, using up energy as if they had an unlimited supply of it. The attention necessary in order to proceed at all had to be directly in front of the body, at a distance of inches or a few feet, and Murray had the same feeling of insulation from his greater surroundings he might have had in a speeding car; the trees, the vistas, slid quickly by, and he hadn't a chance to look at them at all.

He had opened his jacket and shirt, and as he sweated and worked he could feel his moist heat rising above him. Every part of his body was hot, even the top of his head beneath his red wool cap, which he had pushed back as far as it would go without its falling off (but it did fall off several times when little branches cleverly grown into hooks tweaked it into the snow). Once the winter bud on the end of a basswood whip, exactly in the shape of a Q-tip, inserted itself straight into his ear with considerable pain and the noise of thunder. For a moment he thought it had punctured something, but soon the pain went away. He hadn't time to worry about it.

Up and up they went, sometimes holding and pulling with the one free hand, searching for traction with the edges of their soles, and finally Shim began to slow down a little. They had come upon a narrow trail between rocks and small spruce, and here Shim stopped, turned and grinned as if to say, "Some climb!" He managed not to look so hot as Murray knew he himself did. Shim never wore as many clothes, for one thing—always just a green shirt over his various layers of underwear and other shirts, rather than a regular hunting jacket.

"'Bout a half-mile to go," Shim said, "but it's not uphill too much from here on. You been up here before, I think, when you was about sixteen."

Yes, they were on the Cooper Cabin trail, named after some long-gone hunter's shack. Murray remembered his father pointing out a few stones, once, and saying that their vaguely rectangular design meant that they had once been the cabin's foundation. The

Cooper Cabin trail led along a narrow ridge from the top of Gilman Mountain down a gentle curve and then up to the top of Cascom. They must have been nearer Cascom, for the trail slanted up toward the north. The trail was about one foot wide, a little groove in moss and stone, he remembered; now it was a soft line of snow broken only by the marks of partridge feet and one nice walking deer track, according to Shim a doe.

"You got to watch out for springs here and there," Shim said. "You'll hit that ice underneath and go zip down the rock, you ain't careful."

They went on, slower now, and as the trail twisted higher they might have been in northern Canada; the trees changed, the lichens on the few bare faces of the ledge grew strange and arctic, and the few yellow birches among the dense, short spruce were dwarfed and twisted. It was hard for Murray to believe that such a wild northern barren could exist so close in miles to the familiar, comfortable maples and fields of the valleys. They came to promontories where rock jutted out over the beech forest below, and he could look right down the tall trees. At times the trail crossed long, curving spheres of granite, and they went slowly, searching for cracks, holding fast to the few thin trunks—thin as broom handles—of dwarfed spruce. Below would be tangles of trunks and blowdown, the dead and living trees so complicatedly enmeshed nothing larger than a rabbit could have run between them. And then, around a corner as sharp as the arc of a wheel they would come to a cliff, and see the whole white and gray and bluish world curving and heaving out across New Hampshire and Maine, out around over the horizon.

And he would, even while he recognized the beauty of the cold land, ask himself what he was doing here. Where were the noisy plains full of people? He couldn't see them. Where were the cities? All he could see was a frozen lake, far off to the southeast, and over everything a bright blue sky full of cold sunlight. Much more real was the frigid wind—up here it seemed not a wind, which somehow would have had dimensions to it, but the whole cap of the earth's air moving over. Steady, always there, it seemed to move straight through trees and even through sheer walls of the gray granodiorite; they were no protection, and if he stopped against the face of the ledge the air seemed to breathe right out of it, cold as space.

Shim stopped. "Nearly there," he said, and from below they heard two shots. "Now, that was your pa!" Shim looked, and turned his head as if to triangulate the faint echoes. "It *was* your pa, and by the Jesus *he* wouldn't shoot no jackrabbit! He's got something going, Murray!"

They continued at a cautious run, not trusting the snow, ready at each step for violent maneuvers for balance. It was exhausting work. *We'll head 'em off at the pass!* Murray thought hysterically; he had nearly landed on his back, and his riflestock had knocked against the ice, but they ran on, up and down steep little humps, through passages where the trail was merely a narrow corridor at the bottom of a wide crack in the ledge, or between equally impenetrable spruce. Shim fell down once, hard on his knee, got up immediately and kept going, cursing softly and continuously. His boots were older, and smoother on their bottoms, but in certain places this gave him an advantage, for he could half-ski down steep places where Murray had to leap and run with jarring steps.

Finally Shim stopped and bent over exhaustedly. "Now," he said, and took a breath before he spoke again. "This is one place. You git yourself set up on the side, there, facing the wind. I'll be right over that hump. Two places they cross over every goddam time. Nearly every time, anyways." He ran up over the hump and out of sight.

Murray's pass was no more than twenty yards wide, a steep gully running right across the ridge, as if it had been chopped out with an ax to form a V. In the very bottom of it a swampy run had kept the little spruce from sealing it off. He climbed back up the trail, then found a place about ten yards from it to sit; a deer might come down the trail itself, by some chance, even into their scent, and here he would have a chance at it. He had a plastic flap inside the back of his hunting jacket which he let down to form a waterproof seat, and having chosen his spot and broken off a few small branches that crossed his field of vision—and one that would have gouged him in the back of the neck—he arranged his plastic and gratefully let his rear end sink into the soft snow. He shook with weariness, and if a deer had stood broadside to him at that moment he would have had difficulty holding his rifle steady enough to aim.

As he rested and cooled out, his hands steadied and he buttoned up his jacket and let down the earflaps of his cap. Now he was ready, and he hoped that a nice deer—not *too* heavy!—would come by soon and he could shoot it. It would make his father so happy if he got a deer. That was what the Old Man really wanted, and then everything would be fine; he could take off tonight and it wouldn't seem that he was running away from his father. At least it would make it possible for his father to rationalize it that way. If he could only explain it to the man . . .

Bang!—just over the hump. Shim. He sat very still. With a deer you couldn't tell. Another might have chosen this path. The shot had seemed slightly to his right, and if Shim had missed or just wounded it, the deer might come back around this way.

But the deer hadn't: there he was—it was—it didn't matter, right on the trail Shim had taken. There was the chest, white; there was a thin brown leg, a front one. He raised his rifle slowly, carefully, around a pesky twig, took a clear and good sight picture of that shoulder, both of his eyes open. There was the head—it was a doe—no, a young buck, just the right size. *Perfect.* His right hand had been squeezing the rifle, and now the trigger was coming in tight. *Whomp!* The sight picture had been just right. His hand began to come up toward the bolt. . . .

Shim's face, ballooned, Shim's mouth open, eyes bugged out, his red mouth and very regular white teeth like a set of sugar lumps; his mouth open, screaming. No sound, though. Was he deaf?

"Oh, oh, oh, oh!" Shim cried. Well, he wasn't deaf, anyway.

"What's the matter?" he asked Shim, and as he asked, terrible fright came upon him. "What's the *matter?*"

"Oh, Christ, Murray! I shot you!"

"What in hell did you do that for?" But Shim was working like a dog digging a hole. Out of the corners of his eyes he saw Shim working, and he was afraid to look. He was going to be sick, so he'd better roll over to the left and not puke on Shim, whatever he was doing there. Shim wouldn't let him, though.

"What are you doing?" His voice sounded as if it were coming through a tube.

"Your arm, Murray. Oh, God *damn* it!" Shim was that close. Look at that big knife! And then he remembered that the deer hadn't just taken the bullet; he'd shot right back. Ow! Like throwing a tire iron at a tire. It couldn't happen, but that deer rose up and slaughtered him right back! What a counterpuncher that little buck was!

Shim began to get undressed. First he unbuttoned his green shirt, then he pulled up his shirttails, then he took that shirt off, then he took off a pullover—sort of a sweatshirt—then he began to unbutton another shirt.

"You hot or something?"

"Yes!" Shim cried. Nearly bawled, actually.

"Christ, I'm cold, Shim."

Shim stopped getting undressed, and bent down to work again. Murray still didn't want to look to his right, but it did seem as though Shim were turning a great big wheel. And he felt that Shim should let him get his arm out of the goddam thing first, for Christ's sake, but Shim wouldn't.

"Let me get my arm out!" His voice was weak, very weak, mainly because he knew (really did know) that Shim was twisting a stick in a tourniquet, twisting it with both hands, with all his might.

"It hit me in the arm?" he asked Shim.

"Um!" Shim grunted as he twisted.

"I can't feel it much."

Shim took his big knife and slit with it, down out of sight, then put it back in its sheath and began to rip cloth.

"Murray," Shim said as he worked, "you're hit bad. You got to realize it so you won't fight this tourniquet." Shim was wrapping and tying red cloth around the stick. "No! Don't look at it yet!" Shim cried, and put his hand on Murray's cheek in order to keep his head from turning.

Then the snow turned, the trees, the sky, everything turned bright yellow, then gradually darker and darker yellow, then orange, then red like a bad egg yolk with a dead chicken in it.

"What's the matter?" he asked Shim.

"You passed out again, is all."

He was lying flat, and he couldn't move his arms at all, either one.

"I got you all bundled up, now. You don't need your arms, Murray. I don't want you to git cold."

"I don't need my arms?"

Shim was hacking at a spruce trunk with his knife. "I'm going to make a travois and haul you out of here, Murray. I got you all tied up in a bundle, and all you have to do is keep calm."

"OK, Shim."

"It was an accident, Murray!" Shim worked and worked at the trunk of the spruce, and then, suddenly desperate, he crawled to Murray, his knees kicking up snow, and put his hands on Murray's cheeks. "It was the most damnedest freak, Murray! We both shot that deer, you know that? We both hit and killed it dead, but my bullet went on through and smashed your arm. It was a freak!"

"OK, Shim. I know. It's beginning to hurt, though."

His heart was in his biceps, its valves knocking, wanting to get out. *Blum, blum, blum* (split!), *blum, blum* (*split!*) went his heart inside his arm, and it kept splitting the bone into ragged slivers that slid back and forth on each other. The snow turned into tons of orange sherbet, and the sky was jet black.

"Murray? Murray? Murray, listen to me!" Shim's face agonized above him again.

"Yes?"

"Listen, Murray, this ain't going to be a comfortable ride. I got you strapped to two poles, see?" He reached down and lifted Murray up like a wheelbarrow. "The closest road is down the Leah side, understand? We'll find a car, maybe, but we got a long ways to go. If you want to yell out, go ahead any time, OK?"

"OK, Shim."

"I got to stop every so often and look to see how you're coming, or to rest, but I'll get you out, Murray. You can trust me."

"I trust you, Shim," he said, and Shim's face went dark and painful for a second before it moved away. Then Murray's head rose up, and his body bounced awkwardly. His sleeves caught him in his armpits and his pants caught him in his crotch; it was like being on a spit, and his right side was against the fire, his left (would it soon turn?) against ice. But with this new and now bearable pain came an excruciating clarity, and Shim was no longer playing some surrealist game with knives and rope and poles. The trees swayed like masts, Shim grunted and sighed, and he began to feel motion. The little pains helped the big one.

He was badly hurt. His right arm ended in a vise almost where it began. He was tightly trussed, arms and legs, helpless, and someone (Shim) was helping him. Shim was pulling his heart out for him—could it be Shim? Funny Shim didn't just gut him and tag him. Where was his rifle? Who gave a God damn where his rifle was?

The tourniquet was too tight, because his ribs were bending. If only the bouncing would stop, maybe they could get everything straightened out again.

Then clarity returned, and he asked: Why did this have to happen to me? What a stupid piece of luck! His arm was broken, no doubt about that. He couldn't feel it, but maybe the tourniquet caused that. No, Shim's remarks ruled out anything simple; it was smashed, but smashed. That meant he couldn't drive. Oh, *damn* it!

"Ow!" he yelled.

Shim's voice, from ahead somewhere, full of phlegm and air: "Sorry, Murray." Breaths and snores from Shim. "Yell out. Yell right out, you want to." Gasps and grunts. "Remember. Doing my. Best. Help you!"

"Thanks, Shim. I mean it. *Oh!*" He hadn't meant to cry out at the end, there. Shim was taking care of him, and Shim was good at what he was good at. No, don't be facetious. Nobody would be as good in this situation. Granted, Shim had shot him in the first place, but if you insisted upon playing around with guns— No, Shim would now give his life, practically, to save him. If only his father would come, then everything would be fine. His father would get him out, all right. Maybe he would be along—if he hadn't got himself a deer with those shots they'd heard. He'd follow the deer track right up to the ridge, read the whole mess in the snow, and come right along. Of course his father would come.

"Ouch!"

His father would come loping up, and Murray would smile at the O.M. and say: "Slight accident, O.M. Nobody's fault. Just a freak." And his father would say: "Don't you worry, Murray. We'll have you to Doc Silver in a jiffy." Wait a minute. Doc Silver was in New York. Steady, Grimald, we'll have no regression here. And his father would say to Shim, "Let's have a look at it," and they would put him down gently and his father would stop that pain, throw away those awful poles, and pick him up in his big arms and carry him in and put him to bed even though he knew he'd only been pretending to be asleep so that when they got home Daddy would carry him out of the car and upstairs and give him a drink of water.

What am I, a goddam baby? he thought. (*Ow!*) The sky turned from bright blue to an old bruise; the whole sky, the moving, falling trees were bruised flesh.

"You're bleeding, God damn it," Shim said, and grunted out loud as he took two thousand more turns on the winch.

"I really appreciate what you're doing for me, Shim." Shim wore only his green chino shirt on top, and it was wet through except for the shirttails, which were frozen into green boards that knocked woodenly against his legs.

"I ate your sandwich a while back, Murray. You was out."

"I'm not hungry."

"We're gitting there, kid. Don't you fret. I'll git you out of the woods."

Out of the trees, Murray thought dreamily. The dark trees, the night that covers me. Don't ever shoot a deer, or the trees will kill you for it. They bent over him like cold ghouls: birches in antiseptic white; spruce dark executioners with hidden faces; beech gray prison orderlies, arms high, hands clenched, full of knotty clubs. They all bent over him, and when Shim tried to pull him away they ran around and got in front of him again, and were waiting just as before in their threatening, silent postures. Shim wouldn't give up, though. Shim kept going, and you could depend on him. Shim was strong, like his father, and knew about this cold place; lived in it and beat it out of its prizes.

"Shim!" he called.

"Ayuh!" Shim called back.

"Thanks, Shim."

"Take it easy, kid. We got a long. Ways. Yet."

When they next stopped, and his head was lowered, it seemed to him that his life had receded into his trunk, and there it nestled, protected and warm. Sometimes it would sneak up into his eyes and look cautiously out into the cold: above him a maple had been ringed and etched to the bone by porcupines, and the white, naked branches quivered—brittle quiverings against the blue.

Now he could not go on his journey, and it was not fair! Did he still believe that things were fair? How much of the world did a man have to see, how often must he observe his fellow men, how often must he excuse his own filthy ego before he understood the word? The word, the word. Should he pity himself, and cry? he wondered. Then he said, whispering through rubbery lips: "Let's face it, Grimald. Let's forget this man stuff. You're a nasty child, ready to be cuddled." —And convinced. Ready, but no one was there to convince him of the fairness of it all. How did he get to be a man? He outgrew the arms that might comfort, he out-thought the lies that might comfort, and if he found himself grown big enough to comfort others, what if he were unequipped with comforting lies? In the beginning was the lie, and the lie was everything.

Again they were moving, and Shim groaned with each heaving pull; he cried, and cursed the trees that stood in their way. The lurching sky was black behind the sun's orange light.

One fantasy he might allow himself: his father was grown up, and he could no longer be called Daddy. His mother then became a woman, an adult, and the double image of those two, which had been his constant dream image of them, as if they had both been placed against his mind in a double exposure—that double image began to slide apart, and as the two people slid out of each other's ectoplasm they grew into solid flesh, and their skins turned rosy and alive.

Just one more: if the sky were black, and the sun an orange bleeding out that strange nonlight, he might bring to life, no matter the number of ragged wounds and half-healed scars this vision suffered, a time of love and happiness. He didn't deserve it, to be sure, but in this time there was a just and gentle God—somewhat resembling his grandfather, but uglier and ten times as big—and God was a forgiving one. Stern, yes, but you could work off your gigs and be forgiven. All right, but it had better not be too pretty, this fantasy, for in the woodsy darkness the sadists still plotted, and the vain wanted to kill to justify their positions. The only difference between this time and reality was that here the bullies and the stupids didn't run the world, the calm voice was somehow louder than the screams of hatred; an impossibility, but after all, this was a fantasy.

But let's keep it under control, Grimald! Behind the dais were the combined symbols in prismatic juxtaposition—a lack of focus no scientist then present itched to correct; if they bothered you, you didn't have to look at them. Cross and phallus, candelabra and star, syringe and crescent moon, curette and burnished belly and the kind, calm smile, torii and hydra, flute and dancer, etc.—overlapping, diplopic mirror tricks. All right; if you didn't like the queasy feeling they gave you, you could shut your eyes, or look, like a Gothic rubberneck, up, up the slim columnations to a serene blue Universe.

Where were we? Yes. Music; we will this day in the lives of Murray Grimald and Christine Wilson give over this office to the Christians for their melodies and brave hopes, their early lack of sentimentality. Their symbol was a torture device, to remind mankind that sometimes his games were not very funny, "but in the cruellest man there might remain, dry and inactive as a spore, the seed of grace."

Christine: "Hello, Murray," she said, her soft voice full of love and humor. They both thought all this ceremony was rather silly, but they did it for the old folks, and actually they found it rather moving and impressive; at one point they looked at each other and found tears in each other's eyes, and smiled at their own sentiment. They were aware of their parents and grandparents back in the darkness, and knew the pride and love all felt toward the tall young couple. Christine wore white, and she stood, as he did, taller than the religious man who stood making the old incantations and poetry, making with God the garbled and multilingual litanies.

Then, at the proper moment (all this had been rehearsed on Wednesday), Sophie came with the babe, its tiny head and sleeping, rosy face snuggled against the silk, and as they knelt, Sophie, her face dark with happiness, presented the baby to Christine, who took it in her arms as they stood up again. The holy man touched them according to the ritual, and then said the final words: "With this babe I thee wed." They had to kiss each other then, in public, but since it was part of the ceremony they didn't mind. Their mouths met smiling, and the baby cried a little just for comic relief before they walked back up the aisle in the softly radiant light from all those fond faces.

The ugly trees bent down as they passed, then swung up like the heads of angry horses toward the black sky. Shim cursed and labored; each breath was a groan.

<<<<<<<<<<<<<<<<<<<<<<<<<<<<<<<<<<<<<<<<<<<<<<<< 21

AT LAST he had come within sight of the house. His clothes had sweat through, his knees trembled, his arms were about to come loose at the elbows and shoulders. The buck did not want to come out of the woods; if he had been alive he could hardly have managed to hook himself around so many saplings, or to slide his haunches into so many holes. He had, Richard thought, what the automobile magazines he'd been reading lately called "a pronounced oversteer." Now, with his forelegs hooked up behind his antlers so that they would be out of the way, he slid grudgingly along, pushing up snow in front of his brisket. Richard stopped, and leaned against the last sapling before the open slope. The buck's black eye was frosted over—a star pattern of white crystals. With his hoofs higher than his eyes he seemed frozen into a parody of leaping, and in their wake, a deep groove in the snow, were dots and dashes of the bright blood that he seemed never to stop leaving behind him. He, the buck; he, Richard Grimald. He smiled, and weary temblors moved through his thighs. Soon he would be pulling the buck up on the hook, and then he could look at him with no more duty to do, only the victorious telling about it. They would finger the holes in the brown sides—Murray, Shim, and Zach—and read the marksmanship in them. That was the story he wouldn't have to tell!

It was just noon when he reached the barn. Zach and Opal came out to see the deer, and Zach nodded professionally. He'd put on his old mackinaw, and in his unbuckled overshoes he helped Richard hoist the deer up in the barn doorway, then read the holes in its side and nodded again. The buck swung there by the neck, his white belly with the red slash in it exposed, his white tail—his flag—dripping the last of his blood from its now crimson tip.

Opal looked at the deer. She stood away from it and looked at it, holding her coat tightly around her; then she shivered and looked steadily at Richard. She would not congratulate him; she was not a hunter. He couldn't read her expression. Her gaze bothered him a little, and he owed her some of his time, he knew, even though he wanted only to be the victorious hunter—to wait happily for Murray's praise.

"I heard them shoot, too," he said, knowing that she wouldn't particularly care. It disappointed her—he could see it in her eyes— that he put her off with that sort of talk, but then he glanced at Zach, as if to say that he spoke of hunting because Zach was there. He didn't want to hurt her. Now that he was happy again he must not hurt anyone.

She and Zach went back into the house. Before he washed up he had to clean out the rest of the lungs from the deer and tidy up a few ragged edges here and there. When he went inside, Opal was not in the kitchen.

"*Hoach!* Damn fine. *Huch!* Buck," Zach said, nodding from his blue chair. "Runnin'. *Hough!* That second. *Hoach!* Shot?"

"I guess I didn't have to take it, but I sure didn't want to lose him," Richard said.

Zach nodded, his mouth set in an expression of severe approval. "*Huch!* You're a hunter. *Hough!* All right."

Murray and Shim would know that, too! He took most of the blood from his hands with cold water at the sink. He didn't want to change the strong clothes he had been so lucky wearing, but he did go upstairs and wash his upper body. His tiredness had left him already, and he thought he might go out again. There were always bear and wildcat, and a few other animals worth bringing in, and he might, if Shim or Murray had scored, help with the last of the

206

dragging. His shirt and underwear were drying out quickly; he would hang them in his room for a while.

Opal sat on his bed waiting for him.

"I just wanted to talk," she said. "Would you talk to me for a minute?" She was shy, now, and wouldn't look directly at him. She looked around the room, then at the bedspread, which she smoothed gently with her little hand. Then, evidently, she remembered what they had done on that bed, for she drew her hand quickly away.

"I'm not stupid, you know," she said. He saw that she had been crying a little. He turned to hang his shirts on the door, and she ran to him and put her hand on his naked ribs. He felt very strong, but only as a hunter in the woods, and he didn't really want her to touch him. If only Murray had shot a deer! That other young buck, for instance, with the nubbins for antlers.

But even in that little second or two he was communicating his indifference to Opal, and he could not be that cruel. He took her face between his hands and kissed her on the lips. "It was wonderful yesterday," he said. "You made me very happy."

"Happy?" she said dubiously. He knew what she wanted. He was ashamed of his selfishness. She wanted love and permanence, even as she saw by his little hesitations that he would never give them to her. There was a certain point, he knew, when terrible compromises were made, and he hoped for her sake that she wouldn't make this one now, because she wasn't quite yet a cheating wife; she had been in love with more than sensuality. She would be hurt in any case, but if she chose to take him without the faintest hope of permanence then what he had done to her would be unforgivable.

She went back and sat on the bed. "Do you still love me?" she asked.

That was the question he couldn't answer. He sat beside her and put his arm around her. If only he could answer the question. She was passive, waiting. He moved his knife back along his belt so that it wouldn't touch her. "I think you're very sweet and wonderful," he said.

"But you don't love me." A statement of fact.

207

Now she should get up and leave him, and try to make her life out of the materials she had. She got up and went to the window. She could lean her hands on the sill, her legs in her faded dungarees straight, her little waist now looking to him, in his great shame, beautiful and yet used, violated, and his problems with her were no longer exciting. He pitied her, but what a cheap thing pity was! She sniffled like a little girl, and kept her face turned away.

"But I loved you so *much!*" she said unbelievingly. It wasn't fair, of course. How had he managed to make her so unhappy? What sort of person was he, an ordinary man, forty-five years old, to be *able* to hurt this woman so much? But he had heard that past tense, all right, and he shamefully liked that: loved.

She turned her crying face toward him. "What was so 'wonderful'?" she asked. "You said I was 'sweet and wonderful.' What was so 'sweet and wonderful' about me?"

"You're a beautiful woman."

"You don't think so right now."

"Yes, I do."

"But you don't love me."

He was silent.

"You don't even want to touch me."

He was silent.

"You weren't gentle with me, were you? You said you would be, but you weren't. I didn't want you to be."

"I know." He wanted to help her, but he couldn't. He realized that he simply had no resources, and could not communicate. He could only hide behind his smooth face and, in a way, agonize. What could be wrong with him? He couldn't understand it. There must have been a way to try to repair this, but without the energy of excitement his mind was sterile; he had no arguments at all.

"Shim never did what you did. I could never let him." She found a Kleenex and wiped her nose. Perhaps the only thing he had left to give her was the opportunity to repulse him physically. He didn't want to do it, but it seemed all he had to give.

"Come here," he said.

"No." She shook her head as she wiped her glasses, then put them firmly on.

"Don't cry, Opal," he said, and at this she looked straight at him.

He got up and went to her. She shook her head and put her fore-arms together in front of her chest, but that was the only defensive move she made.

"Don't worry about me," she said, and now she wasn't crying. Her hands came around on his back, smooth on his skin, and as it had been before, her real power was one of touch. "Just don't worry about me," she said, and her voice was rough, a little ugly, but suddenly he changed, and held on to her. Her hand was at his belt. She had made the wrong choice, and would give for nothing, take nothing but the brutish moment, the shoddy, sweaty goods he had to give. He was ready, now, without love, and just before his lust became all of him again, he remembered shame. My God, he thought, I could do it anywhere; I could do it on a grave.

Perception, clearing of the mind: her darkness around him, ready to make him mad again, but for a moment out of time they listened to the telephone's faint cries, counting them. It was the Buzzells' ring, and at that meaningful number they rolled stealthily out of bed and were mad this time for their clothes. They heard through their fever of buttons and laces Zach answer the telephone at the base of the stairs, his sucking gulps of air louder than his old voice. They heard him suck some more: "*Hough!* Opal!" Then he went away. Suddenly they thought that he knew, and she turned her frightened face toward him. She said, "He'd never tell," and Richard saw that she was all plotter now. Now, because of him, she would have to be, and she would hate it.

She finished dressing and pushed her hair into place as well as she could. On the way she stepped into the bathroom and flushed the toilet, then opened and closed the door loudly. Zach might not be sure, he might think she'd been in there: there was suspicion, and there was absolute knowledge, and the plotter had to run that knife edge all the time.

"*Mea culpa,*" he murmured to his boot as he laced it up.

Soon Opal came running back upstairs and opened his door. She didn't bother to knock, and that was a mistake. . . . Her face filled him with something very much like dread.

"It was Shim," she said. She kept shaking her head. "Murray's been hurt. He said it was a freak accident. He's been shot. He took him down into Leah and then to Northlee Hospital." Her face was full of pain.

"Where was he hit?" He had asked that question so many times in his life. He was putting on his still damp shirt, carefully tucking it in, now, and buttoning the pockets.

"Shim said his arm—something about his arm."

Oh, thank God! Only then did his hands begin to shake. But a *hunting* bullet. *My son!* The boy's pain made him wince. Murray was there, whole, in his mind—no, there were his strong arms, and the young face smiled at him. He was almost sick; the faint symptoms of shock. Opal had tactfully gone on ahead, and let him pass her in the hall. He ran down the narrow stairs, grabbed his jacket in the kitchen, and ran through the tracked-up snow to his car. He must be there right *now*. But he mustn't panic. He had to drive on snow; he had to be careful; he had to get there quickly and efficiently. Ten miles—five to Leah town square, five or six more to Northlee and the hospital. The main roads would be cleared by the salt, by now, but he must—the car started easily, thank God; the sun had been on it—he must take it easy going down the mountain.

His wheels spun as he backed around. The car itself would be plowing snow until he reached the town road, which by now would be open. "Easy," he said. His speedometer needle swung violently around to forty as his wheels spun in the snow, just out of phase with the tachometer needle. He *must* take it just right; he would go off the road if he tried it too fast, or stick if he were too cautious. Right at the end of Shim's road he would have to speed up and plow through the banking left by the town plow, and then it would be tricky to slide around parallel to the road without shooting straight across into the other embankment. The road was clean snow, gentle curves and luminous blue indentations. It was like driving across a sheet, and the car handled on the soft white stuff mushily, boat-like. It steered from the rear, and the slipping body of the car responded slowly to his nervous work with wheel and accelerator. His hands ached on the wheel, and the cold air came past the side curtains and burned his sweating face.

That part of it went quickly; he mushed through the plow's soft wave—the snow was cold and light—and stopped on the plowed surface to push snow out of his radiator and front wheel wells. Then came the slow descent, where the driving could not take all of his thoughts, and he must live with Murray's hurt.

He turned the wheel when he had to, shifted down and up, felt the car's rear end move out and then catch traction again. The white road curved down between the heavy drooping pines and the rigid hardwoods. The day was cold and bright. Murray's flesh and nerves had been viciously ripped.

He asked God, not knowing who God was, never having had such a need before, please to let it be nothing much. Will You let it be? But he knew that it could not be small. He knew too much about bullets and flesh, and none of the sweet blank spaces of ignorance could help him not to see. He knew too much all at once, and from too much knowledge he could only try to go beyond it— if there were such a place. *I love my son, God. I can't bear to have him hurt!*

Watch it! He'd nearly left the road—had begun in terror to pick an impossible course through the iron trees. He cursed the snow and the bright hard day: his terror was for delay. If he lost the car he couldn't run far enough. He couldn't wait; if he found himself standing, weak in his heavy boots, alone on the white road he would—yes, he believed he would go crazy. He slowed down. There were no alternatives to his getting to his son, none. And so he would have to make it. *Slow, now, slow.*

All he could see, big as the mountain, hovering beyond the road he must steer, was a terrible wound, close to his eyes; there was the tender skin, ripped there, curled, and slivers of wrecked bone. He had seen many such wounds made by shell fragments—vicious because of the random jagged shapes of blown-apart steel, but they were not so fast, those little shards, as a bullet. They had not been designed, like the bright little machine a hunting bullet was, to turn the velocity of a small mass into maximum destruction. *Don't think,* he informed his brain, *drive.*

Murray (soft, the name meant to him—tenderness and bright, precarious intelligence): the boy he saw in flashes of unbearable love was not always twenty years old (last February 10th at one minute past five in the afternoon. "You have a son—a beautiful son," Dr. Silver said on the telephone), but sometimes a younger

Murray in scenes where his right to the boy's company and need was too much taken for granted. Much too much. He had been angry, and spanked Murray! God should whip him with steel for his anger.

Now, hold on, he thought. You never spanked him very much, and only when he really deserved it. *Did he deserve this?* The bullet, whose ever it was—Shim's, Murray's own, some other hunter's —should have hit him, not his son. He could have taken it. He would take it anywhere. But Murray, who didn't even want to be there! Murray wanted to be off on his trip, and had only stayed to please his father. His father, who was in love only with his own selfishness.

Drive.

Hadn't he looked forward to his shoddy triumph with the hung trophy! And then, while he might have been helping Murray, he wasted his energy dragging out his game; he came back gloating and sweating over a dead animal; he used Opal—used her—to prove himself the man still. He hurt her for his selfish lust while his son was in pain, and while the very man he had cuckolded helped Murray down the other side of the same mountain. He didn't deserve to be a father. He'd be in his shoddy, adulterous bed when his son needed him, or shedding blood when it was so precious, so precious. What could he do for Murray now? Perhaps it wasn't really so bad—just a rather deep tick through the muscle, which they could sew up and bandage but had needed stitches and antisepsis and all that. "For Christ's sake, calm down, now," he said, his voice strange with only the empty seat beside him. But it was a relief to put a thought out of his head into the air.

He turned onto the blacktop road, where the salt had worked the snow back almost to the shoulder. Here he began to make better time, but still he kept everything in control. He must have no trouble. The wheels hissed on the asphalt, and the air seemed a little warmer in the valley. It was a beautiful day—perversely so— a day he might have been so happy with Murray in. The blue sky was deep and clear, and the sun shone on the fresh snowbanks— one of those winter afternoons when the cold had turned, begun to lose out, and the world seemed warm and friendly again. Now all this was artificial to him. He was not part of this day, as if he looked out of the small windshield at an overpretty Kodachrome.

Could he face Murray, knowing what he knew, that he had kept the boy near him out of avarice? His watch, his wife, his car, his son. Had he really been worried about Murray's adjustment to Murray's life, or had he been a miser about those things he considered to be *his*? His son comforted him, brought life back together again, made him forget the approach of an age like Zacharia Buzzell's when he would be a man no more, no more, but an old crock with plastic plumbing. He had wanted to take youth from Murray's youth, and to remember good old times when he had his beautiful wife and son. Had them.

"No, I loved them," he said to the buzzing car. "I loved them." No one was there to hear him. He looked guiltily, and no one was there to hear a man blubber to himself. Who the hell was he to blubber out his love to the air and expect an eavesdropper? Who would be listening—God? He had heard men ask the most reasonable questions of that One, men who meant them sincerely, too; what man wouldn't who looked at his own insides or the shank ends of his legs or arms? He had seen too many of that One's handymen at their games to expect Him to watch less interesting phenomena. They loved badly and killed well. They were lousy lovers and good shots. They made good livings and hoarded life, the tough little bastards; you found out about the Father from the sons.

Not Murray. There had been too many times in his life when he had taken sustenance from the boy's love, taken it for granted and used it and gone his own prideful way. Against the pretty winter day, as if in a montage, he saw a winter twilight once soon after the war when they had been skiing at Stowe. Murray was about ten, and had fallen and twisted the ligaments in his knee. He and Rachel had taken the last run of the day on the Nosedive, and when they came out below the chairlift someone had just come by, and told them, and they had raced across to the slopes; there was Murray still on the toboggan, and his pale face, his stern expression of pain. He saw them (had a light been flashed on his face just at that moment?) and he smiled, so relieved—and yet he was confident that they would come—and said as if the pain, worry, all the fuss were now practically over, "There he is! My daddy's here now!"

The light. Someone must have had a flashlight. There on the luminous snow was the complex of objects—the birch toboggan with the guiding handles; he saw it now. A ski—one of the ridgetops that were fashionable then, and the dark blanket, the blocky ski boots. All the tows had closed a few minutes before; the sky was still deceptively bright; yet its final light seemed to end just above the earth, and the snow's whiteness was more remembered than real—cold phosphor, brittle with the turning wakes of earlier skis. It was too dark then for the remembered vision of his son's loving face, which shone now with almost holy warmth in his memory.

Some time after that they had the discussion about the word "daddy." Murray came to him one evening and brought it up. He was quite serious about it, and didn't want to hurt his father's feelings, but he thought he was a little too old, now, to use it any more. He had prepared a list of possible choices, with his opinion of each designated by a system of checks and asterisks:

DAD √ *
PA √√ *
POP √√ *
FATHER √
RICHARD √
DICK
PATER
OLD MAN (O.M.) √√√ ****

It was then Richard realized that Murray hadn't called him anything at all for several weeks, and as he scanned the list with tolerant amusement Murray stood next to his chair fidgeting with embarrassment. His lips were pursed in an imitation of deep consideration, his dark, wide eyes were serious—but couldn't look with serious purpose at his father. Murray preferred "O.M." because, he said, it was "humorous" and he just couldn't *make* himself (after so many years) call his father "Dad"—it sounded as if his father were a grandfather or something. Anyway, it didn't sound right. But "O.M." now—it was sort of friendly, like friendly competition?

And in his pride Richard took everything for granted. His tolerance, his superiority, were colossal. What boy, he must have thought, would not admire such a man as he, and imitate him?

214

Hadn't he had the time to argue with his son what amounted not only to a father's name but to the boy's own counterimage, the image he had of himself, and after that the image of mankind? Shallow, superior in his puffed-up manhood, he had agreed too easily, and never thought that a name was not that important. Murray had gone away without the information he sought.

And hadn't he always? How responsible was the father for the son's despair about the future of the world? Who would kill mankind—the kind of man he had for his very own *father?*

"Oh, God!" he groaned, and drove on as fast as he dared. He went through Leah, past the Welkum Diner where he had stopped such a few days before to call the lodge (a mean figure in a selfish plot), went north on Northlee Street, and soon was out of Leah, past the service stations, again in the hills, the Connecticut River on his left, black water between its sun-white banks. Then into Northlee, past the campus of Northlee College—the hospital was farther north at the edge of the town. He took the wrong way, a newly designated one-way street, his eyes seeing, emergency ignoring the little sign, then around the square. He knew this way; a little street, now, on the left. Then he turned down toward the squat, spreading, yellow brick hospital with its new red brick and glass modern wing, its tall, factory chimney coming strangely out of the bare white ground fifty yards away: steam in puffs along a wall, cars in the parking lot parked in amazing order, all carefully angled against the barrier, all coldly in formation there.

"Murray, Murray," he heard himself saying. He was rehearsing, composing an argument: "Look, Murray. Look how I love you, how I will love easily from now on, without any pride. Don't despair about the world. See? Even your father can change in time to save himself, and maybe the world can, too." But how could he tell Murray? "Look at me. I'm the worst animal in creation, and now you see how I've given up my vanity? We are still a loving family, Murray, and you'll see—your mother and you and I— you just wait and see. When you get out of here (tomorrow?) I'll prove it to you, Murray!"

Stop talking, you fool! He parked the car and ran down the swept gray cement to the hospital entrance. Heavy glass doors— his hand stuck to the cold brass handle and came away with soft, painless reluctance—a ghost of tearing. Modern motel chairs, people crumpled in them like old newspapers, a smell like the lobby of a big apartment house, his largeness, his hunting redness watched by all as he crossed the rubber and the shining floor. The low desk: the girl turned her pretty, institutional face toward him, her hand upon a telephone.

"My son . . ." No. "Murray Grimald, G.R.I.M.A.L.D.—a hunting accident, they told me. They called me. . . ."

"Grimald? G.R.I.M.A.L.D.?" she efficiently asked him, her cool eyebrows raised professionally. Then she inserted a plug in one of many holes, and pushed it home. "Emergency rooms?" she asked. "Grimald, G.R.I.M.A.L.D., Murray. His father is here. Oh." and her eyes sneaked up at him. "Yes, Nurse," she said, calling her eyes home again.

I know it's bad, he thought. Don't pamper me. I can take it. I'm a man, aren't I?

She was careful of him. "The doctor will see you. Will you go down the corridor to the right, please? The first double door at the end of the hall on the left?"

Now she should have smiled, but she did not. He began. Walls grew and corners appeared; he strode in his gross health past wraiths in gray gowns and unnaturally pink faces. He would bring to his injured son strength. His boots tended to catch their thick toes on the smooth floor, and he had to lift his feet high, to stride down toward the double doors. If it were very serious he would have to say to the doctors that Murray must have the very best, and that meant New York, probably. Beth Israel, or Mount Sinai, or Presbyterian. He would find out who was best with bones and muscle repair. That first, but *Murray, Murray, you will see how these animals can also give their love.*

The hall, as he strode down it, became less and less the neighborhood of patients; it grew more businesslike. There were the portholes and gauges of autoclaves—he had bought equipment from the same company. Folded stretchers, the marks of rubber tires on the now blue-painted cement floor. The first double doors on the left were also painted blue, and he pushed through them and stood in a short hallway with three doors leading from it. A middle-aged nurse with gray in her hair got halfway up from her desk, and a

216

young doctor in a short-sleeved green smock turned toward him.

He took three or four steps, and the doctor did too. They met next to a rubber-wheeled table filled with rolled towels and pans and rolls of bandages.

"Are you Mr. Grimald?" The young doctor was blond, and had muscular pink arms, and bad news on his young face.

"Yes. My son . . ."

"Yes, the boy. We're sorry, sir. . . ." The doctor's young eyes faded.

"You must tell him," the nurse said, and came quickly up to them. She put one of her large clean hands on Richard's arm, and her other hand on the doctor's bare arm above the elbow. "You must tell him right away." Her cheeks moved as she nodded; she had fine little hairs on her temples.

"I know it's bad," Richard said. "Don't spare me. Tell me what's wrong with him."

"The boy died on the way here, before we could help him. There was no heartbeat. He was dead on arrival." Each of the doctor's phrases was a breath.

No.

"His arm?"

"There was nothing we could do for him," the nurse said. Her hand was strong on his arm, and her black eyes searched his for understanding.

No.

"You say he's not alive? Murray?"

"We couldn't help him."

"My son."

Yes.

They grew above him, their kind but distant faces. Their arms took him, a chair scraped, a live voice grunted. All this distantly, for he had understood, and believed them. That was not hard; neither was the wave that took his breath out of his lungs, and the blood out of his veins. Murray, Murray. Fainter, fainter; if, if there was a man here, inside him, inside the red jacket, it was a man made of a vacuum. Now die, you. For Christ's sake stop living. Right now. Give it the last twist. Will it.

It almost worked, but the body's will was not his, and the

traitor heart still pumped lustily. The cruel eyes still saw the room in which he had learned. They read for the imprisoned brain a typed list taped to the wall:

1. Jar with dry sterile cotton balls
2. Flask of alcohol 70 per cent
3. Peroxide of hydrogen
4. Collodion
5. Bandage, 1″, 2″, 3″
6. Adhesive, ½″, 1″, 2″
7. Sterile dressings
8. Sterile sponges
9. Sterile applicator sticks
10. Sterile safety pins

"Are you all right?" the voices called, and his ears still heard. "Let him sit there for a moment," a voice said. "It's hard, it's terrible hard." That was the nurse.

"I thought he was going into shock," the young doctor said. "He's not listening to us."

"He's listening. He can't help it, poor man."

"He's sitting up all right."

"He's all right. You'll find out. You keep right on living."

"I don't ever want to find that out," the young doctor said.

Murray was dead. He knew death well; what a strange, lumpish statue it made of a man. But not Murray, who had so much precious life.

"Where is he?" he said, hearing his voice command them.

"Are you all right now?"

"Yes, I'm all right." (Again that stranger's voice.) "Let me see him." He got up, and his knees supported him.

"There," the nurse said, "you've got your color back."

Color of blood.

They led him to the middle door, and all the time it seemed that he did not go into the room at all, was not there, and it was only the traitorous metabolism that would not let him stop breathing and seeing.

It was Murray: he had believed them, hadn't he? On the high

examining table, his eyes insisted, a young man lay on a long piece of butcher's paper they had ingeniously pulled from a roll at the head of the hard table. No blood moved here; the sheet was unspotted green that held his arms to his sides, that was wrapped in a band over the red clothes he hadn't wanted to wear. Crumpling the white paper were his new boots, their good tread still crisp. His shirts were unbuttoned, but had been pulled together over his chest.

Murray.

The strong throat was unlined and white; his morning's beard delicately shaded the square chin, which was now a little slumped; and a white tooth appeared between bloodless smooth lips.

It was Murray, a lifetime of young manhood without the slightest pulse of his nervous strength. No more smiles. Eyebrows of miraculous design. Lashes over the dark hollows below the lumps that were his closed eyes. The face was not sad. The dear face did not express anything at all: a frown that was not anger; upon the barely open lips a sigh that contained no breath.

"His arm?"

"Yes. He bled to death," the doctor said eagerly. "Sometimes it happens. Cold. Shock. The man who brought him out of the woods did just the right things—it wasn't his fault. He applied the best tourniquet he could, under the circumstances. The arm . . ."

Murray's dark hair was creased where his cap had been. On his temple was a little scar; where had he got that scar? Richard didn't know, and suddenly with that deficiency of knowledge came the wave again. He stood through it, welcoming the knife that twisted in his throat. Had Murray cried when he received that cut? Called for his father to help him? How old had he been? What year was it? How many had he then lived of his twenty?

The wave, the knife in the throat.

They turned him around and led him out again. Into the gray hallway, and then—all things now seen through air pellucid yet cracked as ice—the nurse went forward with her hand raised, her stocky legs marching, and she commanded someone, "Wait!"

There were three men: Shim was in green, a bundle of clothes under one arm, his sick face saying, *Kill me, but it was a freak accident;* a state policeman, righteous and big, vengeance in his face; a game warden, whose face did not want to look upon hospitals.

"Give him a little time, will you?" the nurse said angrily.

"Mr. Grimald," Shim cried, stepping forward. "Believe me I'd rather shot myself! It was a freak! You'll see it. The deer's still there. The tracks! Christ, I tried to git him out!"

"He did, you got to give him credit, there," the game warden said shyly. A familiar face—where had he seen it before?"

"In-vestigation," said the state policeman.

"Can't you give the poor man some time?" the nurse asked. "Can't you let him get used to it?"

He heard them all perfectly well, saw them all—those cracks across the air were only fissures in the pure, smooth bell of his life.

Voices: "We can't go up tonight, anyways. It's four o'clock—be dark in an hour." The game warden—young Spooner, whom he had last seen white and stupid under burning magnesium.

"Question is, was it gross carelessness?" the state policeman said.

"You'll see!" Shim said. "It was a freak!"

A freak, a freak. Shim was no freak. Shim was far from being a freak. Richard tried to get a breath. "No, it was an accident, of course," he said. Ah, you reasonable murderer, he thought. Be cool, now. Don't tell anyone who is guilty of a son's despair.

He had things he had to do: murder his son's mother with the news. The world kept on going—was that what the nurse had said? The living kept on murdering each other. He held up his hands, and around each cuticle, as if drawn by the tiniest brush, was a delicate cilia of dried blood. Spots, dark washes of blood were all over his clothes. A yellow bead of lung had dried upon an eyelet of his boot.

He turned toward the nurse, and was vaguely surprised that she still held his arm. "I must make a call . . ." and that strange and ineffectual wave came again. He resented it because it could not complete its work, but traveled past, and only took his breath away.

"Maybe that's best," she said. "You must share your grief. It's easier that way." Her worn face claimed understanding. She still

220

held his arm, and turned to the others. "Now, will you leave him be? He won't be needed! What can he tell you? All he knows is that his boy . . ." She stopped, and stared at them in embarrassment and anger.

It was the thin, weathered, country face of young Spooner that he watched without being able not to, for on the young and unself-protected face came, just for the smallest instant, an expression of softness and compassion that reminded him of Murray.

<<<<<<<<<<<<<<<<<<<<<<<<<<<<<<<<<<<<<<<<<<<<<< *22*

THE NURSE had shooed them all away. She offered him a sedative, but in spite of his indifference to life he had a shiver of terror at the idea of sleep. Death might be all right, but not the terrible consciousness of sleep. She cashed a traveler's check for him, took him to a phone—poor innocent, he vaguely thought, who accepted life as a kind of ability to survive. She admired him for his lack of tears and his steady voice. Her son, she told him, had died in the war. What war? He didn't ask; how could there have been any other war?

She left him alone while he called. How well the efficient memory kept working—he dialed the long-distance code number, then the number that had once been his own. He didn't have a word ready for her, but there was the ring—and again. The phone in New York came off its receiver, and there was half a breath.

"Hello?" It was the voice of a strange woman. All at once he realized that he might have spoken to Rachel, and have heard her voice close to his ear.

"Hello?" He spoke to the stranger in a stranger's voice.

Mrs. Grimald was out. Who had called? Oh. Was there a message? She didn't know when (hesitation) Mrs. Grimald would return.

Message: *Dear Rachel, my dear wife who hates me; you were right all the time, and to prove it I have taken your baby, your sweet, gentle baby, into the dark woods and lost him there.*

"No, I'll call back," he said.

If he had to wait too long he might not be able to call her. Even in shock he could predict that all this would get worse, that only momentum kept him at his duty. The metabolism protected itself in spite of its host—at least until the truth, without pity, rendered justice. And he did not deserve justice; he would lynch himself. The coldest justice in the world could not suffice, and that was why, even though the paternal figure waited in his mind to be called upon, he tried not to think of Saul Weitzner. There should have been no such mountain for him to see; in his world there should have been no friend. But there was—just the one. No one else but his son, and long ago perhaps his wife, had ever claimed love from him, and given it without demanding proof. But he did not deserve comfort or forgiveness. Saul should rise before him like Jehovah and blast him with anger.

No, Saul would give him justice, but the justice in this case would be the sight of an old man bereaved, an old man six million times bereaved. Now, with his beloved grandson—six million and one times. Would Saul try to give comfort?

"I don't want pity," Richard whispered to the black instrument he held in his hand. But he did want it. Not believing in pity, he wanted it. Not believing in mercy, he wanted it.

If he could just see the man again in all his bludgeoned, lovely ugliness, see the kind smile once more, whether he deserved it or not. Maybe then he could confess, before the terrible bell of emptiness descended fully upon him, and for a moment believe what he could not believe.

As he got up from the phone the nurse appeared. He told her again that he was all right, to tell them that he would be back tomorrow to see about—what he had to see about. Then he went out into the winter twilight to his car. He could not return to the lodge—he'd never make it back up the unplowed road, but that was not the only reason. Even to get his clothes and run, could he face Opal, who would remind him of his cruelty, Shim who would cry to him that it was a freak, Zach with his possible knowledge, the cooling body of the handsome buck that was to have been the cause for his and Murray's comradeship and celebration? It would take him five hours to reach the city, and he would have the duty of driving, the blows of oncoming headlights in his eyes to keep him occupied.

On the turnpikes he drove on ice, it seemed, and the danger was that he should slue in his mind into terrible memories of his wife and son. He stopped once for gas, and crouched in the little cockpit away from the light, seeing only a dark hand reach in for its money.

It was 10:45 by the time he found a parking place on Seventy-ninth Street, a block from Central Park West, and walked, his big boots awkward on the cement sidewalks, the two blocks to Saul's apartment building.

His boot caught on the step, and he almost fell. He would have crawled, a child stumbling and crawling in exhaustion toward a loving parent, needing a strong hand even if it were to punish him. "Saul," he whispered. The lobby was too long, the rug shifting like snow beneath his heavy legs. The colored elevator man knew him, and said, "Good evening, Mr. Grimald."

"Yes," Richard said. He tripped again as he entered the elevator, and his shoulder jarred the collapsible gate. "Good evening," he said, but in the rising cubicle his voice died on his lips. They rose slowly to the tenth floor, and the gate and door opened. As he stepped into the high, empty hall, the elevator man closed the elevator upon his back, deserted him there and began his return. Alone, Richard walked on carpet so thick it made him deaf, and stopped before Saul's heavy door. He pushed the mother-of-pearl button, and because he heard no sound, no tolling bell, he had to trust and wait. If Saul weren't there he would have to sit with himself in the ornate little chair at the end of the hall. He would have to sit still in that limbo, surrounded by Murray's death.

The door opened. "Saul," he said, but he looked and it was Orson Gelb—fat, white little Orson Gelb, whose mouth fell open, who looked up at him with aggressive fright.

"Oh! We thought it was . . ." Orson Gelb said accusingly, yet in a hushed, solemn voice. For a moment, unbelievably, it looked as if Orson might try to keep him from coming inside.

"Saul," Richard said again, and pushed by Orson into the wide foyer with its gilt-framed mirror and Saul's paintings, the entrance to a place that had always meant to him wisdom and serenity. There was Sophie Gelb, the girl who had been in trouble two years before; a big homely girl, she had been crying, by the look in her eyes.

"Here's Murray's father," she said, turning back, and there came a harsh sound from the living room.

"Him!" The voice of Ruth Weitzner, full of hate and sharp edges.

He came on, each step an effort because the toes of his boots were awkward as snowshoes, and he could barely lift his legs in order to clear the deep carpeting. Ruth Weitzner appeared before him, then turned like a startled animal and lumbered hippily back into the room. She turned, then, and stood scowling, humming, her arms dramatically akimbo to protect—Rachel. He melted when she was there, really, looking at him. There were her large gray eyes. Worlds, lives, books to him; he saw his whole life in her eyes, the beautiful pale face, her black hair, the body of his wife.

"Rachel," he said, but he could not vocalize. He was dumb in the tones he must use for her name; he had no tender voice. She turned away from him, her shoulders turning, and he couldn't touch her.

Ruth was still shouting—all he heard was the hatred. Saul would shut her up, but where was Saul?

"Saul?"

Mae Gelb came hurrying in from the direction of the bedroom. "Ruth, be quiet! You're making too much noise!" Mae said, and then she saw Richard, and stopped still. "But how did you know?" she asked him. "We were going to call you."

"Saul?" he said, and started toward her.

"You can't go in. The doctor's with him."

"I can't see Saul?"

"No one can see him," Mae said, and then her disorganized face broke up even more, and she began to cry. "Oh, it's very bad," she said, and took several hard breaths. "He's paralyzed on one side." She cried through a whole breath, like a baby, and then said, "He can't even talk."

224

"He's dying," Ruth said in an ugly whisper. She took a step toward Richard and pointed a thick hand at him, her gray, muscular arm quivering, her mouth twisted across her teeth. "How do you like it?" Sound came into her voice, low and ragged with accusation. "Look at him, the *killer!* Straight from murder he comes in his red clothes. My God! He's got blood on him, and he comes to this house!"

"Ruth!" Mae said.

"Ruth!" Orson Gelb said, and turned to Richard. "She's all broken up. Don't mind what she says." But Ruth had always ignored him.

"*Murderer,*" Ruth whispered. "Men like you killed him, you know that? He couldn't stand it because you savages have to kill." Again into her whisper had come voice, grinding and vicious. Richard held his hand up in front of his face as if to ward off all that noise, and looked at Rachel. She wore a dress he knew, an old one. She had gained just a little weight, and somehow looked younger. She looked as she had ten years before.

"Rachel," he said, and because he had no tender voice the word sounded harsh. He tried to wave away the constant noise from Ruth. He could hardly hear himself. "Rachel, I've got to talk to you. I've got to tell you something."

She looked at him once, her pale face unnaturally determined, then looked away and said, in the soft voice she could never change: "I'm not supposed to see you. It's not good for me."

He couldn't touch her, but he took a step closer, and she quivered nervously and shook her head.

"I can't talk to Saul. Is that true?" he asked. She wouldn't answer.

"Leave her alone! Do you want to destroy her?"

He tried to protect himself from that noise.

"Ruth! For God's sake!" Mae said.

"Rachel, I've got something I have to tell you. Murray . . ."

"*He's taken the boy and made a killer out of him!*"

"Ruth, please!" Orson Gelb said.

Between Richard and his tall wife the gray woman postured and bared her teeth, and kept them from understanding each other.

"Can you hear me?" he asked. Rachel shook her head: *No, no, it's all over.* Along the line of her jaw, perhaps, there was the slight softening of age, and yet she was so beautiful. The mother of his son. And with this thought the walls of the high room turned concave, and the lines of the borders of things bent. The wave, that bell-like waste. In his neck the knife twisted, and he tried to breathe. When he got a breath he turned toward Saul's room. Maybe Saul was awake; there must be some little gift left for him, some kind of amelioration. In spite of himself, his body made signals to him in the form of terrible pain, and let him know that the two natures were still bound together, and if one couldn't stand it, neither could the other.

The hallway to the bedroom: Mae was frightened, and moved out of his way. Saul might at least touch his hand, and nod to him.

And then between him and the distant door the gray woman threw herself, making her worst faces and grinding her teeth. That coarse, snapping sow in front of him, threatening and jawing, that lead-colored bitch bumping her bladdered dugs against him. He reached down and grabbed the side of her clayey neck. But he was not mad, and so he asked her for a little consideration.

"I don't want to hurt you," he said reasonably. He should have known, however, that she was alien to reason. Her mouth opened and her teeth appeared. Her eyes were upon his waist where his hunting knife hung in its sheath, and she began to scream as though she were impaled, a shrill, inhuman sound, but quite familiar to him—it was precisely the one sound a rabbit ever made with its throat, and then made only when jaws closed upon its body.

"A *dagger!*" Ruth screamed when her voice returned. "He's got a dagger! All covered with blood! To this house he brings a dirty *knife!*"

Too far. Suddenly these were his only words. A man could be pushed only so far—those too: *so far. Too far.* There was a sweetness in that logic, a sweet, sweet hatred which could find its objects so near. The walls of the room sorted themselves into a little square in which he faced all at once the only makers of his grief. His voice grew strong with this perfect hatred, and was steady, and would be believed. How best destroy his enemies? He needed a

226

word to use with his new voice, and of course it came to him. It came deadly and ready out of an arsenal he hadn't known was his, and would strike them all away from him.

"*You dirty kike bitch!*" he said, and turned with so much cold force that Ruth, who had been pressed against him, fell thumping against the wall and to the floor.

Now he had triumphed over them all, and his victory over ambivalence and complication was perfect. His body was hard again as he walked to the foyer. If Orson Gelb had got in his way he would have smashed him until he splattered. He reached the door and went out, taking care to close it softly; man was so good at his hatred, and made those scenes with beautiful skill.

He would wait for the elevator this time. Oh, he had done a wonderful job. Gloating, freezing, he took several steps toward the stairwell and inexplicably fell down. There was the thick carpet, like pepper in his nose. Quickly he rolled over: thank God they hadn't caught him in this strange weakness!

But one of them had. It was Sophie Gelb, who must have followed him out. Now she knelt down—he tried to get up, and knew that in a moment he would be able to. He cursed his arms that wouldn't push him up. Her flat shoes creaked as she knelt, and her knee pressed the side of his face. She was very strong, and pulled him over so that his back leaned against the wall.

"Oh, you poor man," she said. Her homely face shone at him.

"I just tripped," he said. "I'll be all right!"

"She was so mean to you. Both of them."

"Don't pity me," he said. "I'll be all right."

"I know how you love grandfather too."

"Stop being kind to me!" he said angrily. He tried to get up, but couldn't. "I don't want to be weak like this." In his voice he heard some petulance, and he was afraid of it. Her big, uncontrollable eyes were moist with pity. Her dark face didn't even try to protect itself—even the pores in her nose were too big and open. "Why don't you leave me alone?" he said. "Christ, what next?" And then the question became larger and larger in his mind. "What next?" He didn't know whom he asked: "God, what next? What are You going to do to me next?"

—Because her face was suddenly unimportant, translucent, a

227

shell which gave her a name, and behind its homeliness he saw a blinding generosity that was beyond his understanding. Murray looked out of her eyes, as alien to his own violent humanity as if he were a horned beast looking upon the face of an angel.

PZ 4 .W7275 Ni c.1
Williams, Thomas, 1926-
The night of trees

DATE DUE